Welcome to Jack Snaggler's world, where the only thing ever really crazy is being sane...

"Hilarious Satire – A BIG Thumbs up!"
~ Karen L Prentice, Kindle Reviews ~

"A satirical bird's eye view into the workings of standard home life and Middle America. Deliciously funny and politically incorrect."
~ Tayla Grande ~

"It's a breakneck ride down a steep South American jungle road in the back seat of a 1940's jeep with no windshield and a blindfold on. You know your gonna die but the ride is so freakin' amazing."
~ Readerman Reviews ~

"A clear-cut roasting of modern culture, peppered with sardonic humor."
~ Mark Rook, Rook's World ~

"A hell of a good ride!"
~ Jim Pompa, Soundcheck Records ~

"Pinches a nerve in both business stiffs and romantics alike... a great read!"
~ Euro Travel Addict ~

.

.

NESTING with the LOONS
a novel by Jeff Davis

RAINFIRE PUBLISHING

All Rights Reserved

ISBN: 978-0615838199

Cover Art and Design: Marybeth Cauley

Nesting with the Loons

For my mother and father, who stood beside me through the years with both love and encouragement.

Special thanks to Marybeth Cauley for cover design and insightful input into the project.

Also Ed Caruso and Mark Rainstone for their irrefutable humor and wit, along with Bruce Miette for a lesson in scotch in a rundown little bar in Easton, Pennsylvania.

And of course, to everyone who longs to make an escape from the everyday world to some faraway island called paradise. You know who you are.

Prelude to Paradise
Author's Commentary

Readers sometimes ask, "Where do you get your ideas?" At times I wonder about that myself.

I once heard that Stephen King said of himself, "My writing is the equivalent of a Big Mac and fries." Confidentially, I'm a pizza and beer man.

As a teenager growing up in a small Pennsylvania town, I mopped floors and washed dishes at a local diner. It didn't buy me a Maserati but it filled the gas tank on a rusted '69 Ford Fairlane that I cruised around in on Saturday nights. Life was simpler back then. I didn't worry about company cutbacks, the rising cost of healthcare, national deficits, worldwide terrorism and war in the Middle East. I wanted to meet girls.

In my early twenties, I tended bar at the Little Tiger Cocktail Lounge, a cushy little watering hole on the edge of town. The only hint of life in the place after midnight came in the form of a lopsided neon beer sign that hung in a musty window. Near closing time one night, a customer walked in and sat down at a corner barstool. He had a wrinkled suit and a half-knotted red tie that looked like it went through a meat grinder.

"How's it going?"

"The name is Dave." He nodded. "I'll have whatever."

"Whatever?"

He scratched his chin as if considering. "Yeah, that'd be great."

Whatever turned out to be a shot of tequila, a few beers, and a moat of frustration.

Dave worked as a store manager for a retail chain that sold stereo equipment. With the economy sagging like wilted fruit, sales were sparse and his boss threatened to give him the pink slip. An ambitious man and would-be entrepreneur, he also ran a sideline business distributing gumball machines to malls that nearly bankrupted him. Financial woes aside, he had an irksome wife with a fetish for chocolate cherries and a teenage daughter who came home with a tattoo, a nose ring, and a defiant insistence to go on the pill.

Dave wasn't having a good day.

"It isn't that I don't love my family." He shook his head. "I just can't stand them. Sometimes I think about disappearing to a place they'll never find me. Is that a bad thing? I mean, everyone deserves a little paradise in their lives, right?"

"Disappear to where?" I shut off the neon beer sign in the window.

He shrugged. "Fiji, maybe." Dave drained the last of his beer and set the empty glass on the bar. "I'll send you a postcard." Tossing five bucks on the counter, he nodded and walked out the door, almost as mysteriously as he arrived.

I never saw Dave again. Sometimes I wonder if on a bright sunny morning, driving down the freeway with a takeout coffee and the radio blaring, he made a sudden detour to Philadelphia International and boarded a jet to some far off tropical haven. It would come as no surprise if I found a postcard stuffed in my mailbox with a picture of Dave on it, grinning from ear to ear, lounging on some steamy beach in the South Pacific.

The bartending years are behind me now, as are the untamed twenties. These days I spend my time writing novels, or juggling papers in an office cubicle, or in some cases, taking long walks late at night after most people are sleeping. Those are calm hours, and often I like to reminisce about the old days, and of course, much like Dave on that quiet night in a rundown bar on the edge of town, I like to think about paradise.

For those of us who have staked a claim in that little corner of the world, this book is about 6:00 a.m. alarms and freeway tie-ups. It's about deadlines and overdue marketing reports. It's about boorish husbands, loutish wives, and yes, even falling in love. It's about that island in the sun, where every so often, we all need to escape.

It's about you and me.

So if the kids just scribbled crayon all over the wall, the traffic is bumper to bumper, the boss has you under a microscope, or perhaps like Jack Snaggler, you just saw the girl of your dreams but didn't get a name or number, relax. Help is on the way.

The only thing ever really crazy in the world is being sane.

Nick Crowe

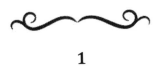

1

Survival Manuals

The instant Jack Snaggler saw the brunette with the beehive hairdo sitting in the '56 El Morocco, it was love, and love was like chocolate and caramel: wonderful but sticky.

That thought filtered through Jack's mind as he pulled into the parking lot for work with a donut crammed in his mouth and coffee spilt down his shirt. When he jumped out of the car, two thugs were crouched down behind a pickup truck, staring at him.

"You over there." He chewed, swallowed and tossed the remainder of the donut on the ground. "Got a problem?"

The men glared but said nothing.

"Are you deaf?"

One of the thugs stepped out from behind the truck. Pulling back his suit coat, he fingered the handle of a pistol stuffed in his trousers.

Gasping, Jack raced in the office door. He got a drink from the water cooler and wiped at a runner of sweat on his forehead. "Those two creeps are back again. What do you think they want?"

Jack waited for a response from his cohorts. None came. Their soggy faces had all the enthusiasm of stale cereal left in a bowl of warm milk.

"Are you listening?" He banged his fist on a filing cabinet. "We're being watched by people with guns!"

Still no answer.

Looking around at the sea of dismal faces, Jack pondered the uncertainties of his own future. In a world of social bias, political injustice and legal quagmires, he was just another hopeless romantic and broken cog on the corporate wheel. People of lesser veracity would have caved under the weight of the pressure.

Only the other day some wealthy investor from Manhattan who made his fortune on lima beans jumped out the window of the 5th floor of a building after the market bellied up. Prior to his demise, his wife eloped with a Tunisian playboy who she met on the internet. It was difficult to ascertain whether it was the loss of revenue from the DOW or a defective prenuptial agreement that finally sent him over the edge. In either scenario, much like the lima bean tycoon, the American dollar and romantic principles were both laying dead on the pavement.

"Hello?" Jack knocked on the wall. "Is there anyone alive in here? Someone needs to call security. For all we know those guys are terrorists."

Ed Shoemaker leafed through a tropical island brochure on his desk. His face had all the glee of a dead fish rotting in the sun. He periodically mumbled rude incantations, words like "obnoxious" and "vulgar", when referring to his not so endearing wife.

"Lighten up." Shoemaker glanced at Jack. "You think those two hoods outside are trouble? Try waking up next to my wife some morning." He dared him. "That's trouble." He looked out the window. "I heard those guys are feds."

Jack raised an eyebrow. "What would the feds be doing here?"

Shoemaker shrugged. "You know how this place does business. Someone probably swiped a candy bar out of a vending machine and the company wants to press charges. Take a lesson from Greene." He glanced across the room. "Relax and do your job. Everything will be fine."

Seated adjacent to Shoemaker, Gary Greene leaned back on his chair and grinned. Stretching his hands behind his head, he kicked his feet up on the desk.

Greene, a former military brat who continually bragged about the combat he never faced, stared dreamily at an airline ticket tacked to a bulletin board. In a few days he'd be on a flight to Las Vegas for a reunion with his old army buddies. As far as Jack could surmise, they'd spend their days rehashing the glory years, drinking beer and soliciting prostitutes.

"You people are impossible!" Jack shouted.

Just then Shoemaker's phone rang. It was an outside call. A jagged line of tension cut across his forehead as he stared at the receiver. "You want to talk about pressure? Listen to this." He put the phone on speaker and picked it up.

"Hello?"

"Edward?"

"Hello?"

"Don't ignore me. Don't even think about ignoring me."

Stress caked Shoemaker's face like dried mud. He smacked the phone down on the desk. "I can't hear you. There must be a bad connection." Frustrated, he shoved the vacation brochure in his desk and slammed it shut. "Didn't I tell you never to call me here? I'm working."

"You call sleeping at a desk all day working?" His wife cackled. "You don't know what work is, you stupid louse. I should have listened to my mother," she droned on. "I should have married John Bickle, the grocer in Elmira. At least he has a respectable job. At least he knows how to treat a woman. At least..."

Shoemaker grew steadily uneasy all the while his wife nagged, moaned, whined, and complained. Finally he threw his hands up and shouted at his coworkers, "She's like a black hole. Every time she opens her mouth everything gets sucked in!"

The telephone went eerily silent. Then, "Keep talking Edward. Just keep talkin'," her nasally voice threatened. "I'll deal with you when you get home."

Click.

She slammed the receiver down. The stale buzz hummed in Shoemaker's ear.

It was no secret to Jack or anyone else in the office about Shoemaker's ailing home life. He complained about it to his cohorts at every opportunity.

Ed Shoemaker was the victim of a neurotic wife who survived on anti-depressants and the father of a defiant teenage daughter with a fetish for nose rings and thong panties. For him, work wasn't just a paycheck, but moreover, a safe haven from the realities of a sagging and fruitless home life. He dreaded Fridays, knowing full well that he'd be forced to spend still another morbid weekend with a morose wife who wasn't happy unless she whined and a daughter that in all likelihood would be pregnant and addicted to drugs before she ever dropped out of high school. Life had become little more than a festival of frozen TV dinners thrown in a microwave, all the while his rude family argued defiantly with him about nothing at all. Often he fantasized about the day that he'd jump in his car for work and then make a detour to Philadelphia International. While his wife vegetated on the couch like a mustard plant and his daughter waited to pounce on him after a hard day at the office, he'd be on a flight to some exotic island, all the while that same dried up TV dinner – perhaps liver and onions – grew into a stale cold lump on the kitchen table.

In the interim, Shoemaker's only saving grace remained the promise of Monday mornings when he could escape the miseries of his unlovable family. It would surprise nobody if he walked in the office one sunny afternoon, almost certainly on a Friday, intent on alleviating the pressures of his daily life by way of an AK47 or some other instrument of destruction. Gary

Greene kept a flak jacket underneath his desk for just such occasions.

⁓

Jack stared out the window at the parking lot. The thugs who hid behind the pickup truck were gone. Shaking off their daunting presence, he retreated to his desk and sipped at a cup of coffee.

Cool Caps Inc., a small bottling company in the Poconos, was in business for decades. Employed by the company for five years, Jack recently got promoted to sales rep in the customer service and development department. In short, that translated into taking orders for bottled commodities such as water and juice. Since most of the clientele were already established, the bulk of the work rested on doing nothing all day long. He took the responsibility very seriously.

Advancement at Cool Caps heavily relied on a person's mindset. Employees like Shoemaker who did the work they were paid to do often became the recipients of verbal and written warnings. It was just a question of time before they'd be asked to resign their position. One day they'd be seated at a desk and the next they'd be gone. Nobody knew where they disappeared to. The only thing certain was that they weren't coming back.

On the upside, unproductive employees got handed quick promotions, the logic being that if a worker doesn't do anything, he or she won't make mistakes. Because of their steady lack of output, these bold recruits often disrupted the labor force by arguing all day long about unreasonable issues like unions, raises, or even the price of eggs. They were troublemakers. To remedy the problem, the company offered generous salaries, private offices, or whatever other distraction helped them avoid the less valuable employees generating the bulk of the work. The less someone produced, the more help they received to complete a task that should have only taken them half the time in the first place.

It was regarded as critical that office personnel have desk dividers that separated them from the rest of the staff. Privacy counted. Without it, people like Eileen Klump, a secretary teetering on a constant cliff of emotional collapse, would see that her peers did little more than maul over crossword puzzles or read the funny papers. She might become insubordinate.

She might refuse to do everyone else's work.

The entire department feared Eileen. Tall and skinny and speckled with freckles, her purse was a pharmacy of modern medicine stuffed with pills from any number of doctors. At the slightest cough she'd fumigate the room with disinfectant. She typically developed any illness suggested to her, and if she wasn't crazy, she wouldn't be working for the company at all.

"What's that noise?" Shoemaker complained one day. "Did someone bring a dog with them? I hear dogs."

The source of the disruption came from the far corner of the room near an empty desk.

"There it is again!" Annoyed, Shoemaker threw his pencil down. "My wife's brother had a cocker spaniel that made a noise like that. I shot that bastard."

Greene glanced at the flak jacket stuffed underneath his chair. It was almost Friday. Shoemaker would again be forced to spend his weekend downtime with his wife and daughter. He could fall to pieces at any moment.

However, the immediate crisis wasn't Shoemaker's unbalanced condition, but rather Eileen's deteriorating mental status. Eileen was never the most stable rock in the foundation; when a wave of hot flashes and the first signs of menopause arrived, the cement cracked altogether. She had three breakdowns in as many months. Usually she cried and kicked at file cabinets, but today proved different. Unable to cope with the pressures of everyday life and the changing hormonal blueprint in her body, she crawled underneath a desk and refused to come out.

Uncertainty flooded the faces of her coworkers. Most of them pretended nothing was wrong. Noticing her would force them to take action. Not unlike unclogging a blocked toilet after a bout with the drips, nobody wanted the job.

Bob Wetterman, a buyer down in purchasing, picked up a half-eaten cheese sandwich that sat on top of the microwave. "Come on out of there Eileen. You're just having a bad spot, right?" He held up the cheese sandwich. "You'll feel better after you eat something."

"Get away from me!" She swatted the foodstuff out of his hand and curled up tighter under the desk.

Help eventually arrived in the form of two gum-chewing young men dressed in white coats. Kicking and screaming, they pulled Eileen out from under the cramped underbelly of the desk. Prodding the woman out the front door, they led her to an ambulance and stuffed her inside.

In the office, coworkers buried their heads in marketing reports strewn across their desks. They silently waited for Eileen to be properly disposed of, at which time they could gossip about her in private and avoid being rude.

Jack watched as the ambulance pulled out and took off down the highway. Over near the corner of the building, he was startled to see that the two goons he had encountered earlier were back again. Dripping with contempt, they stared at him as if he were a terrorist raiding an ammo dump. Rubbing his knuckles in his eyes, he looked again and they were gone.

"Did you see that?" Jack pointed. "Those goons are back."

Wetterman walked over to Jack's desk. "Are you seeing things again?"

"What if I am?"

"Eileen's ambulance can't be far if you need a lift."

"I'm not crazy."

"Of course you're not." Wetterman stepped backward.

"Stop patronizing me!"

From across the office, Shoemaker crumbled up a marketing report he pretended to be working on and tossed it in the trashcan. "You guys sound like old hens. Stop cackling. How is anyone supposed to get work done?"

Taking a deep breath, Jack settled back in his chair. He reached in his shirt pocket and pulled out a crinkled photograph. In the picture, he was seated in a '56 El Morocco with a beautiful brunette. She had eyes bluer than the Caribbean and a smile that could stop a hurricane barreling into the Gulf. For an instant he swore he still smelled the girl's perfume lingering in the air.

Regardless of the goons outside, the chaos of bureaucratic institutions, or even the eccentric characters that encompassed such places, Jack closed his eyes and daydreamed. He found himself momentarily transported back to the carefree days of Hackertown High School. As a second rate football player, he could hear the cheers, and more often boos, ringing in his ears as the senior squad walked on the field of play.

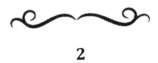

2

Boomerangs

"Eat 'em up, eat 'em up, RAW RAW RAW!" The cheerleaders screamed their lungs out and tossed pom-poms in the air.

Jack sat on a bench in a smelly locker room. The coach delivered last minute instructions. Spit flew everywhere as he barked out orders and pounded his fist on the wall.

The Hackertown football program had been in existence for a proud seventeen years. Within that timeframe, which included some one hundred plus games, the Boomerangs had only managed to produce a total of three victories, two of which came by way of forfeit, and none of which came in the last decade.

Jack never boasted about being a good football player. During many a long Saturday afternoons, he spent his energy warming the bench on the sidelines, waiting patiently for the inevitable ending to another good shellacking by some neighboring district.

The prospects of victory grew even worse during those sporadic moments when he unexpectedly got thrust into the game when key players like Hamburger Kruddle, the

Boomerang's star fullback and only light in an otherwise dank tunnel of talent, sustained an injury.

"Dead man walkin'!" Angry defensive linemen heckled Jack as he stepped up to the line.

Stumbling uncertainly around the backfield, he was pursued by irritable competitors whose only ambition was to smash his face in the dirt. Week after week, sparse crowds gathered on the bleachers and looked on in bitter disappointment as the final gun sounded.

Aside from the Hackertown Boomerangs, the Robbinsville Hoods were the worst football team in the county. Much like the Boomerangs, the Hoods were slapped around by arrogant opponents who spent most of the day trotting gingerly into the end zone. However, if there was any weapon buried in the Hoods empty arsenal of talent, it was their ability to cheat. They grabbed throats, gouged eyes and kicked balls. They were organized criminals in padded uniforms who recognized the true meaning of losing without dignity.

By tradition, the Hackertown Boomerangs and the Robbinsville Hoods were scheduled as the last contest of the year. Up to that point, neither team ever had any victories. Therefore, it always got billed as the biggest game of the season.

"Don't let the Hoods puke on you out there." The coach slapped everyone in the head as a show of love and respect. "Show them who you are."

"Yeaaaah!" The team jumped off their seats, batted around a jock strap hanging off a locker and punched each other's helmets.

Nick Crowe, the team waterboy, sat in the corner of the room chewing on a sausage sandwich that he filched from the concession stand.

"Gimmie that thing." Hamburger grabbed the food out of Crowe's hand. The hoggish sized fullback devoured it in a single bite and pledged victory at all costs. Ketchup and mustard dribbled down his cheek.

From the opening play of the game, it became apparent that the Robbinsville Hoods were in for a dogfight. All talk of fair play was tossed out the window and the doors were bolted shut. Players on both sides of the ball limped on and off the field with bloody noses and aching groins.

"What the hell?" Wetterman's eyes widened. He examined his shoulder after a play. Clear imprints of Pecker Larder's molars were embossed on his skin. "The mangy mutt bit me."

Defense, and defense alone, controlled the line of scrimmage. Like stray mutts fighting over a pork bone, both teams refused to give up their respective positions. Twice the Boomerangs tried to advance forward and twice they were thrown for a loss.

"Nuts and bolts, Nuts and bolts, WE GOT SCREWED!!" The cheerleaders yelled.

After three grueling quarters of play, the game stood deadlocked and scoreless. It wasn't until the final minutes of the fourth quarter that a disgruntled Hamburger Kruddle decided to take matters into his own hands.

"Give me that stinking ball," Hamburger ordered his teammates, disregarding any and all instructions that were shuttled in from the bench.

"It's supposed to be a pass play." The quarterback scratched his head in the huddle.

"Screw you guys. Your hands are butter. I'm taking it straight up the gut."

Quite frankly, it was a thing of beauty. Even before the snap of the ball, Hamburger began pointing – and sometimes spitting – at the weary faces of hesitant opponents whose task hinged on stopping the bruising fullback. Rushing ahead like a bull, he pounded out yardage. Even Skillethead McGuire, the

Hoods best tackle, got carried from the field of play after a fierce collision with Hamburger, who busted Skillethead in the mouth just for the inconvenience. With less than a minute to play and the ball resting only a few yards away from a winning score, victory seemed certain.

That's when tragedy struck.

"Ouw!" Hamburger turned three shades of green.

The star fullback clutched his gut and collapsed on one knee. Mystified spectators looked on in wonder as he was helped to the sideline. The Hoods patted themselves on the back and shook their fists toughly for a job well done, almost as if Hamburger's untimely departure from the field stood as a tribute to their talent.

However, talent had little to do with Hamburger's acute condition. What the Robbinsville Hoods could not accomplish by brute force, Nick Crowe's suspect sausage sandwich did. Hamburger hurried back to the locker room clutching his gut and spent the remainder of the game hugging the toilet.

"You're in the game," the coach told Jack. He whacked the benchwarmer around a little to let him know he meant business. "We only have time for one more play. Run the ball straight up the gut. Don't stop until you hit pay dirt. I know you can do it kid." He sounded confident then warned, "And for God's sake, don't fumble."

Jack strapped on his helmet and trotted slowly down the sideline. Edgy fans shifted nervously in their seats as he walked by. Children with half eaten hot dogs gawked at him, and a young Mexican girl named Rosa Cruz yelled something in Spanish that nobody could understand.

"You ignorant clod!" Norman Cooley, a devout Boomerang fan and heir to the Cool Caps' empire, wailed from the sidelines. "Blow this one and I'll shove your head in a toaster."

Someone tossed Jack a football. That couple of ounces of leather felt heavier than a concrete block. Puddles of sweat amassed on his forehead. He wanted to run. Jump ship. Dig a hole on the fifty yard marker and stuff his head inside where nobody could find him.

"Don't worry." A tender voice unexpectedly reached out of the crowd. "You can do it."

Jack looked up. A dazzling brunette with the smile of an angel approached him. Her blue eyes sparkled in the sunlight. A faint trace of her perfume lingered in the breeze.

Renewed vigor poured over him like mineral water. He stood up straight and thrust out his jaw. For the first time in a long dry season, winning mattered. His level of confidence was measured not so much in talent or ability as it was in the brunette on the sidelines who urged him on.

Hitting the field, rival teams lined up and dug their cleats in the dirt. Pinky Limpet, the quarterback, barked out signals like an angry hound.

"252! 147! Hike!"

Pinky took the snap. He rolled left. Faked a pass and then turned around and pitched the ball to Jack, who circled from side to side, searching for a weak spot. Out of nowhere, Wetterman barreled headfirst into Dirtbag Pegula like a cannonball. Dirtbag crumbled to the ground. The blow created a momentary chink in the armor of the Hoods defensive line.

"NOW!" The coached howled from the sideline with hands prayerfully folded.

Jack lowered his shoulders. He barreled towards the end zone. An angry host of militant Hoods converged on him from all points. Dirtbag Pegula managed to get off the ground. He grabbed Wetterman and started choking him like a wet chicken. All the contestants hurled themselves in a tangled knot of legs and cleats. Jack was buried at the bottom of the pileup with an outstretched hand reaching for the goal marker.

It wasn't until the referee signaled "NO TOUCHDOWN" that the air deflated from the bubble of enthusiasm that surrounded the Boomerang bench.

A sudden hush blanketed the crowd. Stunned fans filed out of the complex. Boomerang players with drooping chins and slumped shoulders limped back to the locker room in quiet disgrace; they were taunted by gloating Hoods every step of the way.

Long after the seats were empty, Jack remained on the ground. He stared at the football that rested not more than an inch away from pay dirt and tapped it across the goal marker with his finger.

"It was a nice try, right?" someone said.

Jack knew who it was. Even through the stink of sweat on his uniform, the scent of her perfume filled his nostrils. He looked up to see the girl's locks of dark hair blowing in the breeze. She wore a purplish blouse and when she smiled, he tingled all over like a Christmas bell. It occurred to him that for a guy who just broke every heart in Hackertown Pennsylvania, he felt pretty damn good about himself.

"Have we met before?"

She shrugged and tilted her head coyly. "Maybe. My family just moved to town, but when I was a little girl, we visited here a couple of times."

The idea of the girl being interested in him didn't just make his heart beat faster. Jack couldn't believe that she acknowledge him at all. He stared at the brunette and stupidly sucked at his lips.

Across the street, an old Chevy squealed its tires, rounded the corner and came to a halt in the gravel just outside the front gate of the football field. An older man, probably the girl's father, tapped on the horn. Disenchanted with Jack's lackluster performance on the grid, he stared a bazooka hole through the kid.

"That's my ride." She slapped her hands at her sides. "Nice meeting you." She turned to leave and quickly hurried off.

Jack got off his knees and watched the girl jump in the car. Despite his denial, he couldn't refute one indisputable fact. It had finally happened to him. Love rushed in on him like a hurricane.

Stripping off his football helmet, he tossed it on the ground. "Wait! I don't even know your name!"

The brunette turned and smiled. "Paradise," she yelled out the window just before the car sped away.

Jack watched as the vehicle turned the corner and disappeared out of sight.

3

Dan Rupert

"Ah!"Jack opened his eyes and screamed.

For an instant he grew confused as to his whereabouts. The last thing he remembered was two goons snooping around out in the parking lot. He got spooked and retreated to his desk cubicle. Somewhere along the way he drifted off and daydreamed about Paradise. Upon opening his eyes again, Wetterman stood at his desk, staring at him.

Jack's eyes darted around the room. "Are they gone?"

Wetterman looked confused. ""Is who gone? You were sleeping at your desk again. Is that what the company pays you to do?"

"Everyone else sleeps. Why should I buck the system?"

Pulling at the undernourished hairs on his chin, Wetterman stared dumbly at him.

Jack stared back. He knew that look. There was a problem.

Wetterman was a staple in the company's purchasing department for years. Outside of an episode that became known as the *Ground Guide Incident*, he was meticulous in his work. Sometimes he suffered from recurring nightmares and woke up in the middle of the night screaming; one in particular involved being attacked by a banana named Paso. If he had one other obsession, it was his unquenchable love for Rosa Cruz, an illegal alien who barely spoke English and wanted nothing to do with him.

Wetterman slumped down in a chair beside Jack's desk.

"What's wrong?" asked Jack. "Your face looks like you just sat in a bucket of wet paint."

"Didn't you get the memo?"

"What memo?"

Wetterman handed him a piece of paper that read:

Effective immediately, ALL VACATIONS are CANCELLED until further notice due to an increase in production of customer orders. Please direct any questions you have to Dan Rupert, our personnel director, regarding the new policy. As valued employees, we hope this inconvenience doesn't conflict with your outside activities or leisure plans.

Have a pleasant day,

Norman Cooley, Proprietor

Wetterman banged a fist on the desk. "They can't just cancel vacations. It's un-American!"

"Canceled?" From across the room, Greene's ears perked up. "I have a plane ticket to Vegas. I'm meeting some of my old combat buddies for a reunion."

"Not anymore," Jack disagreed.

"I am going!" he shouted.

Greene's cheeks turned candy apple red. For an instant he regressed into a state of infantile-like mentality and appeared ready to cry. His right eye twitched so uncontrollably that if it

25

were the pin on a grenade, everyone in the room would have been blown to bits.

Jack regarded Greene as a deranged product of the system. Unlike the typical portfolio of employees who suffered from nervous breakdowns or occasional bouts of attempted suicide, deranged people tended to be dangerous, and at times, even violent. Where one person would put a tack or a dead mouse on someone's chair, people like Greene might favor the use of a machine gun.

Conversely, Ed Shoemaker glowed with enthusiasm at the news regarding the new vacation policy. With no scheduled days off, he could avoid seeing his wife indefinitely during the normal course of the workweek. Smiling from ear to ear, he picked up the memo and tacked it on his bulletin board like a prize fish. Kicking back in his chair, he paged through another pamphlet showcasing a resort in Fiji and quietly snickered about hideaways where undesirables, namely his boorish wife, would never find him.

Jack tossed the vacation memo in the trashcan and then pulled it right back out again. "I'm going to speak to the personnel director."

"Dan Rupert?" Wetterman's jaw dropped. "Rupert never talks to anyone. That's the reason they made him personnel director to begin with."

No truer statement had ever been spoken.

Rupert had no prior experience as a personnel director. That made him the perfect applicant for the job. He was a drifter from the south and made his way northward after being fired from any number of respectable corporations. With so many terminations under his belt he clearly had the upper hand on anyone applying for the position. His duties required him to report the complaints of disgruntled workers to the head office, those people in command who could care less one way or the other and only hired Rupert in the first place under the condition that he never talked to them about the problems of the general workforce. Regardless of the directive, employees frequently barged in on him to complain about insufficient pay raises and poor health benefits.

Determined to escape an onslaught of discontented workers, Rupert began making a steady retreat into the restroom nearest his office. Ducking in a stall, he slammed the door and bolted it shut. Often he stayed there for hours, eating bologna sandwiches and reading scandal magazines between periodic naps.

Unknown to Rupert as he roosted on his porcelain throne, at the other end of the building, Jack grew increasingly agitated about the memo concerning the cancelled vacation policy and was about to pay him a visit.

"Where are you going?" Wetterman pointed as he and Jack hurried down the corridor. "Rupert's office is that way."

Ignoring his crony, Jack pushed the bathroom door open. As expected, the stall door housing the toilet was closed. Someone inside snored like a busted muffler. Jack knocked and cleared his throat. "Dan Rupert?"

There was a shifting noise followed by the rustle of a newspaper.

"Who is it?" a reluctant voice answered.

"Jack Snaggler. I have a few questions concerning the vacation policy."

After a moment, "That's a matter for you to take up with the personnel director."

Wetterman scratched his head and whispered, "What does he mean by that?"

"Begging your pardon," Jack reminded, "but you are the personnel director."

After another awkward moment of silence, the latch on the door clicked open. Seated on the commode, Rupert looked up. Perspiration stains the size of pineapples garnished his shirt. Orange moccasins that could have been mistaken for bedroom slippers cribbed his feet.

Jack glanced at Rupert's shoes. "Are those things standard issue?"

"No more than the bump on your skull." He sneezed. "It's allergy season. My feet swell like balloons when the pollen count goes up. The moccasins help my circulation. Why the hell am I explaining this to you?" He unraveled a few squares of toilet tissue and blew his nose. "I got enough headaches trying to figure out why seventeen-thousand dollars worth of Ground Guide material is buried in the warehouse. I don't even know what the stuff is."

Wetterman gulped at the mere mention of Ground Guides. His expression turned vacant as a nuclear dump. Not even a skilled mortician could have duplicated the look.

Rupert blinked uncertainly. He considered the idea that Wetterman might be having a coronary. God knows the last thing he needed was to get stuck working late and filling out an accident report.

"What's his problem?"

Jack shrugged. "He looks sick. Maybe you should call an ambulance."

"Get serious." Rupert scoffed. "You expect the company to pay for something like that? With the twists and turns healthcare is taking these days, it costs an arm and a leg just to pull a splinter."

Jack crossed his arms. "That's idiotic. How do you know it's not an emergency unless he gets checked?"

Rupert sighed. The conversation was stirring up his ulcer. "Look here." His expression turned sour as warm milk. "I've got better things to do than argue whether or not your buddy is having a coronary. What do you guys really want?"

"We have issues concerning the new vacation policy."

Rupert sucked at his lip. "Didn't you get the memo? We no longer have a vacation policy. How can I discuss something that doesn't exist?"

Jack argued, "That's crazy. What about all the hardworking employees that made reservations to expensive places in hopes of spending enormous amounts of money that they don't have?"

"There's always next year," Rupert considered, "maybe. Besides, not everyone shares your opinion. Just this morning someone came in here. They commended the company's decision to cancel all vacations. I think his name was..." he rustled through some papers in his briefcase," Shoemaker. Yes, that was it. Ed Shoemaker."

"Shoemaker!" Jack laughed. "He just doesn't want to spend time alone with his wife."

"I met her at the open house. Can you blame him?"

"You're being unreasonable. Isn't there anything we can do to rectify the problem?"

"Of course," Rupert said. "You can quit."

"This is ridiculous!"

"Stop whining." Rupert ripped off another square of toilet tissue and wiped his nose. "If you don't like the rules, you can always change things."

"What are you talking about?"

"Alternatives, of course," Rupert said. "Remember Nick Crowe?"

Jack remembered Crowe well. A former employee at Cool Caps, Crowe worked in the IT department and got hired as a PC guru to upgrade outdated hardware. He made daily requests to get the much needed replacement parts, all of which were rejected. Irked by a lack of cooperation, Crowe voiced his concern to the head office. He was promised the problem would be alleviated. Unfortunately for Crowe, alleviation arrived in the form of a pink termination slip the following morning. Indisputably it was Crowe's own fault. If he hid at his desk and took long lunches like everyone else, he would have been quickly promoted. But like so many of his predecessors, he was fired because of his stubborn insistence to do the job the company paid him to do. Out of work and the victim of a sagging economy, he took a job at Alfred's Diner, a rundown eatery on the edge of town. He worked there ever since.

"The guy cleans toilets and fries hamburgers for a living." Jack balked. "What kind of life is that?"

"Don't laugh. Crowe looks stupid as a rock," Rupert agreed, "but is he really that dumb? Tell me something." He switched the topic. "Have you seen those thugs with the dark glasses skulking around the place?"

Jack stiffened. "When I came to work this morning they were hiding behind a pickup truck, staring at me. Who are they?"

"Let's just say they're not here selling magazine subscriptions," Rupert said. "The point is, Crowe saw trouble coming. He got out just in time. He moved on to greener pastures. You guys should think about doing the same. Ha! Everyone knows your entire job is to stare at a blank computer screen and pretend to do a job that doesn't exist."

Jack put his hands on his hips. "It's a living."

"A useless one," Rupert reminded. "Nick Crowe is a friend of yours, right? You should talk to him. Chew his ear. You'll get a new outlook on life." He blew his nose and cleared his sinuses. "In the meantime, all vacations are cancelled."

Jack smacked the wall with his fist. "You can't do that! This is an infringement on our rights. I'm calling my congressman."

Rupert shrugged." Why bother? He's out in the foyer right now delivering a stump speech. Now get out." He slammed the stall door shut.

Fuming like burnt rubber, Jack stormed out of the door. Greene stood in the walkway. His face cold as a block of ice, he kicked open the restroom door and started pounding on the walls, shouting about vacations, constitutional rights, and a nonrefundable plane ticket to Las Vegas.

Just down the hall, Mike Ditsky, a congressman running a hardnosed campaign throughout the state, stood in the lobby on top of a milk-crate. He was finishing up a speech when Jack and Wetterman arrived.

"Always remember, in this great land of ours, you can be anything." He waved at the sparse and non-cheering crowd. "Now if there are no other questions, God bless you and..."

"I don't want to pay taxes anymore," someone from the back of the room yelled.

Ditsky froze. Uncertainty clouded his eyes. "Now that's silly," he answered carefully. "Everyone has to pay taxes. How else would we feed all the other hungry countries of the world?"

Drew Biddle from down in the records department chimed in. "I had a corn removed from my toe a few weeks ago. It cost hundreds in deductibles to rectify the problem. Why the hell should I have to pay hundreds in deductibles for a lousy corn?"

Ditsky glanced at his wristwatch. Perspiration dotted his forehead. "I'm not a medical practitioner, but I'd imagine corns could be a complicated procedure." He paged through some notes in a folder. "We in the political arena believe that every man, woman and child, no matter what race or religion, are entitled to good paying jobs and affordable healthcare for both the individual and his or her loved ones. A happy family is a prosperous family, and a prosperous family is filled with joy, compassion, and yes love, for those people closest to us."

Shoemaker bolted out of the crowd. The veins stood out on his neck, thick as telephone wire. "Tell that to my wife and daughter, you moron!"

Ditsky stepped down off the milk-crate. He backed up two steps. The mob was turning ugly. He looked around the room and searched for an exit in the event of a hostile incursion.

However, no viable means of escape existed, and as if the devil was summoned, the front door of the lobby burst open. Shoemaker's brazen wife and daughter stormed in. Dressed in gothic black, the kid looked irritable and the mother was livid. Pushing people aside, they marched up the center of the aisle toward the befuddled politician.

"Rumor has it that Cool Caps is canceling all vacations this year." Shoemaker's wife's face turned beet red. "I made plans for the Bahamas and have no intention of sitting at home like a bucket of lard while my husband pretends to do work at some cushy office job. I want to go on a CRUISE!" she yelled at Ditsky, who had no clue why anyone was asking him about vacations to begin with.

Ditsky straightened his tie and cleared his throat. "No offense, but I'm just a politician. You can't expect me to be helpful. Maybe the employees of this fine company should voice their concerns to the management. In this great land of ours..."

A pitiful groan sounded out from the back of the room. It was Shoemaker again. He rushed forward and nearly bowled Jack over. "You're being unreasonable." He got up in his wife's face. "I have responsibilities here. Why don't you take the kid and go away by yourselves," he suggested. "Please, just go away."

Shoemaker's daughter didn't care one way or the other. Ignoring the conflict, she flirted with a scruffy reject that worked on the assembly line. He had a ring in his nose and something that resembled a tattoo of a duck on his arm.

"I didn't get married to listen to opinions." His wife scoffed. "You're not staying here like you're on some kind of vacation. You're coming with us."

Shoemaker jumped up and down like a badly behaved child getting a good scolding from a nonnegotiable parent. "You can't make me do anything!"

Jack popped his head up from behind Shoemaker's shoulder. "Everyone calm down. I'm sure we can find a rational solution, like reinstating the vacation policy."

"Never!" Spit flew from Shoemaker's mouth. "I'm not going on vacation with that!"

Shoemaker's wife froze. The atmosphere around her grew thick as black smoke. Even Shoemaker's ill-mannered daughter stopped pawing at the assembly worker long enough to look.

Just before security arrived and escorted her off the property, the incensed woman picked up the milk-crate that the congressman had been standing on. Winding up, she swung it at her husband with all the velocity of a major league pitcher.

Shoemaker ducked.

Directly behind him, Jack was an open target. The last thing he remembered before getting clobbered was Norman Cooley running behind a security guard, pointing at the mad woman and begging them to shoot her.

Jack groaned. Shoemaker's wife smashed him in the head with a milk-crate. Then the lights went out. He might have been dreaming about Paradise, although he couldn't remember the particulars. But when his eyes opened, instead of a brunette bombshell, all he found was Dan Rupert standing over top of him, wearing orange moccasins and holding a handful of smelling salts.

"You ass." Rupert spat. "You had to push the vacation crap, eh?" He checked his wristwatch. "I'll be filling out accident reports until midnight."

Jack pushed himself up on his elbows. Looking around, the place was deserted. "Where is everyone?"

"It's quitting time. After security carted Shoemaker's wife away, everyone went home."

"What happened with..."

"Enough questions." Rupert cut him off. "You got bigger things to worry about." He glanced around and whispered, "You're being watched."

Jack's eyes blinked open. "Watched? I don't understand."

"Keep your voice down, you little lout." Rupert kicked him with an orange moccasin. "The last thing I need is for someone to see us talking. Just stick to the plan and be ready to move. It's almost game time." He turned to walk away.

"Wait!"

Sweating like a walrus in the sun, Rupert quickly took off down the hall and exited into the bathroom.

Fingering the rising welt on his head, Jack got to his feet. He had no idea what Rupert meant. However, much as the personnel director suggested, a creepy sensation of being watched fell over him. He looked over at the open door of the foyer that led into the assembly area. For an instant he thought he saw something move over by the receiving bay.

"Hello?"

Everything remained quiet.

He took a step closer and gasped. Lurking in the shadows with dark sunglasses perched on his nose, one of the goons who had been prowling around the place over the last few days ducked down behind a shipment of Ground Guide material.

"You over there." Jack's heart beat like a hammer. "You're not allowed in here after hours."

A clicking noise, like the hammer of gun poised to fire, echoed in the darkened room.

Jack shivered and hurried out the front door.

4

Katrina's Kitchen

Jack was chasing ghosts ever since he left work. Pacing from room to room in his house, he peeked out the windows from behind closed curtains. The men in dark glasses unnerved him. Once he even thought he saw their darkened silhouettes hiding in the shadows of the back alley. When the telephone rang, he nearly jumped through the front window.

"Hello?"

Someone breathed slowly on the other end of the line. He swore he heard them mumble something about "Fiji".

"Who is this?" he demanded.

The receiver went dead leaving a stale buzz in his ear.

It could have been a wrong number.

Then again, it could have been THEM.

Jack shuddered. The prospects of being stalked by two nameless brutes pricked at his nerves like a needle. Staying locked up in the house all alone didn't help matters. He needed fresh air and even more, some company.

Glancing out the front door, nobody was in sight. He bolted from the house and made a mad dash to his car. Spinning the tires in the driveway, he headed straight for the nearest bar.

Nesting with the Loons

Katrina's Kitchen, a cushy little downtown pub, was a favorite watering hole amongst the locals. A lopsided neon beer sign hung above the front door like a welcome mat. Inside, the place hopped. Captain Jim and the Drunken Sailors, a couple of old rummies playing acoustic guitars and singing calypso songs, performed on stage.

Wetterman was seated at a table near the bar when Jack arrived. He stared dismally into an empty glass of melting ice cubes.

Jack ordered up a drink and sat down beside him. "You look about as cheerless as a dog that just raided a hornet's nest."

"I ran into Rosa at the supermarket. She was standing in the frozen food aisle. I literally begged her to go out with me. Nope." He shook his head grimly. "She just stood there staring."

"What did you expect?" Jack took a sip of his drink "She doesn't speak English."

Wetterman's face split open in remorse like a walnut. "Tell me something I don't know."

Jack studied his friend with uncertainty. His fixation for Rosa Cruz was even more of a mystery than his own fascination for Paradise.

Wetterman's obsession stemmed back to childhood. One day he was hiding up in an apple tree, firing apples at people's heads. A Spanish woman spotted him and started scolding him in a foreign language. The woman's daughter, Rosa, hung tight to her mother's skirt tails. From the instant he saw her, Wetterman's heart melted like butter under a heat lamp.

Years later, Rosa went to work at Cool Caps as a front desk receptionist. Wetterman spent his lunch hour hiding in the bushes. He'd stare at her through the large glass doors leading into the main lobby. Other times he tucked a Wall Street Journal under his arm and walked by her, hoping she'd discern how vital he was to the company.

Love is blind. Actually, it's pretty damn dumb.

"Forget Rosa." Jack leaned forward in his chair. "The personnel director spoke to me today after the incident with Shoemaker's wife. He told me I'm being watched."

"What do you mean?"

"Remember the two goons at Cool Caps? I spotted them snooping around. They hid behind a rack in a receiving bay at work. Later I saw them in a car outside my house."

"That's impossible." Wetterman scoffed.

"Why?"

"Because they're right over there." He pointed.

Across the room, the two men sat at a table and picked their teeth. One of them stared at Jack. Leaning over, he whispered something to his partner.

A wave of heat rushed down the back of Jack's neck. He thought about running and glanced at the exit just in time to see Nick Crowe meander in the door.

Crowe looked spruce in his knitted shirt and kakis. Jostling a cold beer in his hand, he walked the length of the bar, shaking hands and yakking with total strangers. He could have been mistaken for a high ranking politician on the campaign trail as opposed to a fast food chef who cleaned toilets on Sundays for time and a half. Making himself comfortable, he pulled up a chair and sat down at Jack's table.

The two men on the other side of the room stiffened. One of them blatantly stood up and stared. The other tugged his partner's arm and motioned for him to sit back down.

"How's it going?" Crowe asked Jack and tilted his head uncertainly. "You got all the color of a day old corpse. You sick or something?"

"It's those guys over there. Don't look." Jack glanced. "They've been eyeballing me all night."

Crowe sniggered and took a swallow of beer. "You sound delusional. Maybe you should think about a new job. The inactivity of doing nothing all day long has finally rested your brain."

"You were employed by the company until you got fired." Jack pointed out.

Crowe's face turned to vinegar and crusted over with resentment. "Norman Cooley didn't know what he was doing when he canned me. The guy has all the business savvy of a drunken chimpanzee. It doesn't matter." He straightened his shirt collar and thrust out a defiant jaw. "I'm optimistic. The fast food business offers a brilliant career. I was promised a fat raise and a promotion. Salvation is just around the corner."

Jack rolled his eyes.

Crowe had been employed at Alfred's Diner for two years. He insisted that it was just a matter of time before he'd be wading in gold. But gold was scarce these days, and the only advancement he ever got from the owner of the place was to work Sundays scrubbing the urinals and commodes.

"Alfred has been offering you a manager's position for months," Jack said. "The guy is shiftier than a snake. Rumor has it he even worked for the mob."

Crowe brushed the comment off his shoulder. "So he has a few quirks. Is that a crime? Public service is an honorable profession. I think the word I'm looking for is prestige."

"You scrub commodes for a living!" Jack slapped the table in amazement. "Why don't you look for another job? Maybe you could apply for another position at Cool Caps. They clean toilets there too," he reminded.

Crowe sniffed with resentment. "After the way Cooley treated me, I'd sooner do nothing at all."

There was the irony. As far as Jack could surmise, if Crowe would have read newspapers and did nothing to begin with instead of trying to fix the company, he'd still be employed.

Jack sipped his beer and looked back at the two men in sunglasses. They were staring him down. A coil of contempt hung over their faces like a black plague. He slammed his bottle on the table. "You over there!" He pointed an accusing finger. "What the hell are you guys looking at?"

Crowe blinked uncertainly. "What's his problem?"

"He thinks those guys are out to get him," Wetterman answered.

"That's crazy."

"Trust me," Jack insisted. "We're being watched. You know Biddle who works down in the records department? He told me they're feds."

Crowe shrugged. "Would that be so surprising? The owner of Cool Caps is about as cheap as a bottle of outdated cologne. He probably doctored the company's books and the IRS is running an investigation." He took another swig of beer and peered over into the dining area. "Forget about those guys. If you want to see a real pimple that's ready to burst, look over there."

Seated at a table, Ed Shoemaker sniffed hatefully at his dinner. While his rude family picked at their food, Shoemaker boiled like a lobster and stewed in his own juices. Pressured by a tide of unrest among rebel workers, the company opted to reinstate the recently canceled vacation policy. Effective immediately, all employees with ten years or more service were eligible for time off. Shoemaker made it in just under the wire. Instead of basking in a relaxing workweek away from his family, he'd now be forced aboard a luxurious cruise ship, aka the Lovebird no less, where he'd be required to spend his downtime with his miserable wife and cheeky daughter. Instigators like Jack Snaggler and Bob Wetterman were to blame. Refusing to adhere to the rules, they provoked management into giving hardworking men and women the time off they deserved.

Blistered with contempt, Shoemaker pulled a pen out of his plastic pocket protector and spitefully scribbled both Snaggler and Wetterman's names on a used napkin.

"I hate liver," Shoemaker's daughter bellyached. She stuck a fork in a shaving of unsavory meat and flung it across the room. It nearly walloped a waitress in the head.

"Shoemaker is depressed," Wetterman said. "After his wife stormed the company and threatened lawsuits, Cooley folded under the pressure and reinstated the company vacation policy. Shoemaker has to go on a cruise with his family. I think he blames us because we pushed the issue."

Jack nodded at Shoemaker.

Shoemaker made an obscene gesture with his tongue and turned away.

"That poor bastard has a heartfelt love of the tropics." Nick Crowe tapped gingerly on the tabletop. "Sometimes he stops by the diner just to show me his brochures of the Fiji Islands."

"Fiji?" Jack tilted his head. "Someone rang my phone tonight. They mumbled something about Fiji."

"Would you stop with the paranoia?"Crowe set his drink on the table. "All I'm saying is that Shoemaker had some bad breaks."

"What bad breaks?"

"For instance," Crowe pointed a finger, "he married his wife. Maybe all he needs is a change of pace. My guess is he'd make a great bartender. Anyone who can put up with a woman like that could easily listen to the troubles of every souse that ever graced a barstool.

"Shoemaker, a bartender?" Jack pondered the idea and laughed. "That's absurd. His wife would scare off all the customers."

Crowe leaned over and whispered, "Not if she wasn't around."

5

Mika

The two thugs in sunglasses continued to watch them. The weight of their stare was heavy as an elephant.

Indifferent to their intimidating presence, Crowe draped an arm over his chair and leisurely jostled his beer. "Yo man!" He lifted his head up and gave a hearty wave when Lance Sheppard strolled in the door.

Jack eyed Sheppard with contempt. The guy was a self-made entrepreneur and about as honest as a starved wolf. A former sales rep at Cool Caps, he made his fortune the good old fashioned way: disability fraud. One day during a business meeting he developed a severe case of gastritis. Excusing himself, he ran down the hall to the restroom, slipped on a mopped floor in the foyer and banged his head on a water cooler. Sheppard promptly sought medical attention for an imaginary injury that mystified both doctors and surgeons alike.

"The pain in my back comes and goes," he explained. "It doesn't bother me when I'm doing things like mowing the lawn or hanging drywall. It only hurts when I work."

Aided by Fritz Heinbeck, a corrupt lawyer from Philadelphia, Sheppard won $200,000 in punitive damages from the company. He was also awarded disability compensation for the nonexistent injuries he sustained.

"That guy is a shyster," Jack said. "He worked the system for years and never even got a parking ticket."

"You shouldn't bad-mouth him," Crowe defended. "Sheppard is a financial genius. He's considering a business partnership with me."

Jack raised an eyebrow. "What business? You clean urinals and make hamburgers."

"Now you're mocking me."

"Of course I am."

"Go ahead and laugh." Crowe sipped his beer."It won't be funny when the loot rolls in. I might even give you guys a job. The difference is that you'll have to earn your money instead of sitting behind a desk and pretending to do work that doesn't even exist."

Jack crossed his arm. "And when is this going to happen?"

"Don't worry. You'll know." Crowe stood up. "Now if you'll excuse me, I have to tie up a few loose ends with Lance." He nodded and walked across the bar to where Sheppard stood. They grabbed a couple of barstools and retreated into a darkened corner, over by the pool table, where they could talk privately.

A tall blonde leaning against the jukebox stared at Jack and Wetterman. She had all the curves of a racetrack and was built for speed. Sucking at her drink like a sponge, her eyes were about as subtle as a billboard advertisement for legalized prostitution.

Wetterman nudged Jack. "That girl over there just winked at us. I wonder what's wrong with her?"

Sliding her hips off the corner of the jukebox, she wiggled over to their table. "You boys look like you could use some company." She glanced over to a table where her friend sat. "Care to join us for a drink?"

Jack shifted his eyes around the room. The men in sunglasses still looked in their direction. "That might not be a bad idea." He grabbed his drink and stood up.

Following the girl to a nearby table, they pulled out a chair and sat down. Wetterman noticed that the blonde's friend wore far too much makeup. Even worse, she looked nothing like Rosa Cruz, the receptionist at work that he was in love with and wanted nothing to do with him.

"My name is Bob." Wetterman introduced himself.

"Boob?"

"I said Bob."

"Do you prefer Boob or Booby?" the girl asked.

"That would be Bob or Bobby," he corrected. "Either is fine."

"Tell me Booby," she forged ahead, "how long have you been living on the planet?"

Wetterman shifted uncomfortably in his chair. "Pretty much all my life."

"Wonderful." She sighed. "Booby, it sounds as if you've had a lovely life in this world."

"It's Bob or Bobby," Wetterman repeated. Irritability tickled his voice.

"Of course." She nodded. "Now tell me Booby, where did you come from," she paused and glanced at the ceiling, "and are you planning on being recalled anytime soon."

"How many times do I have to tell you, the name is Bob, not Booby." Wetterman growled. He turned and whispered to Jack, "The aliens have landed."

Jack said nothing. He sat idle at the table, stroking his chin. The attractive blonde, late twenties, sat beside him. She flipped her hair saucily over her shoulder and then let it fall back across her face.

"Do that again."

The girl, Mika was her name, looked confused. "Do what?"

"Flip your hair over your shoulder."

"You're becoming aroused." Mika let out a devilish laugh. Once again she tossed her hair behind her shoulder.

Jack took a sip of beer and stared as if in deep thought.

"What's wrong?" Mika looked puzzled.

After a moment of silent deliberation, he answered, "You have a swastika tattooed on your forehead."

"Oh," the girl chuckled, "that old thing?"

"Are you a Neo-Nazi?"

"What if I am?" Mika snapped with mild defiance. "Is there a law against it?"

Jack considered the question. "There might be."

Resentment glistened in Mika's eyes. "You're jealous, yes? There's no room for prejudice in a free society."

"Forget I mentioned it," Jack said, not wanting to add to his woes by drawing more attention.

Mika turned cold. "Forget nothing! Do you think your ethnic background is superior to mine?"

"I really just want to finish my drink and go home."

"You're a capitalist and a bigot." She poked his chest with a bony finger. "You hate me just because I'm a communist."

"Maybe I don't like communists."

"Maybe I don't like you." She spat.

"Have it your way. I love Neo-Nazis. Does that make you happy?" Jack picked his beer up and raised it in the air. "Here's to the master race and conqueror of capitalism. Hail the fuehrer!"

Jack turned his head and froze like a pound of beef in a meat locker. The two men in sunglasses had gotten up from their table and stood right behind him. One of them had his fists clenched so tight that his knuckles went white.

"What are you, some kind of Nazi sympathizer?" He shoved Jack.

Jack cowered in his seat. "You don't understand. She made me say that. There's a swastika on her head."

Mika batted her eyelashes innocently.

"You're lying." He shoved Jack again.

Wetterman cleared his throat. "Her friend thinks she's an extra-terrestrial, if that means anything, chief."

"What do you guys want?" Jack clutched the side of the table.

One of the brutes leaned over and squeezed Jack's cheeks like a lemon. "Don't play stupid. We got you and your friends pegged. Are you working for Nick Crowe?"

"I don't know what you're talking about."

"Sure you don't." The thug snickered and gave Jack a little slap on the cheek.

In the dining area, Shoemaker caught sight of the squabble. He sprang up from the table and waved a fork. "Hit him! Please hit him!"

"I don't understand. What did we do wrong?" Jack asked.

The question was interrupted by an argument on the other side of the bar. Stinky Mason, a nickname passed down from his father who worked as the nightshift attendant at the sewage treatment plant, had a few too many beers. When he noticed Nick Crowe loitering at the bar, he singled him out.

"You work at that diner, right?" He took another slug of beer. "The grease fryers in that place must be dusted with laxatives. When I eat there I get the drips. I hate the drips. It's no wonder the commodes in that place smell like a skunk."

"I resent that." Crowe's cheeks burned. "We give every customer exceptional service in an unsoiled atmosphere. Outside of a faulty electrical system, everything in the place is greased, fried and served to perfection."

"What is this guy, a comedian?" Stinky nudged the person next to him, who seemed moved neither one way nor another by the revelation.

45

From across the room, a braless and brazen Debbie Abernathy stormed over. Her flimsy dress flapped in the breeze from an open window. Flipping her blonde hair – bleached to perfection – over her shoulder, she had her nose stuck up so high in the air one might have thought she was sniffing the exhaust on an airplane.

"I don't like him." She chewed gum and announced to Stinky. "When I stopped at the diner last week, he stared at my breasts." Putting her hands on her hips, she boldly thrust out her goods that threatened to pop out of her blouse. "If you really cared about me Stinky, you'd defend my honor."

As Jack watched the action unfold, it occurred to him that honor wasn't the issue. Back in high school Debbie Abernathy was groped under the bleachers during halftime activities by the entire football squad. The girl had all the innocence of a brothel in the Bronx. She often boasted that if it wasn't for the pleasures of sex and getting free drinks in exchange for showing a little cleavage, the male species should be eradicated from the planet.

"You've got me confused with someone else," Crowe argued. "I have respect for women." He glanced at Abernathy's tight blouse. For an instant his eyes hung there, almost as if considering a pair of prize watermelons at the county fair.

"There he goes again!" Debbie shouted.

"Are you trying to squeeze her melons?" Stinky pushed him backwards. "That's it, isn't it? You want to squeeze her melons."

"Don't be ridiculous." Crowe waved him off. "I don't even like fruit."

Stinky set his beer on the bar. Winding up a fat fist, he knuckled Crowe in the ear. Bent on retaliation, Crowe jumped on Stinky's back and rode him like a bull in a rodeo. Tables and chairs toppled over as both men crashed to the floor. Adding to the melee, a drunken mob loitering over by the pool table started to brawl. Someone even grabbed one of the men wearing sunglasses by his necktie and pulled him into the fight. Barstools sailed across the room and fists flew like bullets. A bartender with muscles the size of bazookas rushed out from behind the bar and tossed patrons around like rag dolls.

Jack and Wetterman cowered underneath a table.

"Quick." Jack grabbed his friend by the shirt. "We need to get out of here."

Crawling on hands and knees, they made their way to the exit door. Racing outside, Jack turned around, certain that he'd find the two thugs in sunglasses running after them.

"Pst." Someone from across the street waved at them.

Jack squinted in the darkness. It was Nick Crowe.

"How did you get out of there so fast?"

"People are barbarians." Crowe brushed off his trousers. Opening the driver's door of a hot pink jeep, he jumped in. "Shoemaker pulled Stinky off me and then pushed me out the door only seconds after the fight started. I owe that guy my life."

Jack marched over and slapped him in the head. "Those two goons were asking questions. They brought up your name."

Crowe popped a gumball in his mouth. "Loosen up. You have any idea how many people die from stress related illnesses? It's tragic." He turned the ignition key and fired up the jeep. "I got to head over to the diner. A couple of buses from upstate New York stopped to use the head. God knows what condition the place is in."

"Shut him up." Wetterman's bottom lip quivered. "Please shut him up. We're being stalked by lunatics and all he can think about is sparkling urinals."

Strain scribbled across Wetterman's face like black ink. It wasn't just the men in dark sunglasses. Other demons were abroad. For one thing, thoughts of Rosa haunted his mind. For another, he was having recurring nightmares about a guy dressed up like a banana, wearing a cowboy hat, who answered to the name of Paso. He speculated that the yellow fruit could be a symbol of some unforeseen sexual tension. Deficient in sleep and unlucky in love, Wetterman was ready to snap.

"You should be grateful." Crowe got snotty. "If it wasn't for me trading punches with Stinky Mason, you'd still be in the bar getting pushed around by those thugs."

"What do you know about them?" asked Jack.

"No more than you do."

"Why are they after us?"

"You tell me." Crowe shrugged. "If they're feds, what would they want with a couple of bums like you? There's worldwide terrorism, global warming and tsunamis in Asia. On the beach of life, you guys are just a couple of broken oyster shells."

The front door of Katrina's suddenly burst open. The two thugs rushed out of the building like a gust of wind. Their dapper suits were crinkled up and sunglasses bent from the scuffle inside the bar. One of them had his hand clenched on what looked like the handle of a gun, stuffed in his pants.

Crowe took a swallow from a bottle of flat cola that was baking in his jeep, swished it in his mouth and spit it out the window on Wetterman's shoe. He reached over and pushed the passenger door open. "Maybe you better jump in. Pick up your cars in the morning. Those guys look pissed."

The men walked towards them. Jack pulled Wetterman by the shirt and climbed in the jeep. Tooting his horn, Crowe peeled the tires and took off down the road in a bowl of dust.

~

"What was that all about?" Wetterman shivered and looked back at the thugs, whose dark presence stood in the middle of the street.

"Relax." Crowe draped an elbow out the window. "Maybe they just had too much to drink." He reached in his pocket and pulled out some candy. "Gumball?"

Jack smacked the candy out of his hand. "Are you an idiot? Those guys were after us."

"Now you're being rude. I just saved both your butts. I'm not going to sit here being abused." Crowe got stuffy. He turned up the radio and refused to speak another word about the incident.

Jack looked in the rearview mirror. He was certain he'd find the thugs racing down the highway behind them. However, the road remained dark and empty.

When they arrived home, Crowe pulled the jeep against the curb and slammed on the brake. Jack and Wetterman jumped out and glanced around suspiciously. Fearing they were followed, they quickly retreated to their houses and bolted the doors.

The events of the day, like fungus on a rock, grew on Jack's every thought. Sleep didn't come easy. He spent the night pacing the floors. About 1:00 a.m. the telephone rang and his heart nearly leapt out of his chest.

"This is creepy," Wetterman said on the other end of the line. "I looked out my window. Those two goons were riding up the street. Maybe they're going to off us."

"You're talking crazy," he told Wetterman. "We didn't do anything wrong. Get some sleep. Things won't look as bleak in the morning."

Jack hung up the receiver and headed up to bed. He pulled the covers around him like a protective shield. Thoughts of the men in sunglasses buzzed around his head like fighter jets.

Outside, a car peeled its tires in the alley. Dozing in and out of nightmares, he stayed there until the morning alarm sounded.

6

Norman Cooley

Norman Cooley glanced at the gold Rolex on his wrist. The soles of his shoes sunk into the plush carpet as he ambled across the office and sat down in a luxurious leather chair. He grabbed a Cuban out of a small wooden cigar box. Striking a match, he lit up and stared dreamily out the window.

"Bah." Harriet Puck croaked from across the room. She sat in a chair, nipping at a glass of wine.

Norman glanced over at the aged woman and grinned.

In her heyday, Harriet was a Miss September pin-up queen. She was the same budding beauty in a picture that hung on the wall of his father's garage when he was a kid. Norman would sneak in, drink his father's stash of homemade hooch, and stare at the pin-up for hours.

After a fleeting career in modeling, Harriet took up residence in the Bronx. Thanks to her business savvy, she built a very profitable prostitution business. However, a couple of undercover cops who enjoyed getting laid but liked making a bust even more, ended the dream. After her incarceration and a stint in the big house, she vowed to cleanup her life. Harriet got a fresh start in a dilapidated halfway house in Delaware. In the years that followed, she spent her time peddling around street corners and begging for pennies.

Fixated with the once flourishing beauty, Norman hired a detective to track down the 1945 dreamboat. It took years, but finally he found her. She was spotted operating an illegal shell game in Asbury Park. He immediately sent for the old woman and offered her a position as chief advisor to the company. Now a decrepit and toothless chain smoker with a fetish for hard liquor, he proudly paraded her around the complex.

Regardless how wilted the flower, love bloomed.

Cool Caps Inc. remained a thriving business for nearly 75 years. The company was founded by his father, Clyde Cooley. Back in the day, Clyde was one of the town's most respected bootleggers. He ran a hooch operation in his garage during the lean years when money was tighter than a stripped screw. The place consisted of little more than a couple of wooden milk-crates for seats and an old pin-up picture of Miss September tacked on the wall.

"Why can't I be rich like the fat politicians in Washington?" he complained to his drinking buddies. Clyde coughed and lit another cigarette, almost as if his lungs might be in danger of clearing. "When I look out the window, all I ever see are dark clouds. Where's my rainbow?"

The rainbow that Clyde so eagerly awaited ultimately arrived and right up to the day that he keeled over from emphysema, he regarded it as an act of God. It came in the form of his thirteen year old son named Norman, a Miss September picture from 1945 that was torn from a girlie magazine, and his neurotic wife named Heidi who suffered from post menstrual syndrome, twenty-eight days a month.

"Ah!" A scream of horror woke Clyde from snoozing on an easy chair one afternoon. He wobbled to his feet, hurried to the garage, and found Heidi standing at the door. Her face was pale as a ghost.

"There's a monkey loose in the house!" she babbled.

The source of the disruption came from Norman. The kid sneaked into the garage. He sat on a wooden crate with a soup can filled with homemade hooch. His trousers were bunched up around his ankles as he gawked at the Miss September picture. Norman's budding red cheeks giggled drunkenly.

"Easy now." Clyde consoled his wife. "Boys will be boys. He's just doing what comes natural." He motioned to his blushing son. "Put that thing away and pull up your zipper."

Heidi sobbed, "He was pulling at it like the starter cord on a lawnmower."

The incident sent Clyde's wife reeling into a pool of depression. She worried that her only child would grow up, move to Miami and become a porn actor, or perhaps worse, a male prostitute who gets paid by desperate old ladies – or envious rich men – for wiggling his manhood in back alley motels. Heidi blamed most of the boy's problems on Clyde's obsession for bootlegging. In a clench of frustration, one morning during breakfast she picked up a frying pan from the stove and conked her husband on the head with it. Scrambled eggs dripped off his nose.

"What in the world has come over you, woman?" Clyde fingered a rising lump on his head.

Unable to cope with the pressure, Heidi began counseling sessions with a therapist named Doctor Ham. She explained to Ham that she had recurring nightmares of her son slobbering over the stout breasts and striking navel of the depraved pin-up queen.

"How would you like to find this staring you in the face every time you climbed out of bed in the morning?" She unraveled the pin-up picture and shoved it in his face.

He examined the evidence closely.

Doctor Ham assessed Heidi's problem as being post-depression brought on by her son's acute masturbation, aided by alcohol and a portrait of Miss September that could give sight to a blind man. He claimed her woes stemmed out of a fear that her son was growing up too fast.

"There's nothing to worry about," Ham assured the woman and passed her a bottle of sedatives. "Kids get curious. Think of it as buying a first car. When a boy finally discovers his little friend hanging around down there, he wants to gas it up, peel the tires and see what it'll do on the open road."

In the end, counseling sessions were fruitless. Heidi insisted that her husband shutdown operations and bolt the garage door shut. The locals were devastated by the news. Happy men on welfare checks who once spent Friday nights swapping lies with drinking buddies were forced to rethink weekends. The bulk of their newfound life rested on spending time with overbearing wives who made unreasonable requests, like going out to dinner. The town mayor went so far as to start a petition to reopen the illegal distillery to get unhappy husbands and useless deviates off the street. Disheartened men of all ages and creeds, much like Moses, awaited a savior to part the rivers of their discontent.

Enter one Marvin Caruso.

Caruso, a shifty neighbor with dealings on the black market, offered to let Clyde setup hooch operations in his cellar in exchange for a cut of the profits. In only a matter of days, business boomed again. Wilted and pruned men required to spend weekends with the women they once loved suddenly bloomed with excitement. Marvin, so impressed with Clyde's business savvy, offered to finance a bottling company with some revenue that he had illegally acquired from diamond brokers on the black market.

"We're going to be rich as a fat walrus drying in the sun," Marvin told his cohort. "Here's a token of my appreciation. Trust me. There isn't another one like in the world."

He handed Clyde a handmade walnut cigar box. Opening it up, it held three vintage Cubans resting on a piece of red velvet. Marvin pulled two of them out, lit up, and with a brisk handshake the Cool Caps Empire was born.

The bottling company took off and money poured in like the surf. Regrettably for Marvin Caruso, so did the feds after they uncovered evidence of his dealings on the black market. Caruso abruptly disappeared one day and was never heard from again.

Clyde assumed that his partner's underworld associates terminated his services – and more likely his life – after they discovered that he secretly filched a fortune in diamonds from them.

Meanwhile, Cool Caps continued to thrive. Clyde erected a World Headquarters as home base for the company. He made a replica of the oval office for his own personal use, complete with a wet bar, from which he conducted operations and day to day business. What began as a lewd act by his young son Norman in the back of a garage, ended in a financial masterstroke.

"Come in here, you little bastard," Clyde hollered to his son one fine morning. "I want to show you something."

Norman stepped in the room. Sitting his son down, Clyde showed him the beautifully handcrafted cigar box that was given to him by Marvin Caruso.

"I just got back from the engravers and had a few alterations made." Clyde held the cigar box up in a stream of sunlight that shined through a window. Across the side of the box, the words *DADDY'S STASH* were etched in gold.

"This is a family heirloom. There isn't another one like it in the world. If anything happens to me, take good care of it." He playfully slapped his not-so-bright son in the head. Pulling out a cigar, Clyde lit up and puffed like a steam engine.

Norman picked the box up and shook it. "What's so special about a box?"

Clyde ignored the question. He grabbed the cigar box out of his son's hand and placed it on the corner of the desk. "Not now, but some day when you're older and show some brains, I'll tell you a secret." He tapped his knuckles on the top of the box. "Keep it safe."

Regrettably, the secret which Clyde spoke of never became known because not long after, Clyde keeled over from emphysema.

Heidi by no means recovered from when she walked in on her son Norman to find him pleasuring himself in the back of a garage with a pin-up picture. She passed on some years after her husband. The coroner listed her death as natural causes, but friends and family alike speculated that she died of a broken heart.

Norman became sole inherent of the bottling business, prominently named Cool Caps. As a tribute to the company's prosperity, like his father before him, he kept that same handmade cigar box, *DADDY'S STASH*, on his desk and enjoyed the daily pleasures of a good smoke.

Life was grand but not without pitfalls, and for Norman, a rise to power meant having enemies. Recently, an audit revealed that money had turned up missing from a company bank account. Someone had raided the depository. He found paper trails and bogus business write-offs that led to places like Guam and Fiji but could never pinpoint the source. With so many disgruntled employees on the payroll, it was impossible to find the guilty party.

Other aspects of his life were equally disturbing. For one thing, he was convinced that Nick Crowe, a computer geek turned fast food chef over at Alfred's Diner, had been trying to kill him.

A former employee at Cool Caps, one day he had the audacity to suggest improvements be made to the networking system and placed a requisition for new computers. Like so many of his predecessors, he disposed of Crowe by way of a pink termination slip and had him escorted off the property. But if Norman learned one thing in life, it was that time never forgets.

One day in a rush, Norman made the mistake of stopping at Alfred's Diner for some takeout food.

"This bun is soggy." He slapped the wet bread on the counter after he received his order.

"Please fill out a complaint card." Crowe impatiently tapped on the cash register behind the counter. "Our aim is to meet the satisfaction of our valued customers. I want to make sure you get everything you deserve."

Rather than squabble over a beef sandwich, Norman grabbed the foodstuff and took off out the door. Later that night, he developed a severe case of diarrhea that left him literally glued to the toilet. Someone dished up some bad meat. He cringed at the idea that Crowe, somewhere between cleaning the fryers and scouring the commodes, might have peed on his edibles.

Nick Crowe wasn't the only troublemaker ever employed by the company. Undesirables sprouted up faster than crabgrass. Norman shunned walking into the development department at all. He feared men like Ed Shoemaker, an unstable worker with a suicidal wife and ill-mannered daughter. In all likelihood and given enough time, Shoemaker would eventually neutralize himself. One day the guy might stroll in the office with a thermos, have his morning coffee, and then jump out the second floor window. The drawbacks to something like that could be enormous. Not only would the company suffer a black eye from unwanted media attention, but more importantly, it could cause insurance rates to rise.

Most of the general workforce loathed Norman, a trait he viewed as a personal asset. It gave him great comfort to know that he could control the lives of the very men who despised him and they couldn't do a damn thing about it. Employees cringed when he walked by. They were fully aware that at any moment he could snap like a rubberband and terminate their lowly existence from the company. Often he dropped pencils or other paraphernalia when he walked by the hired help, if for no other reason than to exert his authority and make them pick it up.

"If that isn't love and respect, nothing is." He gloated in his office and stared out the window.

Conversely, there were rebel employees like Jack Snaggler, a sales rep over in development. Last week when the guy walked down the hall, Norman raced out of his office and dropped a dollar on the floor. Instead of handing the money back, Snaggler snatched it up, stuffed it in his shirt pocket, and kept walking.

Back in high school when Jack Snaggler played football for the Hackertown Boomerangs, he muffed a play and lost a game to the Baskerville Hoods. Norman made side bets all over town and lost a ton of money that day. When his parents passed away and he took over the bottling business, he hired Jack, if for no other reason than to kick him around in the aftermath of a lackluster performance on the grid.

Since then, he often considered moving Snaggler to the advertising department located in a discreet part of the building. At least then he wouldn't have to look at the guy every day. After awhile, he'd quietly terminate him and kick him out the door.

Unfortunately, the *Ground Guide* crisis materialized. From Norman's perspective, Jack Snaggler and his crony Bob Wetterman were the only two people in the company who could alleviate the problem.

7

Ground Guides

Monday morning arrived in the usual manner.

"It's fantastic to be alive." Ed Shoemaker sat down and put his hands behind his head.

Jack sat down at his desk and watched Shoemaker with careful interest. Another weekend at home with his miserable wife and daughter had passed and nobody got killed. Pamphlets of Bermuda and other tropical havens were safely tucked away in Shoemaker's bottom desk drawer. By Wednesday afternoon he'd be leafing through them again and planning an escape from a family he no longer loved, to a place they'd never find him.

On the opposite side of the office, Gary Greene, a war veteran who flew airplane supplies to mess tents in the Gulf, leaned back on his chair and read an artillery magazine. He looked relaxed and evidently sensed that any immediate threat of Shoemaker going berserk stood under momentary restraint. Greene even risked walking over to the stag-line at the coffee pot without his flak jacket.

The telephone rang at Jack's desk. He wondered who would have the guts to call him before he finished his morning coffee. "Snaggler speaking." He yawned. "You got the wrong number."

"Don't hang up!" A frantic voice cackled on the other end of the line. "It's me, Wetterman." He breathed deeply. "Norman Cooley just called an emergency meeting in his conference room."

"What's the trouble?" Jack bit into a bagel.

"I'll tell you what the trouble is. GROUND GUIDE MATERIAL!"

Jack paused. A half-eaten blueberry bagel hung out of his mouth. "Are you sure?"

"Cooley was rooting around the warehouse and found a truckload of the stuff. He wants to know what we use it for. By the time this is over," said Wetterman, "I'll be on unemployment and scrubbing urinals right beside Crowe for slave wages."

Jack nervously bit his fingernails. The Ground Guide crisis emerged two weeks prior when he gave Wetterman a requisition for some office supplies. Rosa Cruz was stooped over a fax machine in a skimpy orange sundress. Mesmerized by the girl, Wetterman inadvertently ordered a wrong number from the supply catalog. Instead of a box of paperclips and a stapler, $17,483 worth of nonrefundable cookie sheets rolled in the door.

"Cookie sheets." Wetterman groaned. "How am I going to explain that?"

Jack slammed a fist on his desk. "If you wouldn't have been eyeballing Rosa like a slice of watermelon we wouldn't be in this predicament! Listen," Jack lowered his voice. "You've got to lie."

"Lie?"

"Pretend the stuff is something else. If you act like you believe what you're saying, everyone else will buy it. It's called suspension of disbelief. There's nothing illegal about it. Car salesmen and politicians do it all the time."

The next morning brought a new attitude of hope to Wetterman. It also brought Norman Cooley storming over to his desk. He wanted to know why over seventeen thousand dollars worth of cookie trays were shoved into the backroom of the warehouse.

"Begging your pardon, Mr. Cooley, they aren't cookie trays."

A wiry vein of discontent danced on Norman's neck. He flapped the purchasing requisition at Wetterman's nose. "Do I look stupid?"

Wetterman said nothing.

"If they aren't cookie trays, then what are they?"

"We needed to replenish our stock of Ground Guide material."

Norman lowered his head suspiciously. "What's that?"

Wetterman paged through a clutter of books on his desk. "I'm not aware of any problem with the item," he lied as Jack suggested. "I thought everyone knew about Ground Guide material. You mean you don't know?"

"Of course I know," he shouted. "Now stop picking your nose and get back to work." Norman hurried out the door, almost as mysteriously as he arrived.

Norman tossed and turned on the bed linen that night. He didn't have so much trouble sleeping since he was a young boy and his mother caught him in his father's garage, lusting over a Miss September pin-up.

Fixated with the thought that he may have been duped by a weasel like Wetterman, he did a snap inspection of the warehouse on the weekend. Buried on a forgotten shelf in the rear of the building, the Ground Guide material jumped out at him like a lost and floating ghost.

Norman called an emergency meeting first thing Monday morning.

Office workers, or deadweight, as Norman referred to them, assembled in the main conference room. They sported plastic pen protectors and tablets, most of which were used to doodle mindless circles or cartoons while pretending to take notes. As a rule, everyone in attendance appeared stressed. When an employee looked dismal and overworked, it promoted the illusion that the individual in question deserved to be overpaid.

The purpose of the Monday morning meeting was to review potential worry spots within the organization. It was an unwritten statute, under threat of termination, that nobody voiced his or her concerns. Therefore, nothing ever got accomplished.

"This is supposed to be a production meeting for the betterment of the company. The last thing I need is people talking about problems," Norman often complained to the meeting's attendees.

On those infrequent occasions when Norman asked for opinions from his managers, the room grew silent. Voicing concerns was considered an infraction of the rules. Those who did it were reprimanded and labeled troublemakers. The result was a room crammed with administrators who resembled mindless puppets on strings. They wagged their heads agreeably to whatever Norman said. If their flowerless faces looked any more wilted, a gardener would have contracted to come in and start watering them.

Norman used meetings as a podium to boast about the success of the company and his father's hard work to build the Cool Caps empire.

However, before passing away, his father joked that if Norman's IQ ever hit fifty, he'd sell everything. As far back as grade school, he set low personal standards for himself and more often than not, failed to achieve them. At select times he showed modest promise, but in the end, while the railroad was up and running, the train was off the track.

Norman failed again.

After his mother caught him in his father's garage with a Miss September pin-up picture, she feared that the boy suffered from a mental defect. She refused to entertain the idea of having a second child who would be born stupid and possibly brainless.

Before their passing, both Clyde and Heidi pondered the mysteries of their son. It was difficult, if not impossible, for them to understand how the very sperm that created Norman beat out over 1,000,000 other contenders.

Jack sat at the conference table and fidgeted at the sight of the two men in the hall. It was the same guys who turned up at Katrina's the night before. Glaring into the conference room, their aura hung in the air like a stink bomb.

"Who are those guys?" asked Jack.

Norman glared. "I don't see anyone," then warned, "and neither do you."

"That's crazy. They're standing right there."

"Really?" Norman looked around the room. "Does anyone else see them and want to get fired?"

Everyone bowed their heads and studied the dust on the table.

Jack stood up, walked to the door, and slammed it shut. "Now they're really not there."

Norman picked at his teeth and eyed Jack with disdain. "Sit down, Mr." He glanced at his notebook and tossed it on the table. "I called this meeting to discuss a shipment of Ground Guide material found in the warehouse. Who can give me a report?"

Attendees at the meeting stared at walls, slapped at imaginary mosquitoes, and rustled through nonexistent notes on blank tablets.

Shoemaker tapped his fingers on the table. "I'm not even sure what Ground Guides are."

"Are you stupid?" Norman suggested.

Shoemaker didn't answer and remained composed. It was Monday, a fresh new workweek away from his family. He refused to allow people like Norman Cooley to ruin it for him. If he wanted abuse, he would have taken the day off and stayed home with his wife.

"I'm not sure you people comprehend the question." Norman snarled. "The next person who says they're unaware of the Ground Guide situation gets fired on the spot." He banged his fist on the table. "I want answers!"

Drew Biddle, the company snitch down in bookkeeping, cleared his throat. "Do we have enough of the stuff?"

Norman answered, "That's the question. The last thing I need is to have our inventory depleted and unable to meet the production schedule."

Wetterman's face turned pasty white. He paged through his empty notepad. "It's a highly chemical treated material, but our supplies should be adequate to meet our demands."

Norman tilted his head. "Chemical treated? Is it dangerous? I don't need any lawsuits from some whining housewife because one of our employees has a low sperm count and goes impotent." He sucked at his lips as if pondering one of the great mysteries of our time. "Do we need some sort of," he paused, "training?"

Wetterman dabbed the sweat off his forehead. "I don't think that'll be necessary. It isn't as if we're talking about nitroglycerin."

"Or nonrefundable cookie trays," Jack mumbled.

"Shut up!" Wetterman blurted out and then took a deep breath. "What I'm trying to say is, despite the risks, if the men remain competent in their work, no accident report forms should be required."

Seated on the other side of the table, Greene scratched his chin in wonder. "Ground Guides. That sounds familiar. I read something about a training program being held in Pittsburgh."

"No, you didn't," Wetterman disagreed.

However, Greene inadvertently tickled the truth.

A recent article in a business quarterly ran a story about the growing trend of jobs in airports. One of those jobs included

Ground Guides, a term used for airport personnel who directed incoming and outgoing air traffic. The article said that a rigorous training program in Pittsburgh was underway to prepare new recruits.

On the morning Norman Cooley approached Wetterman about the suspect material in the warehouse, he had been paging through the article and blurted out the first words that came to mind.

Ground Guides.

Drew Biddle raised his hand. "I'd like to offer some input."

Norman's eyes narrowed. "Since when are we living in a democracy?"

Disregarding the verbal spanking, Biddle forged ahead. "If this is a chemical treated material, it could be unsafe. Shouldn't we have someone certified to work with it? The stuff might not be high explosives, but it isn't as if we're baking chocolate chip cookies. One accident and a lawsuit will be punching us in the face."

If a mortician had been in the room, he couldn't possibly have duplicated the corpse-like expression that painted over Wetterman's face. He found himself wishing that it was Friday. At least then there would be a remote chance that Shoemaker would pull a gun out from under the table and start blasting away. With any measure of luck, Biddle would be killed, or at least severely maimed, and the entire Ground Guide crisis would disappear.

"I'll go to Pittsburgh for training," Shoemaker offered. "Just make sure the seminar is on a weekend. I'm unwilling to leave my family at a time when I'm not at home with them to begin with."

Wetterman hollered, "Nobody is going to Pittsburgh!"
Norman glared.

Jack tapped his friend on the shoulder and begged him to calm down. "What Wetterman means is, all of our staff is too bogged down to attend seminars."

Norman squeezed his fists in contempt. Jack Snaggler was a menace. Even worse, he was friends with Nick Crowe, the bathroom janitor at Alfred's Diner. The cuisine in that place never tasted the same since Crowe got hired. There were more incidents of gastritis than there were crop circles in Glasgow, England.

"I'm just being reasonable." Jack cracked a wad of gum in his mouth. "We can handle all the technical gobbledygook here. Besides, seminars aren't the safest thing in the world. Just last week I read where a helicopter crashed in the desert during some sort of training exercise. One guy nearly got killed."

Greene said, "They were in the army and running a training drill, you idiot."

"Killed?" Norman asked.

"We can't risk it," Jack insisted.

A pencil snapped in Norman's fingers. "Who do you think you're talking to?" he shouted. Spit flew everywhere. Shoemaker pulled out a handkerchief and dabbed at his face in disgust. "I want you and Wetterman to report for Ground Guide training in Pittsburgh immediately."

"But..." Wetterman waved his hand in the air.

"But nothing!" Norman hurled a fountain pen across the room. It bounced off a table and hit Wetterman in the nose. "It's because of rabble-rousers like you and Snaggler that labor relations squeezed me into reinstating our vacation policy."

Shoemaker's eyes opened as if someone just detonated a grenade. Only a minute ago he looked relaxed, almost dreamy, as he stared at the ceiling tiles, undoubtedly fantasizing about some tropical escape away from his wife. In less than a heartbeat, all of that changed.

"You can't give people their vacations back," he spouted off. "My family is leaving for a cruise!"

"And you'll be on the boat with them." Norman slapped back. "Your wife filed a complaint with labor relations. Thank her for that one. With any luck you'll both drowned." He turned his attention to Wetterman. "Double our stock of Ground Guide material. If it isn't utilized properly, I'll have your head on a cookie sheet!"

Norman stood up, flung the conference room door open and stormed out.

Jack was astonished to see that the two men in sunglasses still stood in the hallway.

"You out there!" Jack pointed an accusing finger and pushed his way out of the room. By the time he reached the doorway, the two nameless thugs had vanished.

8

Pittsburgh by the Sea

Norman Cooley was adamant about Jack Snaggler and Bob Wetterman attending a training class in Pittsburgh. Within days, they stood on a street corner, suitcases in hand, poised to embark on a rigid Ground Guide seminar that didn't even exist.

"Ground Guide training in Pittsburgh?" Wetterman stared mindlessly into the blue sky. "I wonder if Rosa will send me postcards in prison."

"You're overacting," said Jack. "Cooley doesn't know anything. I'm more uneasy about the two thugs prowling around the place."

"The word is someone embezzled money from the company. They're going through all the books." Wetterman said. "This is a fine time to get caught up in a scandal. Cooley will hang us."

"Cooley is a lunatic," Jack reminded. "If someone breaks a leg and applies for workman's compensation, he thinks it's a federal offense."

Wetterman's face fell into a sinkhole of depression. "I have a cousin in Pittsburgh. Maybe he'll let us stay in the laundry room for a few days."

"Forget Pittsburgh. I'm not sniffing dirty underwear."

"What are you talking about?"

"I stopped in Alfred's Diner last night. Nick Crowe was there. He has friends that own a hotel called the Sea Sprocket in Ocean City. Crowe gave them a call and made arrangements for us to stay there."

"That's crazy," Wetterman said. "We're supposed to be at a Ground Guide seminar. We can't go on a vacation to the shore."

"Why?"

Why indeed, Wetterman pondered.

It wasn't as if anyone would miss them. Their jobs required no more thought than staring at blank walls or reading newspapers. The worse thing that could happen might be that Greene would steal a pack of cupcakes from their desks or Eileen Klump, released from the local mental facility and prone to outbursts of aggression, would smash their computer monitors with a broom handle.

The debate came to a halt when Drew Biddle drove up the street. His big white teeth reflected off the morning sun. He parked his car and jumped out with an overnight bag.

Wetterman's eyes widened. "What's Biddle doing here? For God's sake, don't let him know what we're up to."

"That might be difficult."

"What do you mean?"

"Cooley has trust issues with us," Jack said. "He thinks we'll pull a fast one and try to duck out on the seminar. Biddle was ordered to come and keep an eye on us."

Wetterman slapped his head in disbelief. "That guy can't come. He'll tell everyone!"

No argument there, Jack thought. Everyone in the office knew the guy was a stoolie.

Drew Biddle was employed as a filing clerk at the company. His office was located in the basement underneath the payroll department and appropriately nicknamed "the morgue". His job required him to update records of employees who had either quit, been terminated or were deceased. In the event that an employee leveled a lawsuit against the company, it was regarded as critical to keep meticulous – if not fabricated – files about the person in question to disprove any and all claims of wrongdoing that might surface.

Like a mole hiding in a darkened corner of a wall, Biddle periodically popped his head of his office to take a look around. One day he walked down the corridor and saw Norman Cooley's office door open. Biddle, not the brightest bulb in the pack, walked in to snoop around. He sat down at Cooley's desk to get a feel of what it must be like to be a big fish in a pool of underachievers. Biddle noticed a beautiful walnut cigar box sitting on the corner of the desk. Picking it up, he admired the fine workmanship. Engraved letters, *DADDY'S STASH,* were written on the side of the box.

Norman suddenly materialized at the door with fists planted firmly at his sides. He marched over and snapped the cigar box out of Biddle's hand. "What are you doing?"

Biddle jumped up like he sat on a nail. He tried to speak but nothing came out.

Norman's face turned fierce as a rabid dog. "You little mole, start talking or I'll stuff your head in a file cabinet and have the metal crunched."

Biddle snapped under the pressure. He cackled about Eileen Klump, a secretary suffering from periodic breakdowns and the detrimental effects it could pose on rising insurance rates. He warned about Shoemaker's secret desire to off his wife and cautioned about Wetterman, who in all likelihood, would be arrested on sexual harassment charges if Rosa Cruz ever figured out what he was saying to her. In one foul swipe, Biddle became Norman Cooley's personal stoolie. And now here he stood, overnight bag in hand and a dapper suit, embarking on a Ground Guide seminar that didn't exist. Trouble closed in around Jack and Wetterman like a pack of starved wolves.

"How much does Biddle know?" Wetterman questioned.

"Nothing. He still thinks we're headed to Pittsburgh for training classes."

Wetterman scratched his chin. "You really think he's stupid enough not to know the difference between downtown Pittsburgh and the beach?"

"Keep your voice down." Jack nudged him with an elbow. "Here he comes."

Drew Biddle sauntered down the pavement. He looked dapper as a penguin in a tuxedo. "It's a beautiful day for traveling." Sweating bullets, he loosened his tie and tossed his overnight bag in the back of a rental.

Jack handed Wetterman the car keys. "You drive and I'll navigate. Biddle can grab some sleep. He looks drained as a corpse."

Cursing and muttering, Wetterman jumped in the driver's seat. A moat of impending disaster dug across his face. Turning over the engine, he tromped on the gas pedal and darted down the road, almost as if he could outrun the idea of getting fired and standing on a bread line. Within minutes, Biddle fell asleep in the backseat of the vehicle and snored soundly.

The miles rushed by, and traveling down 1-95 South, they veered right on Coastal Highway. Soon tall billboard signs sprang up on the road. Advertisements promoted oceanfront bars, seafood shacks and white sands.

Slumped in the backseat like a beached whale, Biddle's eyes suddenly opened. He sniffed at the air. Confusion muddied his eyes. "I smell the stink of fish." He sniffed again. "Look over there." He blinked in confusion. "Isn't that a boardwalk?"

Jack shrugged nervously. "It could be a mirage. I read somewhere that Pittsburgh wants to invigorate the tourist trade by mimicking shore points."

"I read that too," Biddle lied, not wanting Jack to get one up on him.

Wetterman turned the corner on Atlantic Avenue. The highway was flooded with surf shops, nightclubs, and seafood eateries. A college brat rested her curves on the corner by an ice cream shop. She wore nothing but a smile and a sunburst bikini. Wetterman couldn't take his eyes off her and nearly ran over an old lady with a poodle crossing the street.

"Sorry Ma'am!" he shouted at the woman.

"Asshole." The old lady turned up her nose and kept walking.

Wetterman made a sharp turn on Rio Avenue. He came to an abrupt stop outside a seedy hotel called the Sea Sprocket. The place desperately needed a good paint job and a cleaning lady. A mouse ran out of the corner of the stucco and a drunken patron slept on a bench in front of the building.

"The place looks a little rundown," Wetterman said.

"Nonsense," Jack answered. "It's a quality establishment. Nick Crowe recommended this hotel."

Biddle's eyes darted around like a confused rodent. He pulled at his chin stubble. "Is this where they're holding the Ground Guide classes?"

Ignoring him, Jack grabbed his bags. "Park the car and follow me."

A Spanish woman sat at the front desk watching a soap opera and flossing her teeth. The air conditioner blinked out and beads of sweat dribbled down her neck as she fanned herself with a magazine.

Biddle blurted out, "Is there a discount for people in the Ground Guide program?"

The Spanish woman looked miffed.

"The name is Snaggler," Jack announced. "We called ahead."

"Senor, I don't see your name on the list. Your name must be on the list." She shoved the reservation book in front of his nose.

Wetterman grabbed a brochure off the desk and gawked around. Walking over to a snack table in the corner of the lobby, he picked up a stale donut with a dead fly stuck to it. A pot of aged coffee smelled like burnt rubber. "Your brochure advertises a delicious and free continental breakfast," he commented.

"Dig in," the Spanish woman at the front desk said dryly.

Jack twisted around irritably. "Our room reservations were confirmed by Nick Crowe. He's a friend of the owner. We were promised a discount."

"Crowe?" The Spanish woman tilted her head. "No Crowe here."

"There must be a mistake," Jack insisted.

"Senor, the bad news is that your name isn't on the list," she told him. "The good news is we have a room available on the third floor for $475.00 a night."

"That's false advertisement." Jack banged his fist on the desk. "Even without a discount, your brochure says the price is $150.00 a night." He picked up a pamphlet from the desk. "What about this picture of a woman in a bikini by a pool? I don't see any bikinis. I don't even see a pool."

The Spanish woman stuck her nose in the air. "That price is for clientele with reservations."

"But we made reservations!"

"Take it or leave it." She slammed the confirmation book closed. "I've got paying customers to attend to."

Drew Biddle straightened his tie and walked up to the desk. "Arguing is pointless. We're here so let's make the best of it. We'll take the accommodations." He pulled a company credit card out of his wallet and passed it to the desk attendant.

Wetterman tugged at Jack's shirt. "He can't pay for the room with that. The receipt will turn up at Cool Caps. We'll get fired."

"Is that true?" asked Jack. "Biddle has the company credit card. Is it our fault if he overstepped his boundaries in lieu of a day at the beach?"

Pulling a pen out of his spruce suit, Biddle signed for the room. By the time they finished checking into the hotel, the flies had eaten most of the leftover donuts on the continental breakfast tray. Wetterman had eaten the rest.

The elevator was broken so they took the stairs up to the third floor. The room inside was musty and dank. A cockroach roosted in the shower and a scream of horror from Biddle alerted everyone to the remnants of a used condom in the ashtray. He quickly retreated to the outside balcony and watched the waves roll in off the ocean as the wind tugged at his hair.

"I never realized Pittsburgh was so beautiful," he confessed and then turned his attention back to Jack. "Where do we register for the Ground Guide seminar?"

"Stop pressuring me," Jack snapped. "I'll give you the details the minute I think of them."

Wetterman picked a crumbled newspaper up off the night table. "This looks interesting. There's some sort of beauty pageant at Pedro's Cantina on the beach."

Jack snatched up the paper and shoved it in Biddle's face. "This is the place."

"Where does it say that?"Biddle reached for the paper but Jack tossed it over the balcony.

Wetterman slumped down on the bed. His head drooped like a glob of wet dough. "I wonder what Rosa is doing right now? She's probably stooped over the copy machine and wearing that cute little orange number that drives me crazy."

"Stop whining and step on it." Biddle walked in from the veranda and straightened his tie. "We don't want to make a bad impression by showing up late. I wonder if they'll serve lunch?"

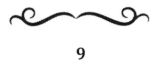

9

Pedro's Cantina

Pedro's Cantina was a hot spot on the beach. A punk band named Stinky Mulligan played earsplitting rock music to a rowdy mob. The singer sported multi-colored hair, a gold nose ring, and spit on the crowd. Everyone banged heads in a mosh pit and had a good time.

Drew Biddle grew agitated after some mope with a pierced tongue, howling like a wolf, shoved him aside.

"Didn't you tell me this was the registration area for Ground Guide training?" Sweat rolled down Biddle's neck. He loosened his tie and drank down a margarita. "You know, I'm no geography expert, but since when does Pittsburgh have oceanfront property?"

Ignoring his cohort, Jack ordered a drink.

Wetterman leaned on the bar and stared off into the horizon. Waves of depression rolled in his eyes. "Do you think Rosa even knows I'm not at work? I doubt it." He answered his own question. "She's out making love to a young stallion in some cheap motel room."

"Probably," Jack said and sipped his drink.

At the rear entrance of the bar, a gang of scantily dressed beauty contestants, mostly college preppies, pranced through the crowd and headed for the stage. The girls sported deep tans and perfect teeth. One of the brazen hussies pinched Biddle's rump as she trotted by.

Minutes later, an MC appeared and the competition commenced. Contestants had far less talent than superficial wares. A girl from Asbury Park even tried juggling oranges with her toes. With such a lack of aptitude hanging in the balance, contestants resorted to showing anything from belly diamonds to breast implants.

"YO BABY!" The crowd hooted and applauded.

The hot afternoon wore on. Biddle continued to slurp margaritas. By late afternoon his lips had the dexterity of a truck tire. He walked around and threatened to sue total strangers unless they directed him to the Ground Guide registration area.

A couple of floozies dressed in grass skirts and coconuts spotted Biddle's company credit card. Cozying up to him at the bar, one of them told him how handsome he was while the other nipped at his ear. Eventually Biddle loosened up. He flung his coat off and even stood up on a barstool and did a jig. Somewhere in the heat of the afternoon he disappeared with the bubbly broads.

"Biddle is more sauced than spaghetti at an Italian cookout," Wetterman said. "He just left with those women. We should find him before he gets into trouble."

A blonde female with an attitude boogied by and jiggled her valuables in Wetterman's face, then moved on. Wetterman scowled as if he got whacked with rotten tomatoes. His expression then turned airless and flat. "What am I doing here? If Rosa found out, she'd hate me." He put his head in his hands. "I thought if I ignored her long enough she'd notice me. It didn't work." He lamented.

Jack stared into the distance as the music roared.

"Are you listening?"

"Shut up." He put his hand over Wetterman's mouth.

"What's wrong?"

"Did you see that?"

"See what?"

"Those creeps from Cool Caps. They were standing by the stage."

Wetterman laughed. "You must be drunker than Biddle."

"I saw them!"

Pushing people out of the way, Jack made his way through the crowd. Finally he caught sight of the two hooligans over by the bar.

"Stop right there!" Jack pointed and shouted.

The men turned in unison. One adjusted his tie. The other peered over his sunglasses. Whispering to each other, they walked towards him. But the crowd, tight as two women in a mud wrestling bout, suddenly shifted and made breathing nearly impossible.

Up on stage, the MC eyed the side entrance of the stage and backed up two steps.

Jack's eyes widened. He wondered if he suffered from heatstroke. Dabbing his face with a napkin, he looked again, hoping the apparition would evaporate in the warm salty air.

It didn't.

From the side of the stage, Drew Biddle made a sudden entrance. Grinning wildly, he walked arm in arm with the two swank females who he met earlier on.

Biddle looked punchier than a boxer in a heavyweight fight. A proud capitalist and corporate wannabe, he spent the bulk of his income on business quarterlies that he never read and tailored suits that he didn't look good in. He was a man dedicated to the prosperity of the company, as long as that prosperity benefited his climb up the stairs of success. A personal stoolie to company powerhouses and CEO's, Biddle would squawk like a duck in a pond full of alligators if it meant a promotion.

Gone was the slick Armani suit he so arrogantly wore in hopes of impressing his superiors. The buttons on his crumpled shirt hung open and his unknotted tie flapped in the breeze. Even more disturbing, his stylish dress pants weren't just ruffled; they were gone altogether. Biddle pranced around in lime green boxer shorts and a black fishnet stocking that clung to his left leg like a leech. His mortifying presence was accented by burgundy panties that dangled around his neck like a string of love beads. If humiliation was a highway, Biddle was a squirrel dancing on the Philadelphia Expressway, about to get run over. Too inebriated to gauge the measure of his own disgrace, he staggered from one side of the stage to the next, laughing and snorting at the patrons.

The spirited crowd turned ugly. They shouted catcalls and waved fists in the air. What began as a harmless prank executed by a couple of impish women, quickly dissolved into a melting pot of anger.

"Have you lost your mind?" Jack shouted at Biddle. "Get off the stage before you're arrested."

The expression on Biddle's face looked no more responsive than a cardiac patient ten minutes after the resuscitation ended. Slopped over a margarita, he put his shaggy hips on display and even had the audacity to swirl them at the crowd. The two rascally women who led him into the spotlight quickly fled the scene. Alone and intoxicated, Biddle stood there, flapping in the breeze.

Making matters worse, Wetterman managed to crawl up on the stage and get to the MC's podium. He began shouting terms of endearment like "baby" and "snuggle bunny" through the microphone. "ROSA, my little petunia!" He poured out his liver. "Why the hell doesn't she love me?" Stomping his foot like a disturbed child, he sniffed back a tear.

"Wetterman!" Jack hollered. "Get down from there!"

Craning his head around, Jack saw the two brutish men from Cool Caps, their faces stiff as hardened concrete, pushing their way up through the middle of the crowd. They headed straight for him.

Jack pulled Wetterman off the stage by his shirt. Screaming Rosa's name every step of the way, he lugged his friend out the rear entrance of the bar only seconds before a squadron of cops in riot gear raided the place.

───

Back at the hotel, Jack was stunned to see a familiar vehicle in the parking lot. Hissing and spurting steam, a dusty pink jeep sat illegally parked in a handicapped spot near the entrance of the building. His worst fears were confirmed when he opened the door of the room.

Lounging on the veranda, Nick Crowe sunned himself in the summer heat. Showcasing knobby knees and skinny legs, he wore purple swim trunks and a hideous shirt that was stained with ketchup and mustard. A decal that read *BURGER ur BRAIN OUT at ALFRED'S DINER* was written on the back of his shirt.

Jack slanted his hands on his hips. "What are you doing here?"

Crowe dabbed suntan lotion on his cheeks. "Alfred gave me the day off. I took a ride to see how you bums were making out."

"How did you unlock the door?"

"The girl at the front desk gave me the key. I'm like royalty around here," Crowe boasted.

"She told me she never heard of you." Jack pushed an ashtray with a used condom in it across the table. "This place is a pigsty."

"You sound dismal."

Jack sat down on a chair beside Crowe. "It isn't just the room. I saw those two goons from Cool Caps. They're trailing us."

Crowe's eyes narrowed with suspicion. "The feds are here? Are you sure?"

"Positive," he insisted. "I spotted them at Pedro's Cantina. It can't be a coincidence."

"That's crazy." Crowe stood up and walked in the room. Jack followed behind him.

Unnerved by the day's events, Jack picked up the TV remote and flicked on the television. The local news reported on a riot at Pedro's Cantina during a beauty pageant. A newscaster cited one of the contestants as the source of the disturbance. Drew Biddle's face ballooned up on the screen. He waved drunkenly at the cameras as police hauled him away.

Jack turned the television back off.

Things were spinning out of control. Biddle's antics at Pedro's Cantina were just added bricks in the wall. Even more alarming was the unforeseen presence of the two federal men from Cool Caps.

Something stunk.

A loud knock interrupted Jack's train of thought. Wetterman was sprawled out on the bed with a wet rag over his eyes. Standing up, he walked to the door and opened it. A couple of serious looking cops with lantern jaws stood at the entranceway. One of them desperately needed a shave.

"Does this belong to you?" The officer stuck a toothpick in his mouth.

Dressed in a yellow rain slicker that said PROPERTY OF THE OCEAN CITY POLICE DEPT., Biddle stood in the doorway in the sweltering 100 degree heat. His pouty lips stuck out like water balloons that were ready to burst.

"This guy is a wiseacre." The cop gave Biddle a little slap in the head. "We don't like wiseacres."

"I'd like to shoot him." The other policeman concurred.

"Keep your friend under restraint. Next time we'll feed him to the sharks."

The cops slammed the door shut and left.

Biddle's face dented in disgrace. He folded his head in his hands. "This is a nightmare. The last thing I remember was having a drink with two women at the bar. After that, everything is a blur." He noticed Nick Crowe and paused. "What's he doing here?" A defensive edge roped his voice. "That guy was fired from Cool Caps. He's not welcome."

"It's good to see you too, Biddle." Crowe eyed Biddle's rain slicker. "What happened? Is the weatherman forecasting storms?"

Biddle flung open the rain slicker. He still wore a black fishnet stocking and burgundy panties draped around his neck. Wetterman gasped at the sight of it. "This is what happened!" He cried and quickly flapped the raincoat back shut. "If anyone sees me like this, I'll be deported to Miami as a male prostitute."

Nick Crowe crunched on a potato chip. "Norman Cooley wouldn't be happy. If word leaked out, it'd be a real blackeye on the company."

The color drained from Biddle's cheeks faster than a squeezed sponge. "He can never find out. I'd be fired on the spot."

"You're overreacting." Jack said. "Nobody has to know. When we get home, just tell everyone that the Ground Guide seminar was a success."

"And if I don't?"

"Things could get messy."

"What do you mean?"

"Arrest reports could turn up. You wouldn't want that humiliation."

"That's blackmail!" shouted Biddle. He blinked stupidly at the rolling waves of the sea. "I don't even think we're in Pittsburgh, let alone a seminar. How are we going to explain this?"

"Why ask us?" Jack picked at his teeth in a musty mirror. "You're the one buying drinks for cheap women and charging hotel rooms on the company credit card."

Biddle slumped down on the bed.

Jack eyed him with a measure of sympathy. Biddle worked hard to gain the respect of his superiors by undermining his fellow coworkers. It was a safe bet that getting arrested for indecent exposure would put a damper on that level of success. Before the week ended, he'd be standing on the breadline.

"I'm ruined," Biddle lamented.

"There's no sense bellyaching." Jack straightened his hair. "We only have one more night here. Make the best of it. Let's do something."

Wetterman wilted in his chair. "Forget it. I'm too stressed to do anything. I already called the front desk at Cool Caps, six times, just to hear Rosa's voice. Maybe I'll just take a walk on the beach and collect my thoughts." He picked up a bottle of tequila, headed out the door and melted into the seascape.

Jack's eyes slid in Biddle's direction, who continually fingered the women's undergarment draped around his neck.

"Would you stop that?"

"Stop what?" Biddle's face turned red as a clown's nose. Releasing the panties, he sheepishly folded his hands behind his back and cleared his throat. "Wetterman is right. We shouldn't be counterproductive by having a good time. I'm a little queasy anyway. Maybe I'll just stay here in the room and read a book or throw up."

Across the room, Crowe slapped his hand on a tabletop and stood up. "I'm up for some action. Besides, I'd like to checkout a few of the eateries on the boardwalk. When it comes to pizza, nobody slings a slab of dough like those Italian boys. I'd also like to take a look at the electrical systems in some of the shops. Confidentially," he lowered his voice as if someone cared, "we're not up to snuff at Alfred's. I wouldn't be surprised if the entire place burned to the ground."

Jack massaged his temples. Life had dissolved into a bowl of discontent.

Wetterman was in love with an illegal alien named Rosa, Biddle wore fishnet stockings, and Crowe, the stupid idiot, agonized over a diner where he served unpalatable food and scoured urinals for minimum wage.

"You're all mad!" Jack shouted and headed out the door.

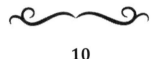

10

Flamingos

The sun slipped behind the sea and night took rise. Thousands of happy vacationers converged on the boardwalk. Kids stuffed their sticky faces with pink cotton candy. Teenagers screamed their lungs out on the rollercoaster, and a couple of hippies played guitars and begged for pennies on the beach.

Jack grew steadily edgy as a steak knife. It hadn't been just the antics of his friends that bothered him. Suspicious men in sunglasses were spying on him.

"What do you think the feds want?" Jack asked Crowe. His eyes shifted suspiciously up and down the boardwalk. "Whenever I turn around, they're hiding in a corner."

"Do you know how crazy you sound?" Crowe asked.

"Don't call me crazy!" Jack jumped up and down in his flip flops.

A woman with a toddler picked her kid up and quickly backed away.

"You're making a spectacle out of yourself." Sniffing at the salty air, Crowe took a deep breath and changed the subject. "Remember that girl you fell in love with at Eddie's Alamo Bar. What was her name, Paradise? What happened to her?"

Reaching in his shirt pocket, Jack pulled out a photo of the brunette. In a world filled with blind lust, Paradise was the only shining star in a muddy trench of fruitless love affairs.

Crowe laughed. "You still carry that picture around?"

Jack took a last look and stuffed it back in his pocket. "I'm not sure where she is, but I never forgot that night we met at Eddie's Alamo. Let me ask you something." He stopped walking. "Did you ever meet someone and get the feeling that you're supposed to be with them? I mean," he paused, "what about love at first sight and all that crap?"

Crowe shrugged. "It happens. People do it in pet stores all the time. They look at the kisser on some mutt and BANG! The next thing you know they're scooping up dog dirt from the backyard for the next ten or fifteen years."

"This is serious."

"I'm being serious," Crowe said. "Tell me the truth. What would you do to be with a woman like that?"

"Anything."

"You mean like, anything?"

"You heard me the first time."

Crowe nodded. "I'm going to remember you said that."

"What's that supposed to mean?"

Crowe didn't answer. His interest already wandered to another part of the boardwalk. The smell of oven fresh pizza carried from an Italian food shop called Cheezeroni's Cuisine. Bold as a winter storm, Crowe marched into the place and started snooping around. He even had the gall to walk behind one of the counters.

The proprietor, a guy with a waxed mustache named Antonio, tramped out from behind one of the bake ovens. "You're not allowed back here, dumbass." Twirling a clump of raw dough around, he nearly slapped Crowe in the head with it. "Are you some kind of terrorist?"

"Certainly not. I'm just here inspecting things." He sniffed the grill. "This is quite an operation you're running.

There's some undo grease buildup on the fryers, but it appears acceptable. What's the condition of your urinals and commodes?"

Antonio settled down. The last thing he needed to do was piss off a health inspector. He offered Crowe a tour of the pizza shop and even threw in a free meal.

"Forget the foodstuff." Jack tugged on his friend's shirt. "We have better things to do."

"Why don't you go ahead without me?" He sat down at a table with a red and white tablecloth. "I'm going to hobnob with the owner. Maybe get a few pointers on the fast food industry." He poured some oregano on a fat slice of Sicilian pizza that a waitress handed him.

Hanging his head, Jack sunk like a rock in a pond. All his friends had abandoned him, not for want of love, greed or raucous fun. He was dumped for a slice a pizza, burgundy panties, and an illegal alien named Rosa who couldn't speak English.

Jack stormed out the door.

Jack meandered along the crowded boardwalk. He stopped to buy a hot dog when a pigeon flew by and pooped on his head. Wiping at the gooey mess with a napkin, he looked up to see a young woman, dressed in black lace, and seated at a fortunetelling booth.

"Hey there." Her witchy eyes blinked. "I'm talking to you, sweet cheeks. Come on over. I'll read your fortune for fifty cents a finger. What do you say, cowboy?"

"The name is Jack."

"Whatever." She snapped five dollars from him and examined his fingers. "Your hands look soft and milky white. Perhaps you don't work for a living."

"I don't work for a living," Jack faced the truth, "but I pretend that I do."

The gypsy woman giggled. "You're grim as a corpse. Not too ugly though. Cheer up," she said, not very enthusiastically. "I see big changes in your life."

No secret there. If Norman Cooley found out they were tramping around Ocean City instead of a Ground Guide seminar in Pittsburgh, he'd be standing in the unemployment line.

"There's romance in your future. Have you ever been in love?" The gypsy picked at a piece of chive in her teeth.

Once again, Paradise danced in Jack's thoughts. "You're the fortuneteller. You tell me."

"A smart ass, huh?" The young woman pulled a handkerchief from her pocket and blew her nose, then grabbed a crystal ball off the top of an empty pizza box. Plunking it on the table, she studied it closely.

"This is a mystery," she said. "I see flamingos."

"Flamingos?"

The gypsy pointed to a darkened spot on the ball. "Right there!"

Jack looked closer. "I don't see flamingos. That looks like a dried up watermelon seed. What did you have for lunch?"

"It's flamingos!"Her nostrils flared with anger. She grabbed the crystal ball and tucked it underneath the table. "Next!"

"Is that all you're going to tell me? What about my five dollars?"

The gypsy's voice took on a southern drawl. "Back in Dallas where I come from, that barely buys a scrap of grits." Stuffing the loot in her bra, she walked away.

Jack trudged along the boardwalk like a lonely lover in the night. Regardless of her crass attitude, the fake gypsy was right. He needed a change. Even more, he could use a new outlook on life. The dream vacation had turned stale as bread and molded over with misfortune.

Out on the south pier, a clown with red lips danced to the music of a hip hop band. Teenage boys with pierced eyebrows chased the high school girls up and down the boardwalk. To make matters worse, some snotty kid whined to his mother about going on the bumper cars and spit out a wad of gum that was the size of a golf ball. Jack stepped in it. He bent down to clean the mess off his shoe with a napkin. When he stood back up, he noticed a fluorescent sign from a nightclub, next to an arcade. The name of the place was the FLAMINGO Bar.

Jack's thoughts instantly digressed back to the gypsy on the boardwalk. She mentioned a flamingo. He wondered if the phony medium stumbled on something by accident.

"Flamingo," he mouthed the word as he stared at the neon sign.

Tossing logic in the wind, he pulled out his wallet and shelled out a cover charge to some brute in a muscle shirt at the front door.

Inside, the bar was painted pink. A hippie with bushy sideburns sat on stage playing a blues tune and an old rummy snored on a corner chair. A woman with bad teeth and a tattoo of a skull on her neck nearly sucked the lips off some gruff guy in a motorcycle jacket. The place would have made a good advertisement for where not to go on a fabulous dream vacation.

Jack ordered a beer and stared at his reflection in a musty mirror. He could have been more entertained at a wake. No sooner than he sat down at the bar, he decided to head back to the hotel, but a new intrusion nearly made him jump out of his seat. Standing in the shadows like malignant spirits, over near the bathroom, he caught sight of the two federal agents again. The weight of their stare hung on him like a cement block.

Jack slammed his beer on the bar. "You over there. Show yourselves!"

"Hello there, lonesome." A blonde Polish woman, mid twenties, touched his arm from behind and made him jump. Her smile sparkled brighter than the gold ring in her bellybutton. "Are you a regular here?"

"No," Jack answered abruptly. Looking back towards the bathroom, the feds were gone again. He considered the idea that paranoia might be setting in. God knows he wouldn't be the first Cool Caps employee to see things that weren't there. Just last week he caught Eileen Klump talking to a water cooler about a sale on cumquats at the supermarket.

Jack turned his attention back to the Polish woman. "I'm on a company seminar to receive extensive training on Ground Guides."

The woman's eyes brightened. "Ground Guide training? That sounds exciting. What is it?"

Jack shook his head. "I don't know." He switched the subject. "Can I offer you a drink?"

"Make it a double." She corrected him. "I'm Cecile. Besides sunning by the water, I run a beauty salon in Deleware. It's nice getting away from all the hustle. The shore is so invigorating." She yawned and stretched. Her perky breasts sprang up in her blouse like ripe oranges.

Up on stage, the hippie playing the guitar finished up and a DJ in a tie-dyed shirt cranked up a sappy love song. The romantic beat hovered over the dance floor like a cloud of stale smoke.

"Would you like to dance?" Cecile nudged Jack.

Before he could answer, she grabbed his hand and pulled him out on the floor.

"I hope you don't think I'm promiscuous, but I need to ask." Cecile spread her curves over him like melted wax. "Did you ever make love to a Polish woman before?"

Jack shrugged. "We have a girl at work who has a fourth cousin from Poland. Sometimes she emails me dirty jokes, but I suppose that doesn't count."

"You're adorable." She smiled and fanned herself. "It's warm enough to broil a lobster. Want some air?"

Nodding, Jack followed Cecile outside.

Although Cecile bore no resemblance to Paradise, for the first time since his arrival, Jack began to relax. They rode the rollercoaster. Tossed balls at a man in a dunk tank. Kissed in the haunted house.

Walking arm in arm, Cecile stopped halfway up the boardwalk at a hotel called The Lagoon. A fake palm tree and an eight foot mannequin of a Jamaican surfer with big white teeth stood at the entranceway.

"This is my hotel. Would you like a drink?" she suggested. "I have rum."

Jack nodded. "That sounds like a plan."

11

Nibbles and the Sea Wench

The bed was covered in satin sheets and pictures of dolphins hung on the walls. Cecile went to the kitchenette and mixed Jack a rum and coke. She set it in front of him and tossed him the TV remote.

"Get comfortable," she said, then stepped into the bathroom.

Jack sat down on the bed and flicked on the television, casually sipping his rum. Things were going okay. Sure, it wasn't a romantic evening by the seaside with Paradise, but certainly better than listening to Wetterman bellyache about being in love with Rosa Cruz. Furthermore, Cecile had a nice wholesome quality. All in all, she was a breath of fresh air rising out of the ashes of the many superficial romances in his life.

A minute later he heard a doorknob turn. Cecile emerged from the bathroom wearing nothing but a fiery red negligee that highlighted every delicious curve of her body. Stricken by the sight, he nearly dropped his drink on the carpet.

She grabbed a beer out of the ice box and sat down beside him on the bed. "I hope I'm not being too forward." She rubbed her naked thigh against him. Taking a gulp from her bottle, she put a hand to her throat and let out a feminine belch.

"I like beer," Cecile announced. "Usually I skimp on meals so I can drink more of it without compromising my figure. Maybe I'm developing a problem."

"There's always AA," Jack suggested, visibly taken off guard by the woman's bold advance. "Perhaps you drink because you don't feel good about yourself."

"I don't feel good about myself," she confirmed.

Jack was stymied. How could he possibly tell the woman all of her problems when she already knew them?

All faults aside, an air of purity surrounded her. Cecile stared at him through half-lidded eyes, still green with purity despite the cruelties of a superficial world. In want of discovering her untapped sexuality, Jack warded off the temptation to take advantage of the woman, who staked her emotional hopes and blameless world of innocence on his every move.

"Maybe we should talk," Jack suggested.

"Talk." Cecile looked confused. "What's that?"

"Like what's your favorite flavor ice cream or perfume. Tell me a few things about you."

"Oh." Her eyes opened as if a light switched on. "You mean talk." She drained the last of her beer and sighed. "I'm suicidal," she confessed. "I lived on anti-depressants before my sixteenth birthday. My parents, both alcoholics, took me to countless psychologists, none of whom offered a solution. I decided to go to college, and just prior to flunking out, I went crazy. Sororities, nude hot tub parties, smoking grass and drinking beer were the norm. It's surprising that I wasn't diagnosed with some rare and deadly sex disease before the merrymaking ended." She kissed Jack's neck. "I guess I'm nothing but a lush and a bum, huh?"

"Yes," he agreed and sipped his rum.

In spite of a dismal past, Jack found himself strangely attracted to the young vixen. For one thing, it was wonderful to know that someone else's troubles were far more depressing than his own. For another, Cecile was so vulnerable and pathetic, if not himself, who in the world would ever want to take care of her if she lived?

"Make love to me," she whispered and nipped his ear.

If the door hadn't opened at that precise moment, Jack, smitten by her miserable existence, would have pulled off his t-shirt and did exactly as she asked.

A bird-like man, at least twice Cecile's age, walked in. He had teeth like a gopher and sucked gingerly at his lips. His anemic face had all the color of a bagged corpse left in cold storage.

"Hello pussycat," he said.

"Hi Nibbles." Cecile winked and turned to Jack. "This is Nibbles. If not for him, there's no telling what disarray my life would be in."

"Pleased to meet you," Jack said, not very seriously.

Nibbles nodded approvingly. "You kids look like you're getting ready to screw. Is that what you're going to do, screw?"

Jack shifted uncomfortably on the bed. He pretended not to hear Nibbles. Picking up his glass of rum, he intently studied a fabric softener commercial on the television.

Cecile belched again.

A hot rush of mortification burned in Jack's cheeks. Something had gone terribly amiss. The lonesome and depressed woman seated beside him wasn't as naïve as he first supposed. Furthermore, Nibbles had all the charm of an anemic frog.

Cecile whispered, "Don't be concerned about Nibbles. He's harmless. A few years ago he had a terrible automobile accident that left him impotent and wilted. He's truly a compassionate and sensitive man who deeply respects all human beings."

"Are you going to screw her or not?" Nibbles sounded cranky. He pulled a beer out of the ice box and flopped down on a chair alongside the bed. "The lighting is horrific in this place." He flicked on another lamp.

"He wants to watch?" Jack was aghast.

Paradise again illuminated the darkened corners of Jack's mind. He wondered what she was doing and dreamed about how nice it would be to hold her in his arms. But reality was a bullet, and bullets hurt. Instead of walking on a moonlit beach with the waves tickling their toes, he was tucked in a room with a depressed alcoholic female with suicidal tendencies as a slippery geezer named Nibbles scrutinized their every move.

"Perhaps I should leave."

"Don't be silly." Cecile licked his neck. "Nibbles, be a sweetheart. Would you mind waiting in another room?"

Nibbles grumbled miserably, walked in the bathroom and slammed the door shut.

Cecile instantly tackled Jack on the bed.

"Take me Romeo. Are we not spawning in a fishbowl, awaiting the fruits and passions of our lusts?"

Jack confessed, "I'm not even sure what spawning in a fishbowl means."

Cecile bit his neck hard.

"Ouch!"

A rustling noise from the corner of the room momentarily diverted Jack's attention. Nibbles again. The feisty creep sneaked out of the bathroom and had a camcorder. An extended zoom lens worked to capture every exotic point of interest.

Jack forcibly rolled the girl off him and jumped up. Cecile grew frustrated at the turn of events. She grabbed a half spent bottle of beer off the nightstand. Sipping at her drink, she dangled a naked thigh off the bed.

"Don't you people have any morals?" Jack yelled.

"No." Nibbles looked puzzled and set his camcorder down. "You're taking this too personal. This just happens to be my wife."

"Wife?"

"It's her birthday. Every year she gets a present. This year it just happened to be you."

Cecile lit a stale cigarette and carelessly blew smoke rings at the ceiling.

Jack threw his hands in the air. "Is there no shred of common decency left in the world? What would possess a man to take videos of his wife having sex with a total stranger? It's madness."

"Don't be such a boor." Nibbles snorted. "Everyone loves home movies. Not to mention, amateur adult videos have a killer profit margin on the streets." He took a swallow of beer. " As long as the monkey was out of the cage, why not make a few bucks?"

Jack made for the exit.

"It isn't as if I asked you to rob a bank." Nibbles grumbled. "At least come back and discuss it. We can order a pizza from Cheezeroni's. I'll even spring for the extra topping."

Bolting out of the room, Jack ran up the boardwalk in the middle of the night towards the Sea Sprocket as if the devil nipped at his heels.

Nick Crowe sat at a desk in the hotel room dabbling with a calculator when Jack burst through the door. His pallid face had all the markings of a man who just made the incorrigible decision to jump off the ledge of a building, headfirst.

"You look zombie white," Crowe said. "What happened?"

Pulling a jug of wine off the table, he drank it straight from the bottle. "A suicidal blonde Polish woman on antidepressants wanted me to participate in an adult movie. Can you believe it?"

"Do you get paid royalties?"

"You imbecile." He set the wine down. "I didn't do it. Some old coot named Nibbles wanted to watch. He even insisted on buying a pizza from Cheezeroni's, for God's sake."

"Well then you missed out," Crowe said smartly. "Cheezeroni's makes the best damn tomato pies on the beach."

"Why am I even talking to you?" Jack looked around the room. "Where is everyone?"

Crowe pointed at the veranda. "Biddle is out there. Don't disturb him. He's contemplating jumping."

Jack walked out on the veranda and found Biddle soaking up a warm wind as ocean waves crashed against the beach. More than once he slipped his hand in his khakis and fiddled with something.

"What are you doing out here?" Jack glanced down at Biddle's pants. "You're not wearing those burgundy panties from the beauty contest?"

"Why do you have to be so gruff?" Biddle shot back. "Don't you realize the embarrassment I suffered today?"

"Never mind that. Where did Wetterman go?"

Biddle pointed at a boardwalk bench. "The poor sap has been sitting there all night with a bottle of tequila. He keeps mumbling something about Rosa Cruz."

Wetterman sat on a bench with his arms folded around his knees and stared into the endless ocean. His eyes looked as directionless as a ship with a busted rudder. A few times he stopped vacationers and poured out his troubles to them, most of whom shunned him like he was an old souse. One guy even tossed him a nickel.

Pulling off his flip flops, Wetterman walked on the beach and into the sea.

"I think he's going to drown himself," Biddle concluded. "Love is a terrible vice."

Biddle was an idiot, but a prophetic one, Jack reasoned. Watching Wetterman sink into the bowels of the ocean only served to remind him of his own romantic woes, namely Paradise, the brunette from Eddie's Alamo. Despite the long passage of time since he last seen her, she wrapped around his heart and refused to loosen.

And now here he was. Instead of stargazing with the woman of his dreams, he found himself slouched over the railing of a balcony, conversing with a man dressed in women's undergarments.

Jack stepped back inside the room. Crowe remained seated at a desk and feverishly worked on something.

"What're you doing?"

Crowe banged his fist on the tabletop. "I'll tell you what. While you were out carousing, I've been productive." He tapped the calculator smartly. "Look at these figures! With the right funds, I could open a pizza parlor on any beach in the world and make a fortune at a buck a slice."

Jack lowered his head like a defeated boxer. The day ended just as it began: unstable. What had been slated as a getaway from the non-pressures of their daily jobs, now dissolved into a condiment of madness. Lying down on the bed, he tried to close his eyes.

Sometime before daybreak, Wetterman staggered back in the room. He carried an empty tequila bottle and sang sappy love songs in praise of Rosa Cruz. More than once he broke down and sobbed like a baby. Sometime during the night he curled up on the floor with the bugs and fell asleep.

Biddle slept stiff as a zombie, and when Jack finally woke, he considered the idea that the guy might be dead.

Opening his pasty eyes, Biddle sat on the edge of the bed as if a tiger crouched at his feet. He stared at a fishnet stocking draped over a desk chair. "Tell me it was all just a nightmare."

Irritable as a loose bowel, Wetterman grabbed the stocking and smacked Biddle in the nose with it. "Idiot. You were dancing around Pedro's Cantina like a wilted prostitute. If word leaks out, we'll all be fired."

Biddle's head shriveled in disgrace.

Crowe, a morning bird, woke before first light. Stuffing his clothes in an overnight bag, he readied himself to leave. He stepped over to the window and opened the curtains. Sun spilled in like the heavens and flooded the room. "It's a glorious day. Pack up. We need to get on the road."

"So get on the road." Jack threw a pillow at him. "You have a car."

Crowe said, "I blew a gasket on my way down. The garage towed my jeep away last night. There isn't a decent rental in town. I need a lift back to Pennsylvania."

Wetterman smacked his lips together. The bad taste of too much tequila clung to his tongue like dried cotton. "We should grab some coffee."

"Coffee?" Crowe stiffened. "There's no time for coffee. I need to get to the diner. The electrical system in that place is a fire hazard. Can you imagine what would happen if it went up in flames and I wasn't there?" He scooped up the keys. "I'll drive."

Within minutes, they were on the interstate. Crowe tromped on the gas pedal, weaving in and out of the passing lane at excessive speeds.

Not long after entering Pennsylvania, an automobile accident turned traffic to a dead stop. Crowe grew so agitated by the delay that he jumped out of the car and started yelling at a victim, even as the paramedics wheeled the guy into an ambulance.

"Is an insect eating your brain?" Wetterman asked. "You can't just run out on the road and start screaming. Jack, talk some sense into this numbskull."

However, Jack had his own problems. A vehicle in the next lane captured his attention. The passengers wore dark sunglasses and serious expressions. Stiff as dead bodies, they stared over at him.

Biddle leaned his head out the window and gawked. "Aren't they the guys that have been snooping around Cool Caps?"

"I saw them in the Flamingo Bar," Jack said. "It's the feds."

Wetterman shivered. "You really think they're following us?"

"Yeah, but I can't figure out why," Jack answered. "We haven't done anything wrong."

"If we weren't doing anything wrong, we wouldn't have been at the shore instead of pretending to attend a Ground Guide seminar," he reminded.

One of the men in sunglasses spit a wad of chewing gum out the window. It slapped Biddle on the nose, hung there for a frozen instant, then dropped on the ground.

"Did you see that?" Biddle wiped his face with his shirt. "He just spit on me. No wonder road rage is running rampant!" He balled up his fist and shook it.

Traffic started moving at a slow crawl. With a look of disdain and venomous as rattlesnakes, the feds pulled away in a ball of dust.

Keeping ample distance but not wasting time, Crowe stepped on the gas pedal and hurried down the highway. Within the hour, they arrived home.

Jack ran into his house and locked the door. More than once he peeked out from behind the curtains, certain that he'd see the two goons hiding in the shadows, but the streets remained empty.

Flopping down on the couch, he turned the television on. Casablanca played on the late movie network.

Jack's mind drifted and he wondered what new turmoil would rear its ugly head in the morning. Despite his dilemma, exhaustion outweighed the heaviness of his troubles and finally he fell asleep. All through the dark hours his dreams were like restless termites gnawing at the corners of his disconcerted mind.

12

Shoemaker and the Lovebird

While Jack and Wetterman were on a hiatus to Ocean City, Ed Shoemaker brewed in a bowl of contempt.

When management at Cool Caps reinstated the vacation policy, Shoemaker wanted to jump off a roof. Thanks to troublemakers like Snaggler and Wetterman, he was officially on leave for an entire week.

It would have come as a surprise to nobody if Shoemaker's wife and daughter had an unfortunate mishap during the family vacation. Bets were cast around the water cooler at work as to the method he might employ to off his wife. Employees and management alike expected to turn on CNN or some other major news affiliate and see his dismal face plastered across the big screen as the authorities leveled charges and hauled him away.

To prevent any mishaps, days before the cruise, Shoemaker secretly visited a psychotherapist. He sought advice on how to survive his wife's insufferable nagging and daughter's continual whining during the weeklong trip.

"Sedatives," Doctor Moon advised. He scribbled his initials on a paper and handed the prescription to Shoemaker.

"Most of my patients refer to them as happy pills. These things could anesthetize a horse."

Shoemaker vibrantly shook the doctor's hand. "I can't thank you enough. My wife has the personality of a stale bean."

"Please," Moon interrupted. "I'm married. Tell me something I don't know."

The cruise ship, named the Lovebird, was scheduled to set sail from Baltimore.

Upon arrival, Shoemaker's daughter insisted they eat at a sushi bar, if for no other reason, sushi made him nauseous. Much like the cuisine at Alfred's Diner, it brought on awkward bouts of gastritis.

After a grueling session in the bathroom, they hailed a cab to drive them to port. Upon exiting the taxi, Shoemaker's wife tossed an arsenal of luggage at him, and then yapped irritably in his ear when he lagged behind.

Still the vacation remained tolerable. The sedatives prescribed by Doctor Moon continued to bolster Shoemaker's endurance and neutralize an onslaught of nagging by his irksome family.

The first several days of the cruise he pretended to be asleep all the time, only sneaking out for food after his wife and daughter retired. Other times he found himself sniggering under the bed covers for no reason at all. He surmised that either the salty ocean air washed away his stress or the medication prescribed by Doctor Moon had further fogged his already anesthetized mind.

Whatever the reprieve, Shoemaker's fragile world of calm came to an abrupt end on the third night aboard the Lovebird when his wife stung him in the head with a bra strap, waking him from a sound sleep.

"What's this?" She held up the bottle of sedatives prescribed by Doctor Moon that she found while rummaging through her husband's personal belongings.

"Medicine," he said. "The ocean water gives me the runs."

"Don't lie to me, Ed Shoemaker," she warned, bra strap in hand.

"Drugs. Is that what you want me to say, I'm taking drugs?"

Shoemaker's daughter burst into tears. "My father is a junkie!"

"Here's what I think about your irritable bowel."

His wife marched over to the commode. She tossed the sedatives in the hole and flushed.

Shoemaker gasped. He raced to the toilet but his efforts were futile. Doctor Moon's happy pills, that minuscule link to an otherwise mournful existence, now rolled through a mass of dirty pipes that would be ultimately dumped in the sea.

The next few days proved more turbulent than the unsteady waves of the ocean. At dinner, his daughter complained to strangers about her father. His wife aided in the abuse by claiming she was married to an insensitive louse with a fetish for illegal narcotics. Any measure of rest became impossible. One morning Shoemaker woke to find that his daughter flung her panties across the room and they landed on his face. Bras and feminine hygiene utilities littered the cabin. He even found traces of his wife's clipped toenails in his shaving kit.

Stress, like a volcano, built.

One night, after his wife and daughter went out for the evening, Shoemaker woke up from pretending to be asleep. Grumbling to himself, he blamed most of his troubles on people like Jack Snaggler and Bob Wetterman. After the company cancelled vacations, the duo of ingrates fought to have the policy reinstated. Instead of sitting back at the office doing nothing, here he was, on the vacation of a lifetime, with a family that sported all the personality of a tree trunk.

Grabbing a pencil off the night table, he scribbled Snaggler and Wetterman's names across the wall beside his cot, then ended the graffiti with a dramatic exclamation point.

Tense as a stretched rubberband, Shoemaker decided to get some fresh air. He took a walk on the deck in hopes of staving off his irritation. Soon he found himself standing at the entrance of Shaky Jake's Rumba Lounge, an onboard dance club.

Inside the door, he caught sight of his tipsy wife mambo dancing on a tabletop. A foreigner with a shaved head and loud kabana shirt swung his hips against her to the beat of the music.

Shoemaker considered the idea that the foreigner might take a legitimate interest in his wife. Perhaps they'd even elope to Switzerland or some other remote part of the world, never to be heard from again. But logic dictated otherwise. After spending any length of time with the woman, who in their right mind would want her?

Making matters worse, Shoemaker's underage daughter stood over by the bar. She flirted with a cabin boy who found it impossible to stop touching her ass.

"Another round of margaritas!" his smashed wife yelled. She flashed a credit card around the room that had been filched from her husband's wallet.

Shoemaker rushed in and snatched the plastic card from his wife's hand. "Have you gone mad? You're draining my bank account!"

"Lighten up, imbecile." She sipped her drink then splashed the rest of it in her husband's face.

Shoemaker wiped himself with a napkin, all the while the festive crowd jeered and mocked.

"I'm leaving," he announced and stormed off like an angry bull.

"Where do you think you're going? You're on a boat in the middle of the ocean, you klutz," his wife mocked.

The foreigner with the shaved head repeatedly grabbed Shoemaker's arm as he made his exit. "I didn't know she was married, pal. She came up to me and wanted to get cozy. It's all good, right?"

"All good?" Shoemaker pulled his arm away. "Take her to a ranch and saddle her up like a mule for all I care. I'm leaving."

Shoemaker's wife stood up on a chair and pointed a finger from across the room. "Don't you dare disobey me and walk out that door."

Refusing to comply, Shoemaker turned and stuck his tongue out then hurried out the exit. His scorned wife dashed after him shouting obscenities every step of the way.

Outside the bar, Shoemaker slipped on a freshly scrubbed floor and did a tumbleset into a public hot tub. Two women in string bikinis drank champagne in the bubbly water. They screamed at Shoemaker's unexpected intrusion. Sopping wet, he quickly climbed out of the tub and kept moving.

Bystanders would later recount seeing a drenched man, giggling madly and answering to Shoemaker's description, run by them while an irate woman with a foul mouth and a lime margarita chased after him.

When Shoemaker's wife arrived back at the cabin, her husband was nowhere to be found. Crabby and drunk, she vowed to deal with him in the morning. Shoemaker's daughter spent the night with the cabin boy who kept touching her ass. She never did come home until after sunrise.

In the morning, after a shower, breakfast, a little shopping and sunbathing, Ed Shoemaker was still counted among the missing. His wife concluded it was time to alert security. The crew doggedly searched every inch of the ship but found no trace of the misplaced passenger.

Alarmed at the prospects of a lawsuit, the captain of the Lovebird notified the authorities about the mishap. Investigators met Shoemaker's wife at the next available port.

"Tell us everything." One of the detectives handed her a tissue to blow her nose. "Did your husband suffer from any emotional problems?"

"Sometimes he grew irritable." She snuffled. "It's almost as if something grated on his nerves. I found a controlled substance in his baggage. He was a non-recovering addict."

Witnesses onboard were detained and questioned. The foreigner with the shaved head attested to dancing in a bar with Shoemaker's wife on the night of the disappearance. "I didn't know his wife. She put the move on me in the bar," he told authorities. "The next thing I know she's balancing a margarita in her hand and chasing him across the main deck. I'm betting suicide."

Standing by the bow of the ship, Shoemaker's wife again burst into tears. Her whiny voice screeched like a wounded seagull.

"We're following all leads." The detective offered assurance and tried to shut her up. "If it's any consolation," he looked into the calm of the sea, "he's probably at peace now."

"Hey chief," the detective's partner hollered. He leaned over a rail around a hot tub near the portside of the ship, just outside Shaky Jake's Rumba Lounge. "I think you better take a look at this. There's something floating in the water."

13

Hill and Rupinski

Word of Shoemaker's disappearance spread like a gas fire in a field of dry weeds. The news speculated on anything from a terrorist abduction to suicide. Talk show hosts ran interviews with criminal psychologists, including a therapist named Doctor Moon who claimed to have treated Shoemaker for bouts of depression, just prior to his disappearance.

"I'm convinced that Mr. Shoemaker took his own life." Moon gingerly smiled at the camera. He repeatedly held up a book he wrote entitled, controversially enough, *Cracking Nuts*. "I'm not at liberty to divulge any of the specifics of our sessions, but it's reasonable to say that despite being equipped with the needed apparatus to survive in an otherwise hostile world, he just couldn't take the pressure." A grim vision of Shoemaker's wife assaulted Moon's thoughts. Who could blame the guy if he jumped?

Back at the office, Norman Cooley was elated at the turn of events. Not unlike Eileen Klump who periodically got locked up in a mental facility, he long suspected that Shoemaker would one day go berserk and inflict casualties. Metaphorically speaking, he dodged a bullet when the guy went overboard. Another pest had been swatted from the payroll.

A knock on the door interrupted Norman's train of thought. Sporting grim faces and black ties, the feds walked in. One of them removed his sunglasses. His granite jaw and stern expression was as uncompromising as a grizzly bear. Wiping off the lenses of his shades, he put them back on again. "We got problems," he told Norman and closed the door.

When Jack's phone rang at the office, Wetterman's shrill voice echoed on the other end of the line. "Are you listening? Those goons are in Cooley's office. They're asking questions. They think we have something to do with Shoemaker's disappearance. Our rap sheets are growing faster than gastritis lawsuits at Alfred's Diner."

"That's crazy."

"Is it?" Wetterman differed. "Shoemaker hated us. He told everyone we were out to get him because we fought to have the vacation policy reinstated just so he'd have to go on a cruise with his family."

"What's your point?"

"Shoemaker left port from Baltimore," Wetterman said. "Baltimore! We were supposed to be at a Ground Guide seminar in Pittsburgh. Instead we went to the shore in Maryland."

"I still don't get it."

"We have no alibi!"

Jack sipped his coffee and laughed. "You sound delusional. Just because we were in the same state as Shoemaker when he disappeared doesn't make us killers." His smile disintegrated when he looked up to see the two grim-faced thugs headed straight for his desk. "I'll call you back," he told Wetterman and slammed the phone down. Folding his hands on the desk, he cleared his throat. "Can I help you gentlemen?"

"Mr. Snaggler." One of the men nodded and removed his sunglasses. A dense fog of suspicion clouded his eyes. "We'd like to ask you a few questions." He pulled out an identification card.

"I knew it. You guys are feds."

"This is Agent Rupinski." He pointed at his partner. "My name is Hill."

"Rupinski and Hill." Jack nodded. "That sounds like a law firm or plumbing business."

Rupinski wasn't amused. Hill looked even less entertained.

They motioned Jack towards the door. "That way."

The feds led Jack into a small conference room at the end of the hall. Minutes later Wetterman and Drew Biddle were ushered in. Slamming the door shut, they stared at Jack.

"Mind if I smoke?" Agent Rupinski pulled out a pack of filterless cigarettes.

"Yes," Jack answered and glared when Rupinski lit up. "What's this all about?"

Hill sat on the conference table and crossed his legs. "What does the name Ed Shoemaker mean to you?"

Wetterman's face turned white as powder. "He wasn't a bad guy, God bless him. Last week he borrowed five dollars off me for lunch. That's money that'll never be recovered."

"Shut up!" Agent Rupinski turned suddenly fierce and slapped Wetterman in the head.

Jack backed up in alarm. "Isn't that police brutality?"

Rupinski and Hill didn't answer. Both eyed him with contempt.

Agent Hill walked around the table and stared out the window. "Three days ago aboard a cruise ship called the Lovebird, Shoemaker vanished without a trace. Can you explain that?"

"Why should I explain? Maybe he jumped. Have you met his wife?"

Hill turned to Jack. "You think you're cute, huh?" He opened his jacket and tapped on the handle of a gun holstered on his side.

Jack's eyes opened wide.

Hill closed up his jacket again and straightened his tie. "We're convinced this wasn't a suicide." Motioning to his partner, Agent Rupinski opened a briefcase sitting on a chair. He pulled out a billfold and slid it across the table.

"You know what this is?"

"It looks like a wallet." Biddle chimed in.

"You idiot," Hill said. "Of course it's a wallet. It belonged to Shoemaker. Along with some soggy vacation brochures, it was found floating in a hot tub outside of a bar on the cruise ship."

Wetterman scratched his head. "I don't see what that has to do with us."

Agent Rupinski grabbed a clump of Wetterman's hair and shook it. "Do you think we're stupid?"

Escaping the feds' grasp, Wetterman retreated and cowered behind Jack.

"You're going too easy on these pukes," Rupinski barked at Agent Hill. "I'd like to twist their heads off with a wrench."

Agent Hill eyed his partner with disdain. Nope. He really didn't like the guy. Rupinski's disposition had all the grace of a hippopotamus in a birdbath. He was most likely one of those kids who wanted to be popular but got eaten alive by his classmates. Ruddy skin and yellow teeth from too many cigarettes couldn't have done much for the guy's sex life, either. He was an angry bastard, alright. Joining the agency was probably his answer to legally shoot somebody.

"Take a laxative," Hill told his partner. "I'll handle this."

Puffing like an Alaskan chimney, Agent Rupinski sat down.

"I want you guys to take a look at something." Hill pulled out a photo taken from Shoemaker's cabin on the cruise ship. Scribbled on the walls were words like

Vacation... Enemies
Snaggler and Wetterman

"Shoemaker wrote this before he disappeared. It's as if he wanted to leave a clue about who snuffed him."

Sweat dampened Wetterman's forehead; he dabbed at it with a handkerchief. "This is a nightmare. Outside of a few friendly football wagers or glancing at Rosa Cruz stooped over the copy machine, I never did anything illegal."

"The same goes for me." Biddle stuck his nose in the air. "I shouldn't even be here. These guys are troublemakers. I wouldn't be caught dead around them."

"Is that true?" Agent Hill held up a tabloid paper lying on the table. "Recognize anyone?"

Like a lost ghost floating out of the shadows, there it was again. The paper reported on a riot at a beauty pageant in Ocean City. Biddle's face was splashed underneath the headline. A black fishnet stocking that added a permanent blemish to his disintegrating life, clung to his lily white leg.

"Degenerate." Agent Rupinski spit on Biddle.

"That isn't me!"

"Don't lie." Agent Rupinski grabbed the paper and swatted him on the nose. "We have a copy of your arrest report."

Jack snapped to Biddle's defense. "So what if he wears women's clothes? It's not like he killed somebody. As for this thing." He grabbed the photo of Shoemaker's cabin and examined the graffiti on the walls. "This doesn't even look like our names."

Wetterman shrugged. "It looks like our names to me."

"Shut up." Jack slugged him in the arm then turned his attention back to Agent Hill. "I'm confused. Why are you guys singling us out? We didn't break any laws. We're just office workers at a bottling company trying to earn an honest wage."

Hill laughed. "You call snoring at a desk all day an honest wage? You should be arrested for impersonating a log." Sucking on a pencil eraser, he stared holes in Jack's head. "Relax," he said. "Nobody has to know about your little seaside hiatus. All we want is some information."

"I told you," Jack said. "We don't know anything."

Agent Hill turned to Biddle. "I'd like to have a word alone with these guys."

Biddle leaned forward in his chair and folded his fingers on the table. "By all means, go ahead."

"Moron," Agent Rupinski said. "He means get out. Now beat it."

Shaking in his shoes, Biddle got to his feet and bolted out the door.

"Why does Biddle get to leave?" Wetterman questioned.

"He's no criminal," Agent Hill said. "He's just stupid and got mixed up with the bad element."

"You keep rubbing our faces in the dirt." Jack slammed his fist on the table and stood up. "While you're badgering us, real killers like Boris Crane are walking the streets."

Agent Hill put his hand on Jack's shoulder and pushed him back down in the chair. "Sit down." He glared as if he wanted to take a bite out of his throat. "There's something I want you to hear." Agent Hill nodded at Rupinski.

Agent Rupinski pulled out a small handheld recorder and slid it across the table. Flipping a switch, Hill turned it on.

"Crowe, you slacker, are you there? It's Lance... Lance Sheppard."

"I told you not to call me on this line. It might be bugged."

"We got trouble. The feds are at Cool Caps. They're going through the books."

"You worry too much. It's better if they're occupied. We got other concerns." Crowe said. "I think I found the package."

"You mean..."

"Don't say it."

"What do we do now?"

"Keep calm. I have a plan. We might need some outside help to pull it off. What do you think about Jack Snaggler?"

"Snaggler?" Sheppard laughed. "He's a desk jockey at a bottling company. You must be crazy."

"Of course I am." Crowe answered.

"Give it to me straight," Sheppard asked. "What's the plan?"

"Not now. Like I told you, the line might be bugged."

"Whatever," Sheppard grumbled, "but you better get us out of this mess. The way things are going I might as well go bunk with Shoemaker's wife. Ha! I heard his family is making him go on vacation with them, the poor bastard."

"Don't worry about Shoemaker. He's resilient as an alley cat. He'll find an escape hatch," Crowe paused, "even if it kills him."

Agent Hill flicked the recorder off. "Heard enough? We recorded that conversation a week before Shoemaker disappeared."

Jack's eyes drooped. Whatever sludge Crowe and Sheppard were playing in, oozed his way.

Agent Hill walked to the window. The sun shined brightly through it in contrast to his dark eyes. "Forget Shoemaker." He shifted gears. "There's ways around that. We might even clear the charges or at least give you a reduced prison sentence. What we're really interested in is your friend."

"Friend?"

"Nick Crowe, the janitor up at that fleabag diner on the edge of town. He turned up in Ocean City when you guys were there screwing the company. What do you know about him?"

Jack's head turned in confusion. "What's to know? He flips burgers and cleans toilets."

"He's pals with Lance Sheppard," Agent Hill said. "If Crowe is a sink, Sheppard is the scum around the faucet. They're up to something. You two cruds are connected." His eyes clicked over Jack and then Wetterman.

"That's ludicrous," Jack said. "I don't know anything about Sheppard aside from him sustaining imaginary injuries on the job. He's been collecting workman's compensation for a nonexistent injury ever since. That's not illegal. Half the schleps in town do it every day. If you want to investigate someone with a real criminal history, go see Alfred up at the diner," Jack continued. "Rumor has it he's in cahoots with the mob. Nobody even knows his last name!"

"Alfred doesn't have a last name," Hill said. "It got canceled."

"Cancelled?"

Agent Hill tapped his foot anxiously. "We're not here to talk about Alfred's genealogy or subpar menu. We need information on Crowe and Sheppard. They're sinking fast. You guys are tied to the anchor."

"But we didn't do anything!"

"You're lying." Hill lurched forward and bared his teeth. "You both smell rancid as rotten eggs."

"I could vomit just looking at them." Agent Rupinski crumpled his face.

Agent Hill walked to the door. Rupinski joined him.

"We'll have to do things the hard way," Hill said and glanced at Agent Rupinski, who fingered the weapon in his pocket. "When the bullets start to fly, you'll be in the line of fire."

"But..."

Hill nudged his partner and they both disappeared out the door.

112

14

Eileen Klump's Secret

With the possible homicide of Ed Shoemaker and a couple of feds shaking up the corporation, anxiety mounted like a hill of rocks.

Office personnel were jumpy. If coworkers were arrested, workloads would shift. People who spent the bulk of their afternoons reading newspapers or talking to their wives and mistresses on the phone would be expected to pick up the slack. Hours once filled with late starts and extra long lunches would turn abruptly productive. Instead of a cup of coffee and a donut on their desks in the morning, they'd find purchasing requisitions requiring immediate attention.

Drew Biddle was so spooked that he refused to come out of his office at all. He propped a chair against the door in hopes of warding off unwelcome visitors. His morbid face, pocked with craters of mistrust, nibbled at cheese sandwiches and waited for the moment when the authorities would break down the door and haul him away.

The only person unmoved by the presence of the feds was Eileen Klump. While the rest of the office buzzed about Shoemaker's disappearance off a cruise ship, earthquakes in San Francisco and unconfirmed sightings of a killer named Boris

Crane, Eileen dusted shelves and made coffee. She had no interest in federal agents and generally speaking, didn't acknowledge their existence. Once she even breezed by Agent Hill and dusted him off with a feather mop.

"What's wrong with her?" Hill wiped at his head. "Right now she's over at the water cooler, putting duct tape around the fountain. She thinks it's a leaky pipe. She's crazy."

"No she isn't," Norman Cooley insisted and turned green with mortification when he heard Hill's comment. "She's as sane as everyone else."

Norman shuddered at his recent encounters with the Klump woman. Recently she sued the company on the grounds that work pressure pushed her to a mental collapse. Lawyers argued that Klump was psychologically pocked before she got hired but the efforts were fruitless. In the end, Eileen was awarded a substantial settlement. The company was also required to provide medicinal support or needed therapy for any future occurrences.

Bitter over the settlement, Norman paced the floor on many of long, sleepless nights. He vowed that if he could ever prove that Eileen Klump was remotely competent, he'd appeal the courts, sue for fraudulence, and have her escorted off the property. In the interim, she'd receive poor performance reviews and no pay raises. If he couldn't get her to quit, he vowed to starve her out by way of attrition.

"She just wants a free ride," Norman told Agent Hill. "She's as stable as everyone else."

Agent Hill looked around the room at a sea of dismal faces. One of them had a pencil eraser stuck in his nose.

"You're making my point for me, Cooley," said Hill.

Jack had his own speculations about Eileen Klump. He assumed that one day she'd be dragged away to some undetermined mental institution, never to be heard from again. All of that changed on the morning he accidentally bumped into her over by the coffee pot.

"Oops." Jack backed up.

Coworkers held a collective breath. Eileen was as predictable as a cornered animal when confronted with any happenstance that breached her unordinary world. They wondered if Jack's inadvertent run-in with the unstable woman would lead to still another outing with the men in white coats and an intermittent stay in wonderland.

Jack froze like an ice cube. "Pardon me."

Eileen said nothing. At first it appeared she didn't notice the intrusion. She stood beside a plastic bottle of non-dairy creamer sitting on top of a microwave jabbering to an imaginary friend about a soap opera.

Following Eileen's lead, Jack went about his business. He ignored the woman. It wasn't until he reached for the coffee pot that she grabbed his wrist.

Her dark eyes swam with sharks, ready to bite. She glanced around the room and whispered in his ear, "I'm not crazy. Don't tell anyone or they'll fire me." Releasing his wrist, she skipped off and disappeared into the supply closet.

Jack stared uncertainly. For an instant he questioned whether or not the woman spoke to him at all or if she was just a hallucination brought on by the pressures of his daily job. Shaking off the incident, he sat down at his desk. A minute later, Wetterman barged in. His eyes were ghosted with dread.

"The feds are back. I saw them walking the halls. I'm telling you, they're going to ride us like mules until we confess."

"Confess to what? They can't lock us up just because Shoemaker decided to take a swim in the ocean," Jack insisted. "We're innocent."

Wetterman looked confident as a squirrel under a truck tire. He sat down beside Jack's desk. Black sacks, the size of rotted potatoes, drooped under his eyes.

"You look awful," Jack said.

"I haven't slept much. It isn't just the feds," he admitted.

"What's wrong?"

"Promise not to laugh?"

Jack chuckled. "Of course not."

"I've been having nightmares." He lowered his voice. "I keep dreaming about being assaulted by a banana with a cowboy hat."

"A banana?"

"His name is Paso."

"A banana?" Jack repeated.

Worry chalked across Wetterman's face. "The entire thing reeks of sexual tension. You don't suppose I'm," he gulped, "gay?"

Jack slid his chair backwards. "Now you're talking silly. You hold the record when it comes to things like falling in love with Rosa, and she doesn't even speak English."

"Did you ever dream about a thing like that?"

"A banana with a cowboy hat?" Jack retorted. "Don't be ridiculous. I just wanted to make you feel better."

Shadows of depression fell over Wetterman's face. "That's what I thought."

The front door of the office opened. Norman Cooley walked in. The feds were with him.

Biting nervously at his lip, Wetterman's eyes darted from side to side, searching for an exit. Finding none, he jumped out of his chair, zipped across the floor and ducked in the supply closet.

Norman peered over the top of his glasses and stared at Jack. "Doing nothing again?"

"Yes sir," Jack answered nervously.

The feds looked around the room. Employees' heads nodded up and down as if they were bobbing for apples.

Absorbed in a hypnotic state, they fought off the compulsion to sleep brought on by the fixation of blank computer screens.

"Doing nothing seems to be the norm around here," Agent Hill commented. He glanced suspiciously at Greene, who sat at his desk, picking his teeth and mumbling something about a cancelled vacation to Las Vegas. "What's wrong with that guy?"

"He's an ungrateful louse." Norman looked over at Greene. The guy was a freaking stick of dynamite. It wouldn't take much to light the fuse. "I suspended everyone's vacation this year but had to reinstate it after Shoemaker's wife threatened to take me to labor relations. I decided to negotiate the issue and make employees with ten years service eligible for time off. Greene missed the mark by two months. He had to cancel his reservations to Las Vegas where he was meeting some buddies, probably to pickup prostitutes. Ha! When he hits the ten year service mark, I'm thinking of raising the magic number to eleven, just to irritate him."

"That ought to do it," Hill agreed.

Norman's cell phone rang.

"Yes?" he answered. "What?" He paused. "Speak English, for God's sake." He ended the call and shoved the phone in his pocket. "There's no talking to that woman."

"Who?" asked Agent Hill.

"Rosa Cruz, the front desk receptionist. You can't understand a word she says. She's Mexican."

"A foreigner?" Hill pulled out a pen and jotted her name down on a notepad. "You might be harboring an illegal alien. Businesses get fined or shutdown every day for that. We'll run a check on her. Maybe have her deported."

An awkward moan came from the direction of the supply closet.

"What was that?" Agent Rupinski blinked. "It sounds like somebody's sick."

Norman wrinkled his nose. "Gastritis, no doubt. There's a fast food place up the road called Alfred's that delivers takeout food. That rat hole caused more bowel disorders than a virus during flu season."

Glancing at his Rolex, Norman hurried out the door.

Turning his attention to Jack, Agent Hill picked up a mug on the corner of the desk that bore the insignia of a Las Vegas casino. "Another crap shooter, huh?" the fed said smartly. "You can forget about rolling any dice for awhile. Much like your pal Greene over there," he pointed, "all vacation plans are terminated."

From across the room, Greene expelled a vulgar noise that sounded like someone with a bad case of gas and then blew his nose in a tissue.

Jack fidgeted in his seat. The feds were needling him like a skunk caught in a garbage can. He'd love to pour ammonia on their heads. "What do you guys want from me?"

"Don't play dumb. Please don't play dumb." Agent Hill crossed his arms and tightened his fists. "You heard the recording of Crowe and Sheppard talking. They mentioned your name and something about a package."

"I already told you," said Jack. "I don't know anything."

Agent Hill opened his mouth to counter, but a tussling noise inside the supply closet interrupted him again.

Agent Rupinski walked over to the door and jiggled the handle. "It won't open. Must be something propped up against it."

Hill turned to Jack. "What's in the closet?"

"Office supplies?"

Agent Rupinski marched back across the floor, picked up a file folder, and swatted Jack on the head. "Smart ass!"

Jack crumpled up in his chair. "What was that for?"

"We do the talking here." Hill popped a breath mint in his mouth. "I don't see the problem, Snaggler." He anxiously tapped his foot. "All we want is a little cooperation, right? Nick Crowe is a janitor, not the president. The last thing you want is a stint in the state pen for a guy like that."

"What do you want me to say?" Jack angrily slapped a pencil down on his desk. "I don't know anything about Crowe or a stupid package. Look at me." He spread his arms open. "Do I look guilty?"

Hill and Rupinski stared like zombies.

Another BANG from inside the supply closet disrupted the steady rise of tension in the room.

Hot coals of infuriation spread across Agent Rupinski's face. He marched over to the closet and pounded his fist on the door. "Open up in there or I'll break it down!"

Everything turned silent. The door creaked open. Agent Rupinski guardedly stuck his head inside.

In the corner of the room, Wetterman was crouched up behind a file cabinet. Eileen stood a few feet away, jabbering to a coat hanger. The sight was so disarming that Agent Rupinski instantly reached for his weapon.

"Nobody move!"

Eileen pointed a stern finger. "You can't be in here. The principal's office is off limits."

"What are you talking about? We're not in high school." Agent Rupinski scratched at the back of his neck and for a moment appeared uncertain.

Eileen picked up a broom and shooed Rupinski over to where Agent Hill stood.

"You can't shove us around." Agent Rupinski jumped up and down on his heels. "We're here on official business. I'll have your job!"

Eileen jabbed the broom handle at him again. "One more outburst and you'll be writing *I AM BAD* one-hundred times on the blackboard. Now get out." She prodded them out the front door of the office, slamming it shut in their faces.

The feds stood outside in a steady rain. Agent Rupinski scratched his head and tried to decipher what happened.

On the other side of the room, Wetterman crawled out of the supply closet on his hands and knees. His hair was mussed like a used mop. He looked like he just inadvertently stepped in a minefield.

Jack pulled his friend off the floor. "What happened in there?"

"Eileen accosted me." Wetterman's cheeks were white as paint. "If the door wouldn't have opened, we'd be making love on a file cabinet right now." He glanced across the room to where Eileen stood. She picked up a feather duster and spruced up the place, all the while fluttering her fake eyelashes at him. "She told me that she's in love with me and wants to elope to Egg Harbor. What the hell is Egg Harbor? She's crazy!"

"She's not crazy," Jack differed. "She's only pretending."

"Why would she pretend something like that?"

"Who knows, but I was over by the water cooler earlier. She told me she was faking it."

"And what did the feds want?" Wetterman asked.

"Information on Nick Crowe."

Wetterman's face morphed into anger. "I knew that creep was involved."

"We need to pay him a visit," Jack said. "Maybe he has some answers. Meanwhile avoid looking suspicious. We don't want to attract unwanted attention."

Eileen walked over with a mop, stopped for an instant and pinched Wetterman's cheek, then continued on about her business.

Wetterman shrunk in a chair like he was kissed by a Medusa. He didn't move again until the buzzer sounded to go home.

15

Nick Crowe

Just after dark, Jack and Wetterman drove to Alfred's Diner. The parking lot was empty when they arrived. Alfred, the owner, featured a menu of gristly meats and imitation caviar. The place bustled with about as much excitement as a fermented corpse.

Inside the building, the tables were wiped clean due to a steady lack of business. Outside of a guy with lopsided sideburns picking his nose, you couldn't buy a paying customer.

Nick Crowe stood behind a counter wearing a wrinkled chef's hat and a white shirt stained with grease. Preoccupied with the condition of the commodes, he strolled over to the restroom, peeked in, then returned to his register. He grinned larger than Texas when Jack and Wetterman walked in the front door.

"Can I help you guys?" he asked. "Today's special includes an Alfred Burger Deluxe sandwich with three blends of burger magic cheese and sauces, including America and Swiss, and a delectable flavoring of..."

"You imbecile," Wetterman said. "We're not here for food."

Crowe tilted his head questionably. "I don't understand. Is there a problem with the menu?"

Jack glanced over at the guy with the lopsided sideburns. He had a dribble of chili running down his chin. Not unlike Eileen Klump, he giggled at nothing and at times engaged in conversations with inanimate objects such as the salt shaker.

Alfred, the proprietor, poked his grey head out of his office. He darted his eyes suspiciously around the room, then much like a gopher, disappeared back in his hole.

Jack whispered, "We need to talk privately. Meet me in the bathroom."

"Can't this wait?" Crowe set down a dirty dish towel. "We're getting ready for customer appreciation night. I'm up to my ankles in grease. It's a big event." He emphasized, "A very big event."

"Forget the diner. We got bigger problems." Jack walked towards the restroom.

Alarm smeared over Crowe's face, almost as if an evil ghost might float up from one of the connecting sewer pipes. He pushed Jack aside and raced in the bathroom ahead of him.

"What's wrong with you?" asked Jack.

Crowe snooped under the stalls, looked around the room, and then tossed his apron on the floor. "I just scoured the place. You're going to mess things up."

Jack leaned on the sink. "The feds are asking questions about you."

Crowe stopped cold. "Me?"

"They had a recording of you and Lance Sheppard talking about some kind of package. Your phone must be bugged."

"Package?" Crowe nervously dabbed at a smudge on the mirror beside the paper towels. "You're delusional. I already told you. Boris Crane was spotted in the area. He's on the hit list for the FBI. They're probably following up on some leads."

Wetterman stomped his foot. "Don't play stupid. Crane has nothing to do with this. The feds are watching us. I even had to hide in a supply closet with Eileen Klump to get away from them."

Crowe dripped with sympathy. "You shouldn't badmouth Eileen. Can't you see how difficult of time she's having pretending she's crazy?"

Jack lurched forward. "How do you know she's faking?"

"All I'm saying is the woman has issues. Okay, so she talks to walls. I blame Norman Cooley for her mental state, that bastard." He spit on the floor in distaste then immediately pulled a rag out of his back pocket and cleaned it up.

Jack rubbed his temples. "Forget about Eileen. Let's try and talk intelligently. We're under surveillance. Isn't any of that registering in your brain?" He slapped Crowe in the back of the head.

"I don't see what any of this has to do with me. Unlike the rest of you flunkies, I work in a respectable business and have a highly regarded position." He unraveled a few squares of toilet tissue and dabbed at a rogue sprinkle on the seat of a commode. "Besides, even if this were true, outside of joining Shoemaker at the bottom of an ocean, what could we do about it?"

The restroom door suddenly opened. It was Alfred. He popped his head inside like a nosy gerbil. "What's going on in here?"

"Nothing," Crowe answered nervously. "The customers were just complimenting us on our facilities."

"I'm running a business here, not a bus stop. Stop lollygagging." Alfred snorted and slammed the door shut.

Crowe put his apron back on. "You're gonna get me fired. That's the last thing I need right now. I'm gaining valuable information here. Trust me." He stuck his jaw out confidently. "Before I'm finished, you'll never have to work at a bottling company again."

"You're talking in circles." Jack fumed. "I need some answers."

The lights flickered from a glitch in the electrical system.

"We'll talk about this later," Crowe said and hurried out the door.

"Don't walk away from me, you screwball!" Wetterman shouted and chased after him.

Jack lingered in the restroom. For an instant the sensation of being watched overcame him. Looking around, the place was empty.

Sitting down on a commode, he tiredly rubbed his knuckles over his eyes. Alone in the privacy of the empty bathroom, he began to appreciate the seclusion that people like Dan Rupert, the HR man at Cool Caps, experienced while roosting in such havens.

The strain of the day wore on him like an old shoe. His eyelids grew heavy. Dangerous thoughts of people like Agent Hill and Rupinski momentarily melted off his shoulders.

Jack remembered being a teenager, green as summer. As a kid he didn't have to think about brutish CEO's or irritable federal agents in mirrored sunglasses. Back then the biggest challenge in life was learning how to effectively waste time by skipping a rocks over a pond or tossing around a basketball in the back alley. It occurred to him that as the years progressed, few revisions were applied to that logic. Now a member of the corporate world, but much as in childhood, he still invented new ways to do nothing all day long.

Seconds or minutes, Jack didn't know how long he sat there, but he began to daydream. If for just an instant, he went back to a simpler time.

16

Life under the Apple Tree

"Pst," someone whispered.

Jack looked up and an apple whacked him in the head. Seated on a tree branch, Wetterman sucked on a piece of bark.

"What's the big idea?" Jack rubbed his noggin.

"Keep your voice down and climb up. I've got something to show you."

Planting his PF Flyer sneakers in a wedge of bark, Jack shimmied up the tree. About halfway to the top he found Wetterman hidden behind some leaves.

"Outside of being a wiseacre, what are you doing up here?"

"Quiet." He peered through binoculars. "You can see right into Debbie Abernathy's bedroom from here. She's with Stinky Mason. The stupid ox is trying to undo her bra."

Jack grabbed the binoculars out of Wetterman's hand.

Inside the house, Debbie had her lilac colored blouse halfway removed. Stinky pulled at the catch on the girl's bra but his efforts were futile. Annoyed with his failed stab at manhood, the girl turned around and whacked him in the head with a bottle of cheap perfume.

"Things are getting ugly in there," said Jack.

A noise from a neighboring yard momentarily distracted their attention.

Jack lowered the binoculars. "What is that?"

"Take a look over there." Wetterman pointed. "That kid is squirrely as a box of worms."

Across the street, Eileen Klump played in her mother's bean garden. She held a rag doll. One minute she hugged it. The next she nearly knocked its head off on the fence. Already flirting with mental instability, she trotted over to a lawnmower and started talking to it.

"I'm miffed." Wetterman swatted a mosquito off his neck. "I bounced apples off that girl's head for weeks. Every time I clobber her she looks a little more unhinged." He plucked an apple from the tree." Watch this."

"Are you sniffing glue?" Jack stayed his hand. "She's more unbalanced than a squirrel on rollerskates. She'll slap you silly if she catches you."

Ignoring his friend, Wetterman wound up like a major league pitcher and fired the nasty little greenie, full force. The apple clunked off the girl's head with a dull thud.

Eileen froze. For an instant she seemed unsure whether the incident happened at all. A minute later she continued playing with her doll and chatting with the neighbor's dog, who looked equally as mystified by the girl's behavior.

"See what I'm talking about?" Wetterman nodded excitedly. "That's not normal. Do you think she's crazy or just stupid?" He plucked another apple off the tree.

"You're being a regular ass and begging for trouble," Jack said. Then after a moment of consideration, "Go ahead. Do it again."

Zeroing in on his target and tied in the grip of temptation, Wetterman fired another apple.

Smack!

Another direct hit.

Eileen turned crimson with anger. She stomped on the ground and let out a dreadful cry.

The boys snickered behind bunches of leaves.

Wetterman picked up the binoculars and turned his attention back to Debbie Abernathy's bedroom window. Stinky Mason still bumbled with the girl's bra. Suddenly it unhooked. Dribbling at the mouth, he removed the straps from her shoulders. Debbie giggled like a young virgin, a condition that would be short-lived long before she ever reached high school.

Wetterman's jaw dropped. "The clumsy oaf did it."

"Really?" Jack's eyes widened. "What's going on now?"

"I'm not sure. There could be trouble."

"Trouble?"

Wetterman's face turned from a bucket of glee to a swamp of doubt. "I think Stinky seen me staring at him through the binoculars."

Jack gasped. "Are you sure? What's he doing now?"

"He's looking back at me and slapping the window with Debbie Abernathy's bra."

In a sudden burst, Stinky raced from the window, bolted down the stairs, and shot out the kitchen door like a cannonball.

Up in the bedroom, Debbie hung out the window holding a raspberry towel over her budding breasts and screamed vulgarities at the peeping toms.

"The bull is on the loose!" Wetterman sounded the alarm.

Stinky barreled over a neighbor's fence. The veins of his neck stood out like telephone wire. Clutching at the empty remnants of Debbie's bra, he waved it angrily in the air. "I'll twist your scrawny necks off!"

Wetterman shivered like a wet dog and scurried down the tree trunk.

Climbing down the tree, Jack accidentally stepped on his friend's head. Both boys tumbled to the ground, all the while Stinky Mason, his arms stretched out and ready for ringing, made his approach.

Nick Crowe, a squirrely kid from over on 4th street, set up a makeshift food stand constructed of cardboard boxes. Counted among his delicacies was a pot of guacamole that he filched from a church bizarre.

"Get your ice cold lemonade and guacamole, fresh off the farm. Guacamole I said!" His voice rang out like a hot dog vendor at a ballgame.

Adjacent the food stand, Ed Shoemaker sat on a bicycle in Bermuda shorts. He picked at a clump of the icky stuff on a paper plate. A girl with a snotty face stood beside him. Bellyaching about something, she repeatedly punched him in the arm and slapped him with a piece of licorice.

In later years, Jack would sometimes reflect back on that day as he observed Shoemaker's sour pus as the irksome girl badgered him. That same offensive little girl would grow up to be an equally obnoxious woman. Shoemaker ultimately married her. Later his wife gave birth to a troubled and spoiled daughter with a fetish for nose rings and thong panties. In the end, Shoemaker's fortune rested not so much in treasuring a family who was about as adoring as a squid in a swimming pool, but moreover, on the day he fell overboard a cruise ship called the Lovebird in the middle of the ocean.

Stinky Mason charged ahead like a loose bull at a fiesta.

Wetterman picked up a rock and hurled it at the bully to slow his advance. It was a clean miss. The stone ricocheted off a trashcan and hit the windshield of a delivery van from Alfred's Diner. The van swerved and collided into Nick Crowe's food stand. The pot of guacamole flew up in the air, splattered everywhere, including on Shoemaker's head.

"Run!" Wetterman hollered.

Out of nowhere, Eileen Klump shot from her yard like a bullet. The enraged girl tackled Wetterman in the street. Kicking and throwing wild punches, her assault continued until a group of alarmed adults dragged her off him.

In the years that followed, Jack later noted, similar episodes would plague Eileen's life. Only then instead of concerned parents stifling an irritable child, the peacemakers would arrive in the form of men in white coats dispatched from the local mental facility.

On the other side of the street, Jack rounded the corner but slipped in a gob of guacamole. He did a tumbleset to the ground and banged his head on the road. Jack tried to stand up but Stinky, hot in pursuit, pushed him back in the dirt with the heel of his boot. The bully angrily snapped the strap of Debbie Abernathy's vacated bra in his face.

A police cruiser with flashing lights rounded the corner and came to a screeching halt.

"You there." A cop with a toothpick in his mouth jumped out of the car. "Lower your weapon."

Stinky stepped back. Mumbling a few threatening words, he kicked a rock in Jack's face and walked away.

Jack pushed himself up on skinned elbows and blinked the fog from his head. Captured in a ray of sunlight, he saw a young brunette. She wore pink knee high socks and rollerskates. A ringlet of dark hair hugged her neck and her eyes were bluer than the summer sky. A faint trace of perfume, perhaps pinched from her mother's vanity, drifted in the wind.

"Are you okay?" The brunette asked. She smiled and Jack grew warm all over.

"I'll live."

"Why was that kid snapping a bra in your face?"

He shrugged. "Probably a salesman."

A glow of emotion strung itself across Jack's heart. One look in her eyes left him speechless. Smitten by the brunette's beauty and given his shyness around the opposite sex, making intelligent conversation was about as likely as eating a bowl of Nick Crowe's guacamole.

When Jack finally mustered the guts to speak, Alfred, the delivery van's driver, marched over and grabbed him by the scruff of the neck.

"You little hoodlum. Did you throw a rock?" Alfred slapped him in the back of the head. "Admit it. You threw a rock."

"No!"

"Don't lie." He slapped him again. "Someone could have got killed. My delivery van looks like a broken sewer pipe!" Gobs of guacamole splattered the windshield.

Ignoring the verbal spanking, Jack looked around.

Across the street, green foodstuff dripped off Shoemaker's nose. He wiped at it with a napkin all the while his rude girlfriend, a portrait of disrespect, nagged him about being a clumsy oaf.

To the left of him, the brunette in the knee high socks and rollerskates looked on.

"Move it along," the cop with the toothpick in his mouth told the brunette.

The girl smiled at Jack and then skated down the pavement. Jack's eyes followed her until she rounded a corner and disappeared.

"Are you listening?" Alfred shook Jack by the shoulders. "Wake up!" he ranted, all the while Jack stared at the empty space that was occupied by the brunette with the blue eyes, only seconds ago.

17

The Great Escape

"Are you listening, you slacker? This isn't a park bench for bums!" Alfred shouted.

Jack's eyes flipped open. For a minute he didn't know where he was. Evidently he had dozed off in the restroom of the diner. The proprietor walked in and heard him snoring.

Alfred kicked the stall door. "I'm not running a hotel for vagrants. Zip it up," he yelled again and stormed off.

Jack rubbed his eyes with his knuckles. The last thing he remembered was talking to Nick Crowe about the feds. Agent Rupinski and Hill were like bloodhounds. They wouldn't stop until they sniffed out a criminal, or in his case, victim.

Regardless of his plight, only one name echoed in his mind. It was the brunette with the pink knee high socks and rollerskates in his dream: Paradise.

Time and again, the girl had slipped into his life and then just as quickly slipped back out again. It seemed inevitable that sooner or later destiny would be on his side. The feds, on the other hand, would not.

Jack's eyes rolled down to the floor to find something even more disturbing. He didn't see it there before. Picking it up, he examined it closely. Someone kicked a tropical island brochure underneath his stall. A cold shiver brushed down his spine. For an instant he entertained thoughts that Ed Shoemaker, shriveled at the bottom of the dark sea, had returned from the dead.

A creeping noise outside the stall door alerted him to the idea that he wasn't alone. Someone must have wandered in the restroom. He heard them pacing the floor.

Jack put his ear against the stall door. "Who's out there?"

The pacing abruptly stopped. Whoever it was walked over and jiggled the door handle.

"Open up," a voice whispered.

Jack froze.

"I said open the door. Don't make me ask again."

Jack heard the hammer of a gun being pulled back. He searched his pockets for a weapon but the only thing he could find was a used tissue and a pack of breath mints.

Just as he was about to bolt out of the stall and run, the wail of police sirens cracked the silence outside.

"We know you're in there," someone shouted in a bullhorn. "Come out with your hands in the air."

Jack's heart raced. Gathering his courage, he stood up and flung the door open. He was about to race out the door but stopped. A familiar face stood across the room.

"Sheppard!" Jack shouted. "Stop right there!"

Turning around, Lance Sheppard winked and gave a wily grin. "You didn't see me here," he said. Without another word, he climbed out the window and disappeared into the darkness.

Jack ran out the door to where Crowe busied himself cleaning spatters of fat off the walls in the kitchen. Breathing deeply, he said, "Lance Sheppard is in the bathroom."

Crowe stared. "It's a restroom facility," he reminded.

Jack knocked his fist against a bake oven. "You don't understand. When he heard the cops coming, he climbed out the window and ran off into the woods."

"Cops?" Crowe blinked. "What cops?"

"Open your eyes." He pointed out the window. "The place is surrounded!"

"That's ridiculous," Crowe insisted. "We serve free donuts to the police like all the other food joints in town. They're here for a handout."

Crowe's logic wasn't only blind; it was nonsensical. If the facts didn't fit he simply pretended they didn't exist. Regardless of a flood of edgy policemen pointing loaded guns, Crowe had a job to do, and by God, the grease fryers were going to get scoured if it killed him.

Jack grabbed him by the apron. "You're hiding something."

"That's nuts."

"What about this?" Jack held up a vacation brochure to the Fiji Islands. "I found this on the bathroom floor. It looks like one of Shoemaker's pamphlets. He must be back in town."

"Shoemaker fell off a boat in the middle of the ocean. It must have been a long swim." Crow laughed and scrubbed a splotch of dried cheese off the pizza oven. "He made regular stops here. He probably dropped it on his last visit before you and Wetterman allegedly shoved him overboard."

"We're innocent!"

"Of course you are." Crowe appeased.

Wetterman plastered his face against the front window. Police cruisers littered the parking lot. Red and blue rotary lights flashed off surrounding trees. The feds had also joined the raid. They barked orders to the local cops.

"They have the place roped off." Wetterman turned to Crowe. "What did you do!"

Crowe chewed fiercely at his bottom lip. His face, once painted with confidence, was now spattered with uncertainty.

"There must be some mistake. We were cited last week for a violation on our electrical system, but that doesn't warrant a SWAT team."

"Don't be brainless," Jack said. "The cops are here to arrest Lance Sheppard, or us, or maybe both. We need to surrender."

Regaining composure, Crowe straightened his uniform and thrust out a defiant jaw. "I'm not going anywhere. You're under investigation for pushing Shoemaker off a cruise ship, but what about me? Outside of failing to report a few electrical problems, I'm innocent." He stuck his nose in the air. "If they want me, they'll have to come and get me. Now if you'll excuse me, I have burgers to burn and commodes to sanitize." Knotting his apron, he went back to work.

Turning his attention outside, Jack saw Agent Hill and his partner Rupinski run to the rear of the building. They hunkered down behind a garbage dumpster near the window where Lance Sheppard had fled.

"We're hemmed in." Jack's heart rattled.

Crowe continued fiddling with a grease fryer. "Remember to keep your hands in a non-threatening position. If you're lucky, they'll only maim you in the leg." He held up a pound of fatty beef that wasn't put away after the last shift. "Now look at this. The meat is spoiled. It's impossible to get good help these days."

Wetterman's face, stitched with worry, yanked in mixed directions of fright. "Tell him to shut up," he begged Jack. "Please tell him to shut up before I'm arrested on another murder charge. He's crazy."

Taking a deep breath, Jack opened the front door and raised his hands in the air. "Don't shoot. We're coming out."

Flanked by Wetterman, the two men walked slowly into the parking lot. The air was stagnant as death and skunked with tension.

A young cop ducked down behind the open door of a police cruiser. A gun shivered in his hand as if he were holding a block of ice.

"Officer..." Jack said.

"Beat it, dweeb." The cop snubbed him. "We got a situation unfolding."

"But..."

A dark figure suddenly bolted from behind a shed on the far side of the building. Graceful as a ballerina, the perp jumped over a garbage can, rolled twice in the dirt, then raced into a wooded area behind the diner.

Spotlights combed the forest. Jack got a glimpse of the unidentified person running into the darkness of the trees. Direct from Alfred's restroom facilities, Lance Sheppard took flight.

"Rabbit on the run!" Agent Hill shouted and pointed.

Flashlights shined in the thick of the woods. A couple of hounds sniffed the ground and rumbled ahead in pursuit. The rookie cop grabbed Jack by the shirt and flung him aside. Spitting out a piece of gum, he ran and joined the chase.

The parking lot was suddenly empty.

Wetterman raised an eyebrow. "What happened?"

Jack scratched his head in confusion.

No logical answer existed. The cops were obviously hunting for Sheppard. But the mud went deeper and like quicksand, he found himself getting caught in the sludge.

Jack and Wetterman jumped in the car. Turning the ignition, the tires spun in the gravel as they took off down the road.

Traffic on the highway was sparse. More than once Jack glanced in the rearview mirror but there was no sign of pursuit. He drove on side roads, often with the headlights off, until they arrived home.

After dropping Wetterman off, a migraine chiseled away at Jack's head. He popped a couple of aspirin and flopped down on the couch. Flicking on the TV, a local news station reported on a mugging downtown, another sighting of Boris Crane, war in the Middle East and a global state of terrorism. Even those misfortunes couldn't make him feel better about his miserable life.

Yawning, he pulled a flimsy blanket off the back of the chair and covered up. Sometime after 3:00 in the morning he fell asleep. Dreams were as fast moving as a river. He envisioned federal agents with dark glasses who went by names like Hill and Rupinski. He screamed out loud twice when apparitions of Biddle sashaying around in fishnet stockings invaded his thoughts.

Still most of his dreams focused on Paradise, the brunette from Eddie's Alamo. Just a passing glimpse of the young woman brightened even the darkest corners of his mind.

When the alarm sounded in the morning, he was curled up on the sofa with a pillow over his face and a blanket twisted around him like a pretzel. The sun gleamed in a musty window and the television was still on. A criminal psychologist with black glasses and messy hair profiled Boris Crane, a notorious killer who terrorized the eastern seaboard.

"Crane had a tortured childhood. He got bullied in highschool. Along the way he lost his grip on reality. People like him act out their sick obsessions." The shrink crossed his legs. "Case in point, last week in Ocean City during a beauty pageant, a man wearing a fishnet stocking with burgundy panties wrapped around his neck walked on stage and..."

Jack flicked the television off.

Unshaved and wrinkled, he heated up some leftover coffee in the microwave and headed out the door for work.

Uncertainty swam in his head like crazed sharks on a feeding frenzy. All indications were that he'd be booked and fingerprinted within the hour.

18

Embezzlers

Norman Cooley paced the floors in his office.

Agent's Hill and Rupinski leaned against a desk. They removed their trademark sunglasses for an instant. Their eyes, immovable and cold as a glacier, stared at him.

"We almost nabbed the little puke last night." Hill said. "He was at that fleabag diner but gave us the slip. Snaggler and Wetterman were there too. Something stinks worse than the food in that place."

Sitting down, Norman looked at a financial report lying on his desk and reviewed expenditures for the last several weeks.

During a company audit, he had stumbled on a major payroll discrepancy. The feds stepped in to investigate. A paper trail led back to Lance Sheppard, a former employee who left the company to pursue greener pastures in the form of disability benefits.

That's when the trouble started.

A computer glitch never removed Sheppard's name from the payroll. He had been collecting a lavish salary, big bonuses, and an unlimited expense account.

"I'm paying this guy like he owns Manhattan and he doesn't even work here!" Norman slammed his fist on the desk.

"God knows how many other people are getting paid to do nothing."

Agent Hill snorted. "My guess is everyone. You got more dead wood working here than there are spuds in Idaho."

Norman pulled at the few strands of hair left on his head. "Can things get any worse?"

Agent Rupinski handed him a newspaper clipping. "Try this."

The article reported on a riot in Ocean City. A drunkard staggered onstage during a beauty pageant. Underneath the headline, Drew Biddle's picture shot off the printed page. Burgundy panties were draped around his neck like a string of love beads.

"Instead of a Ground Guide seminar in Pittsburgh, your boys took a detour to the beach," Agent Rupinski said. "Nick Crowe, the janitor at Alfred's, showed up."

Norman stood up and kicked a file cabinet. "I want them arrested!"

"We can't do that," Agent Hill said. "These guys are shysters. They could even be mixed up in Shoemaker's disappearance. After we nail them, you can boil them in a lobster pit for all we care. In the meantime, play stupid. That shouldn't be difficult."

Norman took a deep breath and sat down. A wire of tension slithered down his neck. "What about the fiasco at Alfred's last night? People will ask questions."

"That's covered." Hill said. "The news has unconfirmed reports of Boris Crane in the neighborhood. He's wanted from Miami to Boston on murder raps. Far as anyone knows, we responded to an anonymous tip about a killer spotted in the vicinity."

"That should keep people happy." Norman sighed in relief.

Hill and Rupinski walked to the door.

"Remember, one slip and the entire investigation gets submarined," Hill warned.

Straightening his tie, he motioned to Rupinski and they both disappeared down the hall.

Jack glanced at Shoemaker's vacated desk. Pulling out the crumbled vacation brochure that he found in the diner, he again wondered if Shoemaker might be alive. More mysterious was Lance Sheppard's exodus out the bathroom window of the diner at the sound of approaching police sirens.

Something stunk.

Wetterman walked in the door and sat down next to Jack. He looked more dejected than a homeless vagrant on a city street corner. Rings of sleeplessness corroded his eyes. "Things are too quiet."

"Don't jump to conclusions," Jack pulled a bagel out of a paper bag and passed it to him.

Wetterman angrily slapped the foodstuff from his hand. The bagel flew across the office and came to a stop in the middle of the floor. "Would you stop with the food? I got something to tell you." He nodded his head hopefully. "Channel 16 News is reporting that Boris Crane was in the area. The feds must have been chasing him last night."

"Get serious." Jack dashed his hopes. "Crane is just a cover story. Sheppard was hiding out in the diner. When he heard the cops coming, he crawled out the window and disappeared in the woods."

Wetterman said nothing.

"Are you listening?"

"Trouble." He motioned towards the middle of the room.

Eileen stood there, hands on her hips. She stared at the bagel on the floor. Aiming a pointy shoe, she kicked the foodstuff across the room like a soccer ball. It ricocheted off Greene's head and came to rest on Shoemaker's empty desk. She glared at Jack, then shifting to Wetterman, her icy eyes thawed. Batting her lashes, she walked over towards the supply closet.

"What happened when you got locked in there with her?" asked Jack. "Did you..."

"No! But she probably thinks we did. Anyone who has conversations with water coolers could easily fantasize about making love in a closet."

Jack shook his head dismally. "That's sad. Eileen didn't lose her virginity and she doesn't even know it. Maybe you should..."

"Don't even think it." Wetterman cringed. "I only have eyes for Rosa."

Jack eyed his friend with sympathy. Wetterman's love for Rosa was solid as a slab of granite; nothing could crack it. Just the idea of another woman trying to seduce him made him feel faithless. More than once he considered confessing all his shortcomings to Rosa, even though she was no more aware of his presence than a fossil buried under the ice in Antarctica.

"Maybe you should tell Eileen that you don't love her," Jack suggested.

"Are you crazy? Last time she nearly pummeled me on a filing cabinet."

Jack shook Wetterman by the shoulders. "Straighten up. She's on the verge of pretending to have another nervous breakdown. If you ignore her, she'll start screaming. Is that what you want, for her to scream? We're already in trouble. That'll only make for more unwanted attention."

Wetterman tilted his head to the left and whispered, "Eileen isn't the only sick duck in the lake."

Jack's eyes shifted in Greene's direction. The guy's hair stood straight up like a crop of alfalfa. When the company canceled all vacations, Greene literally fell to pieces. Stiff as a rock, he sat at his desk and stared at a nonrefundable airline ticket to Las Vegas. At times he giggled sinisterly. Other times he cursed under his breath. Finally he picked up a newsletter with Norman Cooley's picture on the cover and jabbed holes in it with a pencil.

"That guy is a keg of dynamite," Jack said. "He's ready to detonate."

From across the room, a crumbled up piece of paper unexpectedly hit Wetterman on the nose.

Eileen again.

"She's staring at me," Wetterman whispered without moving his lips.

"You're gonna have to talk to her," Jack insisted. "Let her down easy."

Grumbling, Wetterman finally stood up. Like a man walking to the gallows, he approached Eileen. Whispering something in her ear, they both went inside the supply closet to talk privately.

Jack listened.

Everything grew quiet. Eileen either took Wetterman's rejection calmly or perhaps in some other altered state of mind, it hadn't yet registered.

The question was abruptly answered when Jack heard a loud bang as if someone's head got bounced off a wall. The door of the supply closet flew open. Wetterman got tossed out of the room like a sack of trash. He quickly crawled across the floor toward Jack and hid under his desk.

Eileen stormed out of the closet wielding a dirty mop. "How dare you pretend to love me." She poked Wetterman in the ribs with the handle. "I offered to meet you at Egg Harbor, and this is the thanks?"

"I don't even know where Egg Harbor is!"

Eileen swung her mop and smacked Wetterman in the mouth. Jack sat in the line of fire and also got swabbed. The entire office stopped doing nothing and looked up.

Bending down, Eileen squeezed Jack's cheeks like a tomato. Glancing from side to side, she grinned and whispered, "Just remember, buster. This is all part of the PLAN."

Jack pulled away. "What are you talking about? What plan?"

"Don't be an idiot. You know what I'm talking about."

"You're crazy!"

"You think so? Do you?" Eileen giggled. "Why don't you call the men in the white coats?" She dared him. "Go ahead. Call them."

Jack shifted nervously in his chair. "That won't be necessary Eileen. You're as stable as everyone else here."

Across the room, Greene looked up from his desk and mumbled something about Las Vegas. Picking up a ballpoint pen, he fiercely jabbed another hole in Norman Cooley's picture on the company newsletter.

Eileen grabbed a letter opener off Jack's desk and waved it in his face. "You guys are gutless." Reaching past Jack she pinched Wetterman's nose. "I'll be seeing you in Egg Harbor, sweet cheeks."

Tossing the letter opener on the desk, Eileen walked away. She stopped long enough to whisper something in Greene's ear, who regardless of her delicate condition, told her to shut the hell up and get lost.

Wetterman shivered. "She really is crazy."

"No she isn't," Jack disagreed. "She only wants people to think that she is. She practically begged me to call mental health and have her taken away."

"Maybe it's a cry for help." Wetterman guessed.

"Or a plea for disability compensation."

"You really think she's conning everyone?"

"She's up to something."

On the other side of the room, Greene left out a loud groan. Submersed in anger, he milled his teeth together like a meat grinder. He picked up the newsletter with Cooley's photo on it, tore it to shreds, and tossed it in the air like a ball of confetti. Getting up from his desk, he kicked the front door open and stormed off.

Wetterman stood up and stuffed his hands in his pockets. "Everything is snowballing around us. The feds are moving in for the kill. Even Rosa Cruz thinks we're guilty, and she doesn't speak English."

Jack bit the skin around his fingernails. It was true. He and Wetterman were victims of a malicious system. The feds didn't view that as an alibi. Agent Hill and his partner Rupinski were convinced that they were involved in Shoemaker's disappearance.

It occurred to Jack that in the end, nobody really knew what happened to Shoemaker on that night aboard the Lovebird. The only thing certain was that without his obnoxious wife breathing down his neck, he had to be happier.

"Don't talk stupid," Jack said to Wetterman. "The feds don't have any concrete evidence. They can't arrest us." Doubt flaked in his voice.

Wetterman's chin drooped to the floor. He looked up to see Eileen lingering over by the water cooler. Puckering her lips, she blew him a kiss.

Looking like a snowman left out in the rain, he trudged out the door.

19

Gary Greene

Jack stood in a convenience store and grabbed a cup of coffee. A cold lump settled in his gut like a cement block. After a week of downbeat events, not unlike Shoemaker's desk that sat empty and gathering dust, employees returned to a normal state of depression and a lack of productivity. Even the feds kept a low profile and stayed out of sight.

The cashier, a gum-chewing blonde with dimples, rang up the coffee. "Care for anything else, a donut or cigarettes?"

"Did I ask for anything else?"

"No, but..."

"Thanks," Jack replied, and walked out the door.

The morning sun shined brightly. Birds chirped happily in the trees. Still a feeling of impending doom hung over him like an iron mallet ready to drop.

Jack walked to his car but stopped short when he saw a classic automobile cruising up the street. The car was an El Morocco, the same model showcased in Eddie's Alamo, on the night he fell in love with Paradise. A smile crossed Jack's lips at the thought of the brunette girl. It was the first one he had in days.

Pulling out on to the highway, he turned on the radio. An old Springsteen song wailed over the airwaves, making him reminisce back to happier times.

Jack had his share of romances over the years. Lately he thought about all the pitfalls and conquests when it came to love. People met in bars, supermarkets, on the internet, and at the gas pumps. They went out to dinner and movies, sent flowers and had drinks. Sooner or later they shared that first magical kiss; the one that spells forever.

Looking back, people weren't as bitter back in his younger days. They hadn't yet been beat up, slapped silly, banged around, or punched hard enough to grow cold. Back then, they didn't care about job cutbacks, paying the rent, mortgage and taxes, or any of the other many responsibilities that landed on the doorstep of their lives. They hadn't figured out that sometimes you have to be stone cold and hard as a brick to survive. Youth was magic, and the magic kept life vibrant and full of colors.

That same magic for Jack came in the form of an elusive brunette named Paradise on a hot summer night at Eddie's Alamo. Whenever Jack thought about her, the unkind world, the one filled with corporate bureaucracies, conniving lawyers and crooked politicians, blew away like a feather in a windstorm.

When Jack turned the corner into the parking lot for work that morning, it didn't take long to remember it again.

A squadron of police cruisers surrounded the administration building at Cool Caps.

Jack looked around at the chaos. The source of the disruption wasn't immediately clear, but the police had guns pointed at the office building. With so many unbalanced employees, anyone on the payroll could have fallen to pieces and wreaked havoc inside.

On the far side of the parking lot, Norman Cooley stood beside a disconcerted cop. His face was stitched with tension. "What do you mean I can't enter the building?" He glanced at the cop's badge. "Officer Bobbles, is it? I have a production schedule to meet."

The cop stuck a toothpick in his mouth and shut him down. "Look pal, you're starting to grate on me. We got a hostage situation here. Why don't you take the day off?" he suggested. "We'll handle things on this end."

"Have you lost your mind?" Norman shook with anger. "We have a quota to meet. Greene is a maniac. Take him down so we can get back to business."

Unable to cope with the rising pressures of the crisis without smashing Norman in the face, Officer Bobbles stepped off and pretended the guy didn't even exist. The last thing he needed on a day like this was some blowhard whining in his ear.

The cop sipped at a takeout coffee and pondered the gravity of the situation, including that of his own life. At times he thought about resigning from the police force. But his duties required little more than eating free donuts at the local convenience store and flirting with the cashiers.

Then this happened.

Stymied, the cop picked up a bullhorn and shouted, "Give it up, you ass. We have the place surrounded."

"Come and get me, screw!" The suspect yelled out the window.

Jack hurried across the parking lot to where Officer Bobbles stood. "What's going on?"

The cop stared a hole in the office building. "Some freak is holding the personnel director hostage. He keeps whining about Las Vegas and nonrefundable airline tickets."

Jack gulped and stepped forward for a closer look.

Hunkered down at the office window and poised for self-destruction, Gary Greene stared at the growing conglomerate of law officers converging on the property. Dan Rupert, the company's personnel director, sat stiffly in front of him. Greene had a pocket knife at his throat.

"Don't try anything stupid or the guy in the orange moccasins gets it," Greene warned. He tightened the blade against Rupert's fat neck.

Pacing in the parking lot, Norman Cooley's face was cratered with dread. He thought back to that pivotal day when Greene first walked in the door and filled out an application for a job.

Greene, a helicopter pilot during the Gulf War, transported supplies to soldiers in the desert. While he never saw any real combat, one morning before flying a mission he stopped by a mess tent and grabbed some breakfast. In a freak accident, a splatter of grease from a slab of bacon hit him in the eye and damaged his retina. Greene never quite recovered from the wound and was awarded the Purple Heart for his wartime injury.

Upon discharge from the service, time after time and appeal after appeal, his many requests for disability compensation were refused. Unlike Lance Sheppard who was handed a fortune in disability compensation after pretending to slip on a wet floor, Greene was forced to seek other means of financial support.

Greene worked in car washes. Dug ditches. Shoveled manure. Once he even got a job as a bouncer at a strip club in Milwaukee. Eventually he landed on the doorstep at Cool Caps seeking employment.

Norman eyed Greene with mounting skepticism. The guy looked unstable. If he refused to hire him, he might go berserk, pull out a weapon and start blasting away before a 911 call could ever be placed. Given the injuries that might be incurred, workmen's compensation premiums would skyrocket.

"I've had some difficulty finding work," Greene explained. He sat across a table from Norman during a job interview. His tense fingers drummed the tabletop. "If you don't hire me," he drew a slow breath, "I'm not sure what I'll do."

Norman shifted backward in his chair. It was uncertain if Greene packed any weapons, but clearly things could get ugly.

"There's no need to do anything rash." Norman nervously giggled.

Confused, Greene stared at him. After a minute, he stood up and reached in his pocket for a folded up resume.

"Let me just give you this..."

"No!" Norman shouted and ducked down underneath the table.

Greene was hired on the spot. Norman offered him a fat salary that required him to do little in return for his services. Most of his days were spent reading gun magazines or eyeballing people like Ed Shoemaker, an unhappy gloat with a vulgar wife and an obsession for tropical islands; Fiji in particular.

With such unstable employees as Greene, Norman often worried about a critical moment arising in the business's history. Now just a few months short of ten lackluster years of service to the company, a terminated vacation policy, and a nonrefundable airline ticket to Las Vegas, Greene had figuratively speaking, blown a head gasket.

At least when Eileen Klump had a nervous breakdown she had the decency to do it without the benefit of an outside audience. A couple of guys in white coats, dispatched from the County's mental health facility , turned up on the doorstep and carried her away, case closed.

This was different.

Word leaked out that a possible terrorist incursion transpired on company grounds. Within minutes, news stations crawled on the property like termites on wood. By early evening, the shootout (or perhaps suicide) would be broadcast on every major network across the country. The entire incident would be a real blackeye on the company.

Stomping his foot angrily, Norman took a few steps forward and hollered to the personnel director, "Rupert, what do you think you're doing in there? You're supposed to be the HR man. Now disarm that fool so we can all get back to work."

Rupert looked about as calm as a duck flapping its wings in a tornado. "For God's sake, Greene has gone bonkers. Give'em what he wants."

"A plane ticket to Vegas?" Norman scoffed. "Maybe we could throw in a free room at the Mirage."

"Just keep talkin', tough guy." Greene tightened the knife against Rupert's throat.

Sweat poured off Norman like a broken fire hydrant. "Do something, you idiot!" He barked at the cop.

Officer Bobbles leaned against his police cruiser, took a sip of coffee, and stared at the scene unfolding in the administration building.

Earlier that morning, he had been loitering around the pastry section of Jed's Market. Then the call came in over the radio. Some whacko at the Cool Caps Bottling Company went bananas and was holding the personnel director hostage. Things spiraled downhill ever since.

Setting his coffee down on the hood of the police car, the cop shouted, "Take a look around. You're surrounded. Nobody has to get hurt here. We can talk it over, pal. Now put the damn weapon down before I blow your head off, you little puke."

"Don't bully me, sucker," Greene yelled at the cop. "Norman Cooley, that bastard, took away my vacation time. I'm not going anywhere until my demands are met."

Officer Bobbles checked his wristwatch. Time was pressing. He was captain of the bowling team over in Mahoning and the team had an afternoon match for the league championship. At this rate he'd never make the game.

Bobbles shouted through slanted teeth, "Last chance. I don't have all day. You gonna surrender or what? We both know you're bluffing."

The knife in Greene's hand fidgeted underneath Rupert's flabby neck. "You think I won't do it, donut boy?"

Officer Bobbles paused and stepped back. "Take it easy." He reconsidered. "I'll make a few calls."

"You got ten minutes." Greene's voice was tense enough to snap a telephone pole. "After that, things get ugly. One more thing," he said. "I wanna speak to Nick Crowe."

The cop tilted his head uncertainly. "Who?"

"He works at Alfred's Diner. Get him down here. And tell him to bring food with him. We're starved in here."

"You there." Officer Bobbles turned around and pointed at Wetterman. "Get on the horn and call the diner. Have them send Nick Crowe down here, pronto."

Wetterman pulled out his cell phone and nervously punched in the number. "You heard me. The cops are here. We need Crowe to come to the administration building at Cool Caps. Have him bring food," he said, and then quietly added, "Throw in a breakfast bagel on the side."

Officer Bobbles leaned over and whispered, "Make it two."

20

The Delivery Boy

Traffic was tied up in knots for blocks. Frustrated drivers sat in cars in the sweltering heat, beeping horns and cursing.

In what resembled a funeral procession, a squadron of police cars escorted a pizza delivery van up the shoulder of the road. A colorful caricature of Alfred, the diner's owner, was painted on the driver's door. Turning into the parking lot nearest the administration building, the van came to a stop. Nick Crowe jumped out with a pizza box.

"Morning, gents." Crowe sniffed at the early morning air and beamed at the mouth. "Beautiful day. What's the problem?"

Stress caked Norman's face like dried mud. He tugged at the cop's arm. "I have a restraining order against that guy. He isn't allowed on the property."

"Back off." The cop dusted Norman's hand away. "This is a police action." He straightened his uniform as cameramen from news stations rolled their films in hopes of what would be an exciting, if not violent, outcome to the standoff.

Just down the road, a car with a flashing light skirted up the side of the highway. It came to a screeching halt outside the administration building. Garbed in dark glasses and black ties, the feds jumped out of the vehicle.

Agent Hill glanced at the cop's badge. "Officer Bobbles?"

"You got it."

The fed flipped his badge at the cop. "I'm Agent Hill. This is Rupinski. What's going on?"

Officer Bobbles set his coffee down and wiped his mouth with his sleeve. "We got a hostage situation. Some whacko named Gary Greene has the personnel director held up at knifepoint inside the building. He's demanding that we give him a plane ride out of here."

"We'll give him a plane." Agent Rupinski spit. "Right up his ass."

Bobbles added, "He asked to talk to some guy named Nick Crowe who works at the diner up the road."

"Crowe?" Agent Hill removed his sunglasses and tilted his head suspiciously, then turned his attention back to the cop. "Who's in charge here?"

"I am." Officer Bobbles crossed his arms toughly.

"Not anymore." Hill dialed a number on his cell phone. "Get everyone in position. I want a sniper on the roof. We're not giving this bastard an exit ramp."

Compliant with Hill's orders, men dressed in SWAT gear materialized from behind hedges and the corners of the building. Armed and dangerous, sharpshooters pointed weapons at the office window where Greene was held up.

Agent Hill turned his attention to Crowe. "We got a terrorist situation. The guy's name is Gary Greene. You know him?"

"Maybe." A line of perspiration formed on Crowe's forehead.

"He wants to talk to you. Why do you suppose that is?"

Crowe's face puddled up with resentment. "Are you accusing me of something?"

"Yes."

"That's crazy. Greene comes over the diner when I'm working and tells me his problems. He has issues."

"What issues?"

"Are you serious?" Crowe pointed at a policeman ducked down behind a Subaru, targeting his rifle. "For one thing you got more cops here than there are mosquitoes on a pond of scum. With the government spitting out that kind of payroll, no wonder the federal deficit is rising. Greene is no criminal." Crowe laughed. "He's just going through some difficult times with all the company cutbacks, not to mention that bastard, Norman Cooley, cancelled his vacation. Maybe the guy just needs a little attention."

Agent Rupinski pulled a weapon out of his car and cocked it. "He's getting it."

"Hold up." Agent Hill stayed his partner's hand. He squinted through his binoculars. "Someone else is in there."

"Another hostage?" Agent Rupinski shoved some chew tobacco in this mouth.

"What the hell?" Hill lowered the binoculars, rubbed his eyes, and then raised them again.

The scene was cryptic. Sharpshooters circled the parameter. Police lights gleamed in the bright sunlight. Newscasters crawled over the perimeter and reported on what would inevitably be still another bloody chapter in American history. Those particulars were bizarre enough, but this?

"It's that secretary, Eileen Klump," Hill said blankly.

"What's she doing?" Rupinski asked.

Hill paused. "She's making coffee." His face clouded over in confusion. "Is she crazy?"

"No!" Norman Cooley, standing nearby, blurted out. "The woman hates me. She's making a spectacle out of herself to give the company a bad rap."

Inside the administration building, Greene popped his head out of the office window. "What's all the jabber? Send Crowe over here." He paused. "Tell him to bring Jack Snaggler with him."

Agent Hill turned his head and glared at Jack. "Why is Greene asking for you?"

Jack gulped. "I don't know, but I'm not going over there. He's dangerous."

"We're dangerous." Hill tapped the handle of his gun. "We need to buy a few minutes to get our team in position." He glanced up at a sniper on the roof who crept around by a drain spout. "Go talk to Greene. Try reasoning with him. At the first sign of hostile action, hit the dirt. Bullets will be in the air."

"What if I refuse?"

"People get snuffed in friendly fire every day, Snaggler." He gave him a push. "Move it."

Jack took a deep breath and slowly advanced towards the building. Nick Crowe had his hand wrapped around a pizza box and walked beside him. From the window of the office, Greene scrutinized their every move.

"This is psychotic," Jack told Crowe. "There's no telling what Greene will do."

"Stop whining. I'm knee-deep in grease at the diner and had to drop everything to deliver a takeout order."

Jack stood speechless as he tried to comprehend the confused workings of Nick Crowe's unbalanced mind.

Crowe graduated with honors from a respectable college in the northeast. He gained the admiration of his peers and majored in computer science. It was difficult to imagine that someone with such a natural talent for education, confronting a madman no less, would be preoccupied with the glories of flipping burgers and sanitizing toilets.

"Are you an idiot?" asked Jack. "Greene is crazy."

"That's no revelation. Everyone at Cool Caps is crazy."

"This is different. Greene stepped over the line. He's holding Rupert hostage. For all we know he has a bomb."

Crowe laughed out loud. "That's absurd. Greene isn't such a bad guy. His instability stems from the constant pressure of working in an office environment."

"What pressure? He sits at a desk and does nothing all day."

"Exactly," Crowe said. "Greene is an army brat. He flew planes in the war and needs the challenge of stimulation. He's oppressed by the lack of productivity in his life."

"I'm telling you, he's crazy."

"You really think so?"

"Don't you?"

"He's just a little unsettled."

"What does he want from me?"

Crowe shrugged. "Greene went ballistic when the company cancelled everyone's vacation. You tried to get them to change that, didn't you? He trusts you."

"He's going to get us killed," Jack said.

"You worry too much. Stick to the plan and everything will be fine."

"What plan?"

"I'm talking about our partnership."

"We don't have a partnership." Jack stopped walking and poked Crowe in the chest. "You're up to something. Even the feds know it."

Peering out the office window, Greene's face looked as white and crumbled as a crushed marshmallow. "Are you guys having a class reunion? Snap it up!"

<hr/>

"How goes it, Greene?" Crowe asked as he and Jack approached the office window.

"What are you, stupid?" Greene growled. "Take a look around. The place is surrounded."

Crowe confessed, "Things look a little grim."

"You told me there'd only be a few cops. It looks like they called in the 3rd Infantry Division!" Greene sweated bullets. "Did you get the package?"

Jack raised an eyebrow. "What package?"

"I'll handle this." Crowe politely told Jack to shut up and then turned his attention back to Greene. "The feds sealed off all the entrances to the buildings. We have to scrub the mission and take an alternate route."

Jack eyed Crowe with mounting suspicion. It was impossible to discern what he was conniving, and considering the welcoming committee surrounding the place, staying alive to find out looked more and more in doubt.

"What do you want with me?" Jack asked Greene.

"Shut your trap. You're lucky we even let you in the loop."

"I'm not in any loop!"

Rupert, his neck jiggling under the blade of a knife, looked like he was on the verge of a coronary. "Stop agitating him, for God's sake. Can't you see he's crazy?"

Greene chewed at his fingers. The enormity of his dilemma hung over his head like a black cloud, ready to burst. Looking from side to side, he scrutinized the landscape. Federal agents coordinated operations on their cell phones. Cops bent down on one knee behind the open doors of police cars and targeted their weapons. A heavy trollop of boots ran across the roof, undoubtedly snipers, poised for killing and ready to fire bullets in every orifice of his soon-to-be dead carcass.

Reaching through the window, Greene grabbed Nick Crowe by the shirt. "You got me in this!"

Crowe pushed Greene away and backed up a step. "You're falling to pieces. There's still a way out. Listen to me. There's a large air duct in the cafeteria. It leads to the rear of the building, near the woods. Someone could easily slip out of there unnoticed."

"There's an air duct?" Greene blinked. A glimmer of hope flickered in his eyes.

"All you need is a diversion. A good smoke bomb should do the job." He handed Greene the pizza box he was carrying. "I think you'll find everything you need in there, made to order."

Greene shook the box. "Is this what I think it is?"

"What do you think?"

"You really think I can make it out alive?"

"You tell me."

Greene examined the parking lot. A big lug with a granite jaw hid behind a parked car and pointed a rifle at his head. Men dressed in SWAT gear concealed themselves in hedges up on the ridge of a grassy hill. A police helicopter even did a flyby. In what stacked up to be a fierce shootout, the waters of salvation were sparse, and instead of a river leading to safety, he found himself trapped in a moat of desperation.

Greene's face drooped like a clump of mud. "They're going to crucify me."

"Put yourself in my shoes," Crowe said. "The feds are convinced I'm in league with you, and not only that." He glanced at the pizza box. "I'm going to end up getting stiffed on a takeout order."

"Would you shut the hell up about the pizza and quit making jokes!" A wave of panic surfed Greene's eyes. "We're in serious trouble."

Unable to contain himself any longer, Norman, his face hot as a bake oven, walked boldly up the center of the parking lot. "Greene, you screwball, come out of there and get shot like a man!"

"You'll never take me alive!"

Compliant with Greene's wishes, Agent Hill waved his hand and sounded off. "Open fire!"

Jack and Crowe hit the dirt. Snipers and local cops alike let out a barrage of bullets. The men in SWAT gear rushed towards the entrance of the building.

A huge puff of smoke suddenly erupted from inside the administration office. Heavily armed lawmen in gas masks raced to the front door and kicked it in. Intent on taking no prisoners and with guns drawn and blazing, they riddled the walls with bullets.

Agent Rupinski led the pack on the excursion. He ran from room to room, firing at will. When the smoke finally cleared, he stopped his assault and stared at the empty walls of the vacated building.

"Where's Greene?" Rupinski looked from side to side.

A cop holstered his weapon and scratched his head."He must have escaped."

Agent Rupinski kicked the copy machine and then in a fit of rage opened fire on the water cooler. Water shot up in the air and ran down the floor.

Over by the coffee machine in the office room, much to Rupinski's surprise, Eileen Klump continued to brew fresh coffee. A couple of befuddled lawmen approached her with caution and grabbed her by the arms. Cackling like a crazed parrot, they dragged her out the front door and put her in an ambulance.

Jack lifted his head off the ground and looked around. The last remnants of a plume of smoke drifted out of the office building. He started to stand up but Agent Hill rumbled over like a fullback and pushed him back down in the dirt.

"Where's Greene?"

The memory of Crowe talking about an unguarded air duct flashed in Jack's mind. Crowe all but drew Greene an escape map. Still he couldn't reveal that information. It'd only give Rupinski and Hill one more reason to implicate him in a crime.

"I don't know what happened to him. One minute he was here. The next he was gone."

Agent Hill's eyes shifted to Crowe. "What do you know about this?"

Crowe's cheeks were smudged with dirt. He stood up and dusted off his shirt. "Who cares what happened to Greene? You almost got us killed."

Fuming like a leaky gas pipe, Norman Cooley walked over. "Are you blind?" he asked the feds. "These guys are crooks." He pointed at Crowe. "That one wants to kill me. I fired him from the company and he's been out to get me ever since." His eyes turned to Jack. "This one is his accomplice. They both stink worse than a dead rat in the wall."

"I'm innocent!" Jack claimed.

"Shut up." Agent Hill kicked dirt in Jack's face then turned to Norman. "Don't sweat it. Greene won't get far. When we find him, it'll make Gitmo look like a swim at the YMCA. He'll crack under pressure and take everyone down with him." He looked back at Jack. "Maybe you should revise your statement."

"I'm being framed!"

Hill cracked his knuckles. "It's your funeral, Snaggler. But if I were you, the last thing I'd want to do is a stint in the state pen for the sake of a guy whose idea of a great Saturday night is sniffing commodes." He glared at Crowe. "Hey Rupinski." He called his partner, who paced back and forth in front of the office, waiting to shoot someone. "Let's hit it."

Smashing his fist angrily against the wall, Agent Rupinski walked over to the car and jumped in. Spinning the tires, the feds tore out of the parking lot.

Across the street, Jack cringed at an all too familiar scene. The guys in the white coats were again dispatched from mental health. Eileen Klump offered little resistance as they loaded her into the back of an ambulance. Before they slammed the doors shut and pulled away, she stuck her head out, looked over at Wetterman, and hollered the words, "Egg Harbor!" and then disappeared down the road.

21

Postcards from Fiji

Word of Gary Greene's bold flight from justice spread quickly. National news hounds rehashed the details of the escape. Criminal psychologists were divided as to whether Greene was a terrorist programmed by foreign powers, or in another scenario, psychologically damaged by an abusive childhood. No matter what the presumption, Jack sat under a growing umbrella of suspicion.

Jack hunkered down at his desk and looked at his coworkers, who stared back at him distrustfully. It was the worst kept secret in the company that the feds were watching him. The consensus of his peers was that the authorities would march into the office at any given moment and drag him away to some undetermined location. Much like Greene, he'd disappear and never be heard from again.

Stress levels thickened. Under strict orders from Norman Cooley, supervisors roamed the halls like venomous snakes, ready to strike at the smallest infraction of the rules. Someone even stuck a written warning on Shoemaker's desk for taking an unscheduled day off work, and as far as anyone knew, he was dead. Tension screamed louder than a hot kettle. By the time the afternoon mail arrived, it blew altogether.

"Ah!"

Jack picked up a ruler and poked at a postcard that arrived on his desk. It had no return address but was postmarked from Fiji. The picture on the front of the postcard sported an unshaved beach bum in fluorescent shorts. He waved a tropical island brochure in the air. An island girl with a dark tan clung to his flabby arm. An insignia across the bottom of the postcard read:

Splash it up in the Islands
PLAN your GETAWAY Now!

Mesmerized by the postcard, Jack might have stayed there for hours if Wetterman wouldn't have barged in the room.

"Just when things look bad, they get worse."

"What do you mean?"

"Eileen," Wetterman said. "On her way to the mental facility, she jumped out of the back of the ambulance at a traffic light. Nobody saw her since. Do you suppose they'll blame us for that too?"

Chewing his fingernails, Jack pondered the growing trend of conspiracy. Shoemaker vanished. Green disappeared. Lance Sheppard was missing. Now Eileen Klump jumped out of an ambulance en route to the mental hospital.

Jack calculated the odds that aliens might be abducting people but quickly dismissed the notion. If little green men were kidnapping humans, the last thing they'd want aboard the mother ship would be a bunch of pests.

"Forget about Eileen," Jack said. "Take a look at this." He slid the day's mail across his desktop. "This came this morning. It's from Fiji."

Wetterman studied it closely. "It looks like a postcard."

Nesting with the Loons

"You idiot, of course it's a postcard. Don't you see who this is?" He tapped his knuckle on the picture. "It's Shoemaker."

"Shoemaker?" Wetterman laughed. "That's crazy."

"Maybe he's trying to send a message that he's still alive."

"Shoemaker fell off a boat," Wetterman reminded. "Even if he isn't fish food, he'd never risk sending a postcard. His wife and daughter might find out where he is and make him come home." Pencil lines of stress crisscrossed his forehead. He dabbed at a runner of sweat with his shirt sleeve. "The feds must have sent this. They're trying to mess with our heads."

"It's not the feds." Jack angrily pounded his fist on the desk.

Coworkers napping in their cubicles got jolted awake by the thud. Looking around, they quickly recovered and went back to sleep.

Jack lowered his voice. "I think Greene and Crowe are trying to steal something from the company. I overheard them talking about a package just before Greene disappeared. Whatever they're planning, the feds think we're mixed up in it."

Wetterman's face cracked with alarm."Are you serious?"

"We're being setup."

"Setup for what?"

"Who knows," Jack said. "But every time I turn around the noose around my neck gets a little tighter."

Wetterman looked beaten as a boxer in the twelfth round. "We'll be doing time at San Quentin before it's over!" Black circles crusted around his eyes. "I haven't slept in days. I got problems."

Jack raised an eyebrow. "You're not still dreaming about the dancing banana?"

"His name is Paso." Wetterman sheepishly stared at the floor. "Do you think something's wrong with me? Who dreams about dancing bananas?"

"Pull yourself together." Jack put a sympathetic arm around his friend's shoulder. "Between Rosa rejecting you and a piece of fruit with happy feet, you're losing your grip on reality. We've got to stay alert. The feds have their eyes on us. Don't you realize that?"

"I'm trying not to."

Wetterman stuck his hands in his pockets. Worn as a used dish towel, he walked away and out the office door.

Driving home that night, Jack blasted the radio, almost as if hoping the beat of the music would ward off any bullish ghosts that traveled in the form of federal agents, namely Hill and Rupinski. When he pulled into the driveway and doused the headlights, he half expected to find them lurking behind a hedge.

Inside the house, the dishes were piled up in the sink. A ripe canister of strawberry yogurt fermented on the kitchen table and an empty beer can sat atop an overstuffed trash bag.

Everything appeared normal.

Jack flopped down on the couch and ran his hands tiredly over his face.

Trying to ward off the ghoulish visions of the feds, he pulled the picture of Paradise out that he carried in his shirt pocket. Caught in a swamp of quicksand and sinking fast, she was the only cord of hope to hold on to in his otherwise dismal life. He closed his eyes and for an instant could almost taste her lips on that magic night in the El Morocco at Eddie's Alamo. Her touch, soft and wet as summer rain, melted his every emotion.

The phone suddenly rang and startled him out of the daydream.

Jack picked up the receiver. "Hello?"

No answer.

"Who's there?"

Still no answer.

For a second he heard someone mutter something about Fiji.

"Shoemaker, is that you?"

After a moment of silence, the phone went dead. An instant later, it rang again.

Jack grabbed the receiver. "Shoemaker! You're lower than a fly on manure. Are you alive?"

A voice on the other end of the line started cackling. "Are you on drugs? It's me, Nick Crowe. You're late."

"What are you babbling about?"

"Don't play dumb. It's customer appreciation night at Alfred's Diner. The place is mobbed. Why aren't you here?"

"Seriously? The feds are crawling down my spine and you want me to go toast marshmallows?"

"You're not seeing the big picture."

"I'm going to sleep." Jack lowered the receiver.

"Wait!" Panic crouched in Crowe's throat. "Big things are happening here. Don't you know how much planning goes into a thing like this?"

"There's that word again." Jack snapped. "Before you helped Greene escape, I heard you spilling your guts to him about some plan. The feds even have a recording of you and Lance Sheppard talking about it. You have a plan?" He angrily banged the phone's receiver on the wall. "What plan!"

Crowe breathed deeply. "You really don't know what's going on, do you?"

"You tell me."

"Not now," Crowe said. "The feds have everything bugged. That's illegal, you know." He pointed out. "Jump in your car. Meet me at the diner. I'll put you in the loop. Trust me. It'll be a life changing experience." He sniggered and abruptly hung up the phone.

Listening to the stale buzz of the receiver, Jack's world took a turn into the dark. Everyone was disappearing. If the feds had any say in it, he'd be next. His life, like a cheap magician's trick, would vanish. Down in the records department at Cool

Caps, Biddle would file him away in one of the cabinets and slam the drawer shut. Case closed.

Jack frowned at the thoughts of his own demise. It was hard to imagine, but even Nick Crowe, a minimum wage toilet concierge at a fleabag diner, was happier than him.

Glancing outside, it was getting dark. On any other night, he'd be down at Katrina's Kitchen, jiggling a glass of rum in his fingers and reminiscing about Paradise. Instead, he sat in his house, staring at the walls as the world disintegrated underneath his feet.

Against his better judgment, Jack decided to pay Crowe a visit. If nothing else, he might get some answers to the questions that plagued him.

Flicking off the light, he hurried out the door. Outside, except for the steady buzz of electric filtering through the streetlamps that lined the pavements, the neighborhood was eerily silent.

Starting up the car, he pulled out and headed for the diner.

22

Alfred's Diner

When Jack pulled into the parking lot of the diner, frustration pinched at him like a lobster. The feds were on the prowl and convinced he committed a crime. He hoped Nick Crowe might be able to provide insight as to why he was under investigation.

The place hopped. Like pesky flies, the locals buzzed around a huge pot of chili strung on a wire over an open fire. Alfred, the proud owner of the establishment, greeted people as they arrived. Recently turned ninety and despite insufferable drinking and smoking habits, Alfred still kicked like a mule. He hosted the gala event in the diner's parking lot in hopes of drumming up business and went to great lengths to secure superior pricing on outdated meats and subpar side dishes. Combined with cooking the books, the day delivered one hell of a profit margin. Even if sales bellied up, he could claim a loss on the books at tax time. In either scenario, it was a successful business venture.

Despite Jack's troubles, his mind drifted back to Paradise. He touched the crinkled photograph of the brunette that was stuffed in his shirt pocket. The picture was the only thing that kept him afloat in an otherwise decimated world.

Jack walked around the grounds but couldn't find a familiar face. He poked his head inside the diner. Except for a couple of young punks in blue bandanas, the place was empty.

The door to Alfred's office stood ajar. Someone rustled around in there. Glancing inside, he saw Nick Crowe leaning behind a desk and fiddling with a container that sat on the floor.

"What are you doing in here?"

Crowe jumped like a sprung mousetrap. Guilt stenciled his face. "Are you talking to me?"

"Is there anyone else here?" Jack sniffed. "What's that smell, gasoline?"

"What if it is?"

Jack looked at the container on the floor. "What are you doing with that?"

"Is this an inquisition?" Crowe got snippy.

"Why did you call me?"

"Stop badgering me. You're just an office flunky from a bottling company."

"So what? You clean urinals and commodes for a living."

Crowe raised his pompous head. "And do a damn good job." Picking up an ammonia bottle, he exited the office and hurried out the front door. Jack trailed behind him.

Outside the diner, a portable toilet sat near the front entrance to accommodate customers in the parking lot. Getting down on one knee and armed with a can of disinfectant, Crowe scrubbed at the commode with a rag.

Saturated with dejection, Jack sat down on the ground beside him. A constant pressure of criminal allegations hung over his head. All doors of happiness, once secure, now creaked on broken hinges. He couldn't even find comfort in thinking about Paradise, nor did he have any clue as to her whereabouts. Not unlike Shoemaker, she vanished without a trace.

"I got a confession." Jack kicked a rock across the parking lot. "Remember Paradise, the brunette from Eddie's Alamo?"

Crowe didn't answer. Spraying the can of disinfectant, he wiped at the toilet seat with all the gusto of someone polishing a Bentley Continental.

"Sometimes I dream about her." Jack forged ahead. "That sounds stupid, right?" He left out a dramatic gulp. "I think I'm in love with her."

Crowe popped his head up. "There now." He got off his knees and slapped his hands together at a job well done. "That's one sparkling piece of imitation porcelain."

Jack glared. "I'm pouring out my liver and the only thing you can think about is an unsavory toilet seat?"

"Whether you're watering the flowers or fertilizing the field, we aim to make it a memorable experience." Crowe's proud face beamed. "Confidentially," he lowered his voice, "my only real complaint is our shoddy electrical system. Can you imagine what would happen if there was a fire?" He grinned. "Can you?"

Jack stared at Crowe.

The need to replace the faulty electrical system in the diner had been a budding fixation for Crowe ever since a local health inspector uncovered the problem in a snap inspection. According to Crowe, Alfred paid the inspector off and the violation was swept under the rug. However, given the bad circuitry, it was just a question of time before the place went up in flames.

"Why are you concerned?" Jack asked. "So what if the building goes up in smoke. The place dished up more bad meat than there are crazy people at Cool Caps."

"What's your point?"

"Stop evading the real topic." Jack said. "Why did you help Greene escape from the feds by telling him about the air duct? That's aiding and abetting a criminal."

Crowe said, "I was just making an observation. Can I help it if he followed up?

"You're impossible." Jack shook his head in frustration. "I'm going home."

A sudden gush of mortification burned in Crowe's cheeks. "You can't do that! You'll ruin everything. Can't you smell it?" He sniffed. "Things are in the wind."

"What's so important about a half price sale on burnt cheeseburgers?"

Crowe leaned against the exterior of the portable toilet and smirked. "What would you say if I told you I could get her for you?"

"Get who?"

"The brunette, of course. Paradise."

Jack froze at the joints. Paradise's face flashed in his memory. He hadn't seen her for years, but when he closed his eyes, he could still smell her perfume and taste her kiss. "You know where she is?"

"Not now," Crowe whispered. "We're being watched."

Just across the road, Alfred stared and sucked at his withered gums. His grey head and sharp eyes pivoted around the property.

"That guy gives me the creeps," said Jack. "Rumor has it he was in the mob. Nobody even knows his last name."

Crowe shushed him. "Keep your voice down. The old geezer has ears like a hawk. The rumor is true. He was a player in the underground. He bought and sold hot merchandise on the black market until he got nabbed by the feds. Later he turned state's evidence against the mob in exchange for enrollment into the witness protection program. He's been in the restaurant business ever since."

"Crowe, you slacker," Alfred hollered. "This is a business, not a social club." He walked over, bent down, and sniffed the toilet. "Finish up here. There's foodstuff that needs attending to." Glancing at Jack, he hurried off.

"Time to go." Crowe began walking away.

"Wait!" Jack pulled at Crowe's shirt. "Why are the feds riding me, and what about Paradise?"

"We'll talk later." Crowe tied up his apron and brushed a few stands of sweaty hair out of his eyes. "Things are heating up." He rushed off.

Jack hurried after Crowe but got sidetracked when someone tapped him on the shoulder.

"What are you doing here?" asked Jack, surprised to see Wetterman skulking around.

"Crowe called me. He said it was urgent."

"He called me too. Something isn't right."

Jack turned his head towards the bonfire. Crowe had taken up a position at a large pot of chili. Picking up a wooden mixing spoon, he stirred the tub of slop and sang campfire songs to annoyed patrons who wanted nothing more than to put a muzzle on him.

"Greetings comrades," he yelled to Jack, all the while dishing up bowels of brown muck to customers.

"Shut up, you stupid louse." Wetterman grumbled. "We're here because you called us. What's so important?"

Crowe slipped a hot dog on a bun from a grill beside the bonfire and passed it to Jack. "We have a big night planned." He leaned in and repeated, "A very big night."

The headlights of a passing car illuminated a cluster of trees bordering the diner's parking lot. Jack saw someone skulking around in the shrubbery.

"Did you see that?" Jack pointed. "Greene. He's hiding in the woods."

Crowe laughed. "You must be smoking something good. Greene isn't even in the same state as us by now. The next thing you'll tell me is that Shoemaker is still alive."

Jack threw his hot dog on the ground and tromped on it. "Shoemaker is alive!" He pulled the postcard from Fiji out of his pocket that landed on his desk, earlier that day. "Anyone in the picture look familiar, hmm? It's Shoemaker. He's in Fiji." He nudged Wetterman. "Go ahead. Tell him."

Wetterman stood motionless.

"Are you listening to me?"

Wetterman pointed and stared. His face was as immobile as a corpse. "Over there."

Bathed in flickering firelight, Rosa Cruz sat on the opposite side of the bonfire. The woman's purple sundress flitted in the warm summer breeze. Her dreamy eyes, distant, focused on the fire as she picked at a plate of chili with a plastic fork.

"Look at her." Wetterman sniffed back a tear. "She's the most stunning illegal alien in town and nobody even has the decency to talk to her."

"What's the mystery?" asked Jack. "She doesn't speak English."

Crowe cleared his throat and stopped stirring the chili. "I don't want to brag, but I had a little Spanish in high school. Buenos sties stet," he said, and then dished up another gob of muck to a patron.

Wetterman's eyes opened wide. "You speak the language?"

"Maybe you could be an interpreter," Jack suggested.

"Get serious." Crowe wiped back a strand of oily hair. "Between dishing up chili and unclogging commodes, I'm neck deep in sludge. Even worse," he licked his finger and stuck it in the air, "the wind is picking up. One rogue ember from this fire and the entire place could be toast."

Wetterman frowned. If his face was plaster, it would have cracked up the middle.

"The guy looks like he just swallowed a hot pepper." Jack said. "How can you deny him?"

"Enough!" Crowe threw down his mixing spoon. "You bastards know I'm a sucker for love." He paused. "Okay, but we need to hurry. I got things to take care of."

"What are you talking about?" asked Jack.

"Would you stop with the questions?" Crowe unknotted his grimy apron and tossed it on a picnic table. "Let's go."

23

Rosa Cruz

(Burn Baby Burn)

Rosa sat at a picnic table beside the bonfire at Alfred's Diner. She stared dreamily into the crackling fire. A crème colored blouse hugged her proud breasts. Wetterman's knees buckled at the sight of them.

When Rosa looked up, Jack Snaggler, Bob Wetterman, and Nick Crowe, froze stiffer than sides of beef in a meat locker.

The girl slid her dark eyes in Wetterman's direction.

"Tienes una haba entre tus dientes," she said.

Translation: *"You have a bean stuck in your teeth."*

Wetterman bristled with excitement and tugged Crowe's arm. "What did she say?"

"She said that she loves your smile and that you have nice white teeth."

"Can you believe this?" Wetterman pivoted around in a circle and shook hands with everyone. Tears of joy watered his eyes.

"Easy," Jack warned. "Don't let her think that you're too eager."

Wetterman turned his attention back to Crowe. "Tell her I'm in love with her and want to invite her for a glass of wine and a romantic walk on the beach. Go ahead." He shook him by the shoulders, "Tell her."

Crowe chose his words carefully. "El quiere consequirte un Dos Equis y chingarte en la playa."

Translation: *"I want to get you drunk with beer and screw on the beach."*

Rosa turned abruptly sour. She wagged her finger and scolded Wetterman in a dialect none of them could understand. She then picked up a paper plate full of chili and flung it at him. The foodstuff splattered in his face and the sauce dripped off his nose.

"What happened?" Wetterman grabbed a napkin and wiped himself off. Confusion puddle his eyes. "Should I take that as a yes or no?"

Crowe shrugged. "Who knows? Maybe it's a tradition to throw chili in Mexico when a girl gets asked on a date." He crinkled his nose at Wetterman. "That stuff smells rancid."

Jack sniffed the night air. "Alfred's food isn't the only thing that stinks. Something's burning."

Looking over at the diner, the men saw smoke pouring out the windows. At that precise moment, Greene ran out of the kitchen door and hurried across the parking lot, nearest the woods. He wore army fatigues and camouflage paint. Greene laughed as each fresh puff of smoke erupted from the premises.

"Greene!" Jack pointed. "I see you over there!"

Crowe swatted Jack on the arm. "You see nothing. Greene isn't there and that's not smoke pouring out the windows. We just hired some undergrad for the summer as a cook. He probably overloaded the grease fryers."

"Are you a moron?" Jack shook him. "The place smells like a landfill where they burn old tires."

Crowe snapped back in defense, "The place always smells like a landfill. It's nothing more than grease spattered on the wall. Why in God's name would you think it was anything else?"

Alfred suddenly bolted out of the diner. His big eyes bounced around so fiercely in their sockets it appeared they'd burst out of his skull. "FIRE!" he screamed. "Call 911!"

Crowe stiffened. Regardless of the drama unfolding, he paused to watch the ever growing flames rise in the night sky. After a minute, he jumped atop a nearby picnic table.

"Don't panic," he advised the crowd. "We have the situation under control."

Onlookers, however, showed excitement, but little signs of alarm. Some patrons watched with almost holiday-like spirit, "awing" and "owing" at each fresh burst of combustion that shot through the doors.

Crowe jumped off the picnic table and made a mad dash towards the rear entrance of the diner.

Seconds before Crowe slipped inside the burning building, Jack grabbed his shirt and hauled him backwards. "You can't go in there. The diner is going up in smoke. Greene just ran out the kitchen door. He must have lit the place up."

"Why are you following me?" Crowe pulled away from Jack's grip. "You're still not getting it, are you?"

"What are you talking about?"

Crowe leaned over. He picked up an empty container of gasoline that sat inside the doorway. "This is the culprit. Someone doused the place with petrol. It must have hit an exposed wire in the electrical system and ignited the place. There should be a law against that kind of stuff."

Jack's eyes widened. "That's the same container you had in Alfred's office. Did you have something to do with this?"

"Do I look like an arsonist... hmm?" he asked, all the while a jumble of faulty wires above one of the bake ovens sparked. He turned toward the door. "I have to get inside."

"You'll be incinerated!"

Perhaps it was the smoke in his eyes, but Jack swore he saw Crowe grin.

"Just remember," Crowe shouted over an explosion that blew out the remaining windows. "You did say anything, right?"

"What?"

"Paradise. You said you'd do anything to be with her."

"The place is burning down and you're talking love connections? You're nuts!"

Crowe slapped Jack in the cheek. "The only thing really crazy in the world is being sane. Good luck. You're going to need it."

Shoving the empty container of gasoline in Jack's hand, Crowe disappeared into the clouds of black smoke that emanated from all orifices of the diner.

Another explosion sounded off on the inside of the kitchen area and rocked Jack back on his heels. Spitting up sooty air, he regained his balance and ran from the flames.

The world shifted into slow motion. Again he saw Greene, circling the area, moving from tree to tree. Agent Hill and Rupinski also arrived on the scene. They waved guns over their heads and pushed bystanders away from the fire.

Coughing, Jack ran into the middle of the parking lot and saw Biddle worming his way through the crowd.

"Snaggler! You're an arsonist!" Biddle shouted.

Jack's face bent like a question mark. Everyone stared at him. He looked down to discover he still carried the container of gasoline that Crowe handed him. He raised the container in the air. "This isn't what it looks like. I'm innocent!"

Agent Rupinski shot through the crowd. He wrestled Jack to the ground. Grinning like an alligator, the fed rolled him over and ripped a pair of handcuffs off his belt. "I got you now, petunia."

A gas stove inside the building suddenly erupted. The explosion was deafening. The crowd rushed from the property like a gang of mad bulls. Rupinski and Hill were both trampled on by the stampede.

Escaping Rupinski's grip, Jack crawled away on bruised knees.

Within seconds, the feds were back on their feet and sifting through the crowd like hungry vultures in search of a carcass.

"Snaggler." Jack heard someone call. "Over here."

Wetterman sat on the side of the road in his car with his engine revved. He flung open the passenger door. Hacking up grey spittle, Jack crawled in. Not wasting time, Wetterman peeled the tires in the dirt and pulled out.

"Can you believe this?" Jack looked out the rear window. The diner, engulfed in flames, lit up the sky like the sun. "Crowe will never make it out of there alive."

"They'll probably find his remains guarding the commode, the stupid ass." Wetterman said. "What were you doing with that container of gasoline?"

"Are you insinuating I had something to do with this?"

"Everyone thinks you had something to do with it."

"Crowe handed me the container before he jumped in the fire."

"You want me to believe that?"

"I don't like your tone," Jack told him. "I'm no criminal. Even if I were, you're driving the getaway car. That makes you an accomplice."

178

Wetterman's face melted.

Jack understood his friend's anguish. The future – hell, what future – looked bleaker than an approaching tornado. All Wetterman ever wanted was to make love to Rosa Cruz. But the dream, like a winter storm, quickly turned dark and cold. The feds were on the hunt. When they found them, the closest Wetterman would ever come to an intimate encounter with Rosa would be sharing a 4 X 8 cell with a depraved gorilla sporting a bad attitude.

Wetterman's facial muscles wilted. "We're going to jail."

"The cops can't prove anything," Jack insisted. "So what if they saw me run from the diner with gasoline. Does that make me an arsonist?"

Wetterman mopped at his forehead with a handkerchief. "Maybe you're right. What can they really prove?" He flicked on the radio.

A local newscaster broke into the middle of a song. "This just in. A fast food diner up on 903 is going up in flames. Two men were seen fleeing the scene. Jack Snaggler and Bob Wetterman are being sought for questioning in connection with a fire being labeled unusual and suspicious." The newsman switched gears. "Talk about unusual, did anyone catch the story in the tabloids about the guy in fishnet stockings at a beauty pageant in Ocean Ci..."

Jack reached over and flicked off the radio.

"We're fugitives!" Wetterman banged on the steering wheel.

"Get a grip. We need to keep our wits." Jack glanced at the fuel gauge. "We're almost out of gas."

"You should have thought of that before you dumped it on the diner." Wetterman slapped his empty pockets. "I'm broke."

Jack pointed to the left. "Turn the headlights off and drive up the alley."

Wetterman doused the lights and turned up the back street. Halfway there, he pulled over and cut the engine. Things were quiet. There was no sign of pursuit.

"We need money," Jack said. "I'll grab some from the house. We'll disappear. Maybe leave town until we can figure a way out of this mess."

Jack looked up and down the street. Getting out of the car, he ran across the lawn and slipped through the kitchen door of his house. Running upstairs, he hurried through a darkened hall to his bedroom where he kept an emergency stash of money on the nightstand.

For an instant he grew lightheaded and wobbled on his feet. Grabbing a bedpost, he sat down on the bed.

Jack rubbed his fingers over his temples. Faster than a grease fire at Alfred's Diner, his life had taken an abrupt change. Everyone in town, including a couple of bad-tempered feds, wanted him dead. If any shred of light was left in the darkened corners of his mind, it came in the form of Paradise, the brunette from Eddie's Alamo.

Scared stiff and beaten down, Jack yawned. The pressures of the day weighed heavily on his shoulders. Disregarding the dangers, he momentarily closed his eyes and began to drift back to a place where federal agents with dark glasses didn't exist.

If only for an instant, Jack returned to happier times. He went back to that night at Eddie's Alamo, when visions of Paradise danced in his head.

24

Eddie's Alamo

Wetterman laid on the horn of his '69 Cougar.

"Are you in there?" He beeped again. "We're late."

Jack ran out the door with his shoelaces untied and corn chips stuffed in his mouth. Wearing a white t-shirt and tight cuffed jeans, he flung the passenger door open and jumped in the car. Wetterman hit the gas and took off down the road.

"What's the rush?" asked Jack.

Wetterman checked his hair in the rearview. If it was any more slicked up with oil someone would have called a plumber to clog the leak. "I just want to be on time, that's all."

"I'm never on time."

Wetterman snorted. "That's no secret. You're always late for work. Everyone in the office talks about it. You know what your problem is?"

"I don't care what my problem is."

"Exactly." Beaming with self-importance, Wetterman slapped his hand on the dashboard. "Now take me. I want to do a good job for the company. You know, make an impact."

Jack crunched another corn chip and stared at Wetterman.

Like so many go-getters, Wetterman wanted to make a difference in the workplace but was about to be consumed by the mediocrity of the corporate world. He didn't recognize that advancement rested on learning how to effectively waste time. Morning coffee superseded pushing a purchasing requisition out the door to meet a deadline. It was as simple as that.

"Maybe you should do what everyone else does at work," Jack suggested.

"Like what?"

"Like nothing."

"Nothing?"

"Nothing."

Confusion clouded Wetterman's eyes.

Jack had summed up corporate America in a single word. Forget about dedication and rising up from the trenches of the industrialized world by hard work and determination. When it came to business, it was all about political favors, bigwig CEOs taking kickbacks, trickle-down economics, outsourcing and globalization, the disintegration of the middle class, and screwing the American taxpayer. It was about capitalism in progress, the big fish swallowing the little fish, bank bailouts, rising gas prices, healthcare costs and wealthy executives making more money than the entire payroll of all the third world countries combined. It was about welfare fraud and manipulating the system. It was, in fact, about the ninety-eight percent of the population whose only recourse in an economically oppressed world was to take whatever they could get, even if whatever they could get amounted to Jack's final conclusion.

"It's all about nothing," Jack repeated.

"You're crazy," Wetterman said.

"What's your point?" asked Jack.

Wetterman went blank. It was difficult for him to accept that all the fruits of his labor, all the perseverance and commitment, boiled down to eating a crummy blueberry bagel on company time. Doing nothing promoted the absence of mistakes, and the absence of mistakes resulted in profitability. It was the first of many lessons that Wetterman would learn during his tenure in the corporation. He would later regard it as some of the most valuable information of his life. Sloth pays.

Wetterman pointed. "We're almost there."

The lights from Eddie's Alamo glowed in the night. A neon sign that read, "*Remember the Alamo, 2'fer One Drink Specials*", blinked on the side of the road. Wetterman veered his car to the right and pulled in the parking lot. He began driving around the grounds.

"What are you doing?" Jack checked his hair in the mirror. "Park the car already."

Wetterman's pouty lips hung down to his knees. "I don't see Rosa's car."

"Would you stop? You're living your life around a fantasy. Besides," Jack said, "we have more illegal aliens around here than a bullfight in El Paso. If you can't have Rosa, find another one."

"Stop mocking me!" Wetterman punched the steering wheel. A weed of depression took root in his heart. "Can't you see the pain I'm in over that woman?"

Not only couldn't Jack see the pain; he didn't care. Time was wasting. He didn't want to spend Saturday night listening to Wetterman bellyache.

"We'll talk about this later. I'm headed in." Jack shoved a comb in his back pocket and jumped out of the car. "Ready?"

Ambling through the parking lot, both men entered the bar, each with different hopes of what the future might bring.

In the fifties, Elvis was king and transistor radios were hip. Only rich people had color televisions and the average household income was about four-thousand dollars a year. There were no cell phones, internet or TV remotes. Kids emulated Davey Crockett, little girls yearned to be Barbie and Dick Clark introduced the coolest new groups on American Bandstand.

Eddie's Alamo, a hotspot for locals, was celebrating that golden decade of rock-n-roll. An archway decorated in white and pink balloons stood at the entrance of the building.

Inside, sock hop signs were plastered on the walls. Women in beehive hairdos and poodle skirts swiveled their hips. The dance floor was covered in black and white poly vinyl laid out in a checkerboard pattern. Tables were sprinkled with confetti, float candles, and pink napkins. A soda fountain stood behind the bar, only instead of Root Beer Floats, the machine spit out butterscotch rum.

A classic 1956 El Morocco was showcased on a makeshift stage that had been built to hold the metal monster. The car's sleek black exterior gleamed like the sun under a neon beer sign. A surfboard mounted on the wall above the vehicle had the words, *"Lover's Lane"* spray-painted on it.

Nick Crowe, a computer geek from the IT department at Cool Caps, sucked on a cold beer. Wetterman sat down on a stool beside him and Jack leaned against the bar.

"How goes it, Snuggler?" Crowe asked.

"The name is Snaggler."

"Whatever." Crowe took another swallow of beer and glanced at Wetterman. "What's wrong with your buddy? His face looks like a pimple ready to burst."

"He thinks he's in love with Rosa Cruz, the receptionist from work."

Crowe laughed. "Wetterman doesn't know what love is. Take a look over there." He pointed at Jodi Frick, a local Catholic girl from the Marian district. She had a mole on her cheek the size of a grape. "I had a thing for her back in high school. She thought I was a nerd. Whenever I talked to her she snubbed me." He nodded. "Someday when I'm rich, she'll beg for another chance."

"Why don't you just ask her for a date?" Jack suggested.

Crowe blinked in amazement. "Are you out of your mind? Can you imagine the humiliation I'd suffer if she rejected me?"

He took a swig of beer, swished it in his mouth and swallowed. "You don't understand women. If you want them to love you, ignore them. They like the challenge."

"Isn't that the truth." Wetterman shook his head and angrily slammed his drink on the bar. His sunken eyes waded in a pool of self-pity. "I asked Rosa out last week. All she did was look at me with a blank, stupid stare. It's almost as if she doesn't speak English."

Jack scratched his head. "She doesn't."

Wetterman nodded. "That's what they say."

Across the room, Debbie Abernathy pranced on the dance floor wearing nothing but a velveteen pencil skirt and a black halter top. A faint breeze from an open window flapped at her dress, accentuating every delicious curve of her body. Turning her head in Jack's direction, she winked.

"Did you see that?" Jack slapped Crowe on the shoulder. "Debbie Abernathy just noticed I'm alive."

"Isn't she dating that big ape, Stinky Mason?" Crowe took another sip of beer.

Debbie winked again.

Crowe whistled. "Man, she got hot eggs for you."

Reaching in his pocket, Jack pulled out a breath mint and popped it in his mouth. "I'm gonna talk to her." Straightening his shirt, he took off across the floor.

Crowe sniggered and nudged Wetterman. "Someone should grab a fire extinguisher. Snaggler will be shot down in flames before he ever reaches flight altitude."

Minutes later, Jack raced back across the room and found Wetterman sulking at the bar. Jack's face blazed with anticipation. "Debbie Abernathy wants to meet me outside."

Wetterman's eyes opened wide. "You think she wants to..."

"What else could she want?" He paused. "She has a friend."

Wetterman shrunk. "Don't look at me. I'm a one man woman."

"Rosa again?"

Wetterman lowered his head and sniffed.

"You're being ridiculous. Rosa doesn't even know your name. Forget her."

"If you want the Abernathy girl, go ahead." Wetterman held firm. "You don't need me."

"She won't come unless I square her friend away with a date."

Wetterman eyed Jack with suspicion. "Is she attractive?"

"Perhaps." Jack coughed and stared at a stain on the bar. "Debbie is attractive. Don't they travel in packs?"

Wetterman drummed his fingers on a glass of rum.

The premise sounded reasonable. Back in college, cheerleaders cheered together. Football players reveled with each other. It only made sense that dazzling women with loose morals would align themselves with women who were equally dazzling and loose.

"You're sure about this?" asked Wetterman.

"Would I lie?"

"Where are these women?"

"In your car."

Wetterman put his drink down and jumped up. "I have all my valuables in there!"

"A stale cup of coffee and discount coupons from Alfred's Diner aren't a winning lottery ticket." Jack told him.

"Why do I let you talk me into these things?"

Jack slapped Wetterman on the shoulder. "You won't regret this," he said as they hurried out the door, all the while Fat Robbie and the Hubcaps smashed their way through a Chuck Berry classic.

25

Blind Dates

Giggling like teenagers, the post-pubescent duo stepped into the parking lot. The darkened silhouettes of two females sat in Wetterman's car. One was in the front seat and the other in the back.

Wetterman chewed fiercely at a stick of gum. "I'm not good at blind dates. Tell me the truth. Is Abernathy's friend really a knockout?"

"Quiet." Jack staved off the question. "We're here."

Jack jumped in the backseat. Not wasting time and with little resistance, he started mauling Debbie Abernathy's neck.

Wetterman grinned nervously and slid into the driver's seat. When he turned his head to find out what captive fate awaited him, the smile melted off his face like snow in the desert sun.

In the backseat, Debbie peeled Jack off her. "Hello, Bob." She greeted Wetterman and squirted perfume on her neck. "You remember Lillian? She graduated with us. Lillian won an award in home economics for a pot belly soufflé. She also majored in..."

Debbie's voice disappeared under an alarm signal that to Wetterman sounded like an air raid siren going off in his head. This wasn't the beautiful and sumptuous woman that Jack promised to deliver. The girl wore so much pasty makeup that at a distance she could have been mistaken for someone who got hit square in the face with a cream pie. One other notable feature came in the form of a pair of black horn-rimmed glasses that sat aboard her thin nose that routinely offered an unpleasant snort.

"You remember Lillian." Jack draped his arm around Debbie. "She was in our dental hygiene class back when we were seniors in high school."

Wetterman faked a smile. "Nice to meet you," he gulped, Lillian."

"A little music might be a good mood swing," Jack suggested.

Wetterman reluctantly flicked on the radio.

"Love songs... nothing but love songs," the DJ announced and cranked up a sappy record.

Wetterman quickly flicked the radio back off.

Debbie tapped him on the shoulder. "Don't be shy, Bob. Go ahead. Kiss her."

Wetterman's face shattered. He stared at Jack through the rearview mirror with eyes cratered in dread.

"Yes Bob, go ahead." Jack ran his fingers through Debbie's hair. "Make it a wet one."

Wetterman glanced over at Lillian and she snorted at him. "Maybe we should go home," he suggested. "I have to get up early."

"What's the rush?" Jack asked. "There's a full moon tonight. Drive up to the lake and we'll watch the submarines."

Debbie pulled a pallet of strawberry lipstick out. She snobbishly painted her lips. "I don't think so."

"What's wrong?" asked Jack.

Debbie pointed a finger at Wetterman. "That's what's wrong. He doesn't like Lillian."

"That's not true," Wetterman lied. He dug in against the driver's door so tight it would have taken a chisel to dig him out. "Like I said, I have to get up early."

"Get up for what?" Debbie asked doubtfully.

Wetterman paused. "Church. I have church."

Lillian sniffed. "He hates me."

"I didn't say I hate you."

"Then why won't you kiss me?" She puckered her lips like a fish.

Wetterman rolled the window down and fanned himself. "Is it getting warm in here? Maybe we should go back to the bar."

"If he doesn't kiss her," Debbie slapped Jack away, "then you don't kiss me."

"Maybe he doesn't want to kiss her," Jack argued. "I don't see why I should be penalized for that."

"What's the problem, Wetterman?" Debbie poked him in the back of the head. "Do you think you're better than her? All you are is an office lackey with a pimple crisis working in a bottling company." She poked him again. "Give me one good reason why you won't kiss Lillian. Go ahead. Tell me."

Jack's eyes widened. By the expression on Wetterman's face, he sensed that a bomb was about to implode and his best laid plans would fizzle like yesterday's warm beer.

"Because it's LILLIAN BLACK!" Wetterman shouted. "There. Is that what you want me to say?" He punched the dashboard. "She has so much makeup on it looks like a vat of vanilla ice cream!"

Lillian broke into a shower of tears. Makeup dribbled down her cheeks in soggy lumps with every wet sniff.

"Pigs!" Debbie took off her high-heel and whacked Jack over the head.

"Are you crazy!" Jack covered up.

Wetterman looked like a man who just woke from a nightmare and still hadn't decided if it really happened. "I don't know what came over me." Trying to defuse the damage, he reached up under the visor and pulled out a discount coupon for Alfred's Diner. Handing it to Lillian as a peace offering, the girl slapped it away and broke into a fresh shower of tears.

"Come on Lil." Debbie stuck her nose in the air. "If I want abuse, I'll date Stinky Mason."

Flinging the doors open, the girls climbed out. A warm breeze tugged at the fringes of Debbie's skirt and exposed her slight panties.

Jack leaned out the car window. "He didn't mean it. Come back!"

"Shove it, Snaggler," Debbie yelled as both females walked back in the bar.

Wetterman dabbed at his forehead with a napkin. "You're crazy! What were you thinking by pulling a stunt like that?"

Jack settled back down in his seat. "You don't have to apologize."

"Me apologize!" Wetterman's jaw dropped.

"I have a tendency to attract the bad element."

Wetterman rummaged through his glove compartment for an antacid tablet. "I got a mouse in my stomach the size of a gorilla. I'm going home."

Jack shrugged and looked out the window. A shooting star streaked across the sky. He wished that just once he could find someone special; that missing spoke in the wheel of his life.

"Tell me something," Jack asked. "Do you believe in love and all that mush?"

"I thought I did." Wetterman stared into the darkness. "Then Rosa came along. I asked her on dates countless times and she turned me down. Love stinks." He curled his lips down in a frown. "Now let's get out of here."

"I promised Nick Crowe that we'd give him a lift home," Jack said.

"Snap it up then. I had enough fun for one night."

Jack and Wetterman got out of the car. Dejection dripped from their faces as they walked back in the bar.

Inside, the crowd cheered the band, who sounded better as alcohol levels increased.

"You see Crowe anywhere?" Jack asked.

"There." Wetterman pointed. "If this was a mule farm, he'd be the head ass. Why doesn't he say something?"

Near a pool table, Crowe stood beside Jodi Frick. After a cordial "Hello", Crowe froze solid. He studied the tips of his shoes and at times pointed at a cobweb on the ceiling.

Jodi Frick giggled. The girl found Crowe's awkward mannerisms cute, or in another scenario, was amused by what she viewed as an idiot showing compulsive signs of sub-moronic behavior.

Jack walked over to Crowe and tugged him by the shirt.

"What are you doing?" Crowe asked.

"We're leaving."

"You're ruining everything. I decided to take your advice and was about to ask Jodi Frick for a date," Crowe said. "I also told Lance Sheppard I'd have a drink with him."

"Sheppard?" Jack's eyes rolled. "That guy is a crook. He just won a huge settlement from Cool Caps for faking an injury and pretending he needs disability compensation."

"What's wrong with that?" Crowe asked. "Everybody's doing it these days. He's as entitled to illegal benefits as the next guy."

"You're impossible." Jack walked towards the exit door but stopped short. Something caught his eye from across the bar.

Puffing on a half-spent cigarette, Stinky Mason listened intently as Debbie Abernathy angrily flapped her lips. Stinky turned his head and glared in Jack's direction. Throwing his cigarette down, he tromped it out, cracked his knuckles, and marched across the floor towards Jack.

Wetterman's eyes bulged. "He's gonna murder us!"

Running for cover, Wetterman headed out on the dance floor and ducked behind a gang of raucous women dressed in poodle skirts who were doing the jitterbug.

Snarling and muttering curses, Stinky circled around the bar and headed straight for him. Jack turned from side to side, searching for an exit.

A guy with a beer gut and a goatee stood beside the '56 El Morocco, parked in the middle of the bar. "She's a beauty." He wiped a smudge off the hood of the car. "Rumor is James Dean owned this thing." He turned to Jack. "Five bucks puts you behind the wheel. All proceeds go to a new pool table." He pointed at the billiard room where some hotshot banged around a cue ball.

Jack glanced around the room. With fists curled and a face sour as vinegar, Stinky marched around the far end of the bar. Craning his head over the crowd, he temporarily lost sight of his target, but was still closing fast.

"What do you say, buddy?" the guy with the goatee asked again.

Jack hurriedly pulled five dollars out of his wallet and stuffed it in the guy's hand. He jumped inside the El Morocco and slammed the door shut. Looking into the crowd, he breathed a sigh of relief as Stinky passed by.

The sugary scent of perfume alerted Jack to the idea that he wasn't alone in the car. Given his luck, it wouldn't have been surprising to find Debbie Abernathy seated next to him and holding a loaded shotgun.

Turning to look, Jack's hands started to sweat and a romantic twinge knotted up in his gut.

The girl seated next to him, her eyelids set at half mast, had the bluest eyes he had ever seen. When she smiled, he could have died in her arms.

"We've met before." The brunette tilted her head bashfully. "I'm Paradise."

26

Lance Sheppard

"Ah!" Jack yelped when he opened his eyes.

Lance Sheppard stood in a darkened corner of the room. Dressed in a grey hooded jacket, he picked at his teeth. "You were grinning like a clown. It must have been a good dream."

Jack retreated to the far corner of the bed. "What are you doing here?"

Sheppard shrugged. "I couldn't sleep." He looked around the room. "Nice place."

"You have to leave," Jack insisted. "I'm already under investigation for arson and murder. If the police find you here, it'll get worse."

"Loosen up." Sheppard sat down on the bed and crossed his legs. "Nobody knows I'm here. I made a fortune on disability fraud and embezzling company funds. Outsmarting a few cops whose priority in life is getting a free jelly donut from a convenience store isn't exactly magic."

Jack sniffed. "You smell like gasoline. Did you set the diner on fire?"

Sheppard leaned back on his elbows. "I didn't, but according to the feds, you did. Witnesses saw you run from the place with a container of petrol. That's called incriminating evidence."

"I'm being framed!"

Sheppard waved his hand at Jack. "Stop whining and get in the game with the rest of us. You think I'm not taking any risks being here? We're all in this together. Look at Crowe. He scrubbed more urinals than there are oil wells in Texas so that people like us could reap the rewards."

"What are you talking about?"

"Crowe hated the idea of you working at a dead-end job for the rest of your miserable life." Sheppard fingered the dust on the top of a dresser. "Call it a premonition, but just the other day, he asked me to check on you in the event of a tragic accident. Then what happened? He got smoked in a fire. Ha! Considering the electrical system, it's amazing that diner didn't go up in flames years ago."

Jack clenched his fists. "It wasn't the wiring. Gasoline started the fire. Besides, Crowe might have made it out alive."

Sheppard shook his head. "The place is an inferno. No survivors are walking away from that one."

"My guess is that you had it planned that way," Jack charged.

"You should be more appreciative." Sheppard locked his fingers around his knee. "Regardless of what people say, I'm an honorable man with an impeccable reputation."

"You're wanted for embezzlement and disability fraud!"

"Is that a bad thing?" Sheppard asked. "I worked hard to reach my financial goals. Do you have any idea how much planning it takes to make that kind of money in illegal assets? Stand in my shoes for a minute."

Jack shook his head. "No thanks. I'm perfectly content working for a company and doing nothing."

"Not anymore," Sheppard reminded. "You're a fugitive, Jack. The feds are moving in for the kill. Maimed, alive, and preferably dead, they always collect on their corpse."

Jack exhaled and slumped on the bed. "What do you want from me?"

Sheppard stood up and walked to the window. The curtains fluttered in the warm breeze against his dark figure, outlined in a muddy light. In the distance, sirens echoed as he sniffed at the night air. "Outside of a little smoke inhalation, it's a beautiful evening." He turned around and stared at Jack. "My associates are interested in having a job done. You, on the other hand, have to avoid getting shot. We could help each other. All I need is a favor."

Jack eyed him closely. "What favor?"

"Not now. The feds probably have the room bugged. You need to go."

"What are you talking about? Go where?"

"Sam Bales' Family Campground. You know the place, right?""

"Yes, but..."

"When you get there," Sheppard cut him off, "head for the boat launch down at the lake. Somebody will be there to meet you. Do what he says."

"You're not serious."

Sheppard impatiently tapped his foot. "Does it look like I'm joking? The thing is, if you don't listen, people could get hurt. You wouldn't want that on your conscience."

"Are you threatening me?"

"What do you think?" Sheppard reached in his pocket.

Jack cowered behind a cover. "Is that a gun?"

"You tell me." Sheppard smirked.

Doubt swam in circles around Jack's face. Sheppard was dirtier than a broken sewer pipe but the cops never indicted him on weapons charges. Still, he worked at Cool Caps, and people employed by the company had a tendency to be unbalanced. That made him dangerous.

"You're despicable." Jack spat on the floor. "I wouldn't even be surprised if you pushed Shoemaker overboard."

"According to the police, you pushed him," Sheppard reminded. "Besides, nobody should bellyache about him. His wife had the manners of a tarantula. Regardless of how Shoemaker met his fate, he's better off now."

Jack lowered his head. It was the final shot fired. After the feds saw him race from a burning building with a jug of fuel, coupled with Shoemaker's disappearance, there'd be only one conclusion.

"They're going to hang me!"

"It smells suspicious, doesn't it?" Sheppard agreed. "But there's still a way out of this mess. I have friends in low places. They could hide you. Maybe even get you out of the country." He pulled a roll of money out of his pocket and flapped it in front of Jack's nose. "This'd be enough cash to keep you stockpiled in margaritas on some shitty little island in the South Pacific for the rest of your life."

"I've heard enough." Jack stood up.

Sheppard reached in his pocket again.

"Don't shoot!" Jack's heart banged.

Sheppard pulled a piece of candy out and popped it in his mouth. "Gumball?"

Jack slapped it out of Sheppard's hand. "I don't want anything from you. You're a crook. There's nothing you could say that would make me help you."

Sheppard walked towards Jack. Reaching out, he snapped the crinkled photograph of the brunette out of his shirt pocket. Eyeing it carefully, he left out a long whistle. "That's a beautiful piece of real estate. Paradise, right?"

Jack grabbed the picture from Sheppard's hand. "How do you know her name?"

"Does it matter?" Sheppard walked back to the window. Sticking his foot up on the sill, he tied his sneaker. "What's important is that she stays healthy. I don't see any reason to punish her for your sins."

Jack gripped the night table. "Don't even think about it."

"It's nothing personal." Sheppard popped another gumball in his mouth. "Collateral damage happens every day. Think of it as an incentive plan. Strictly speaking, I got no beef with the brunette, but my associates? They can be real bastards." He nodded. "You should do the right thing."

Jack sat immobilized on the bed. The weight of the crisis fell on his shoulders like a slab of granite. "I'll be a fugitive."

"Hello?" Sheppard rapped his knuckles on the wall. "You're already a fugitive. You have a list of priors longer than an elephant's snout. I got to give you credit, Jack." He shook his head. "A lesser man would have crumbled. You got spunk."

Jack stared into the darkness. He no longer was just a suspect for arson and murder. The authorities had him targeted. If he didn't move fast, long before sunrise, he'd be arrested and interrogated for hours until he confessed to all the crimes he didn't commit.

Glancing out the window, Sheppard peered down into the alley. "Isn't that Wetterman sitting in his car, the stupid mope?" He turned back to Jack. "You might as well take him with you. The cops saw him driving the getaway car when you fled the scene at the fire."

"You won't get away with this." Jack pointed accusingly

"I already have." Sheppard stuck his sneaker out the windowsill. "Stick to the plan, Jack. You'll be slopping on suntan lotion in the tropics before you can say "Fiji"."

Grinning wildly, Sheppard crawled out the window, shimmied down the drain pipe, and vanished into the night.

27

Sam's Family Campground

Near midnight, Jack and Wetterman arrived at Sam's Family Campground. Concealing the car behind some trees outside the entrance gate, they walked down a path that led to the camping area. A full moon hung in the sky like a yellow balloon. Glowing campfires and laughter wafted in the wind as vacationers dabbed the woods.

"Explain this to me again." Wetterman stumbled in the dark. "Why are we here?"

"How many times do I need to tell you? Lance Sheppard was hiding out in my house. He told me someone's going to meet us here, down by the boat launch."

Wetterman blinked a June bug out of his eye. "So why are the police chasing me? I didn't run out of Alfred's with a gas bomb."

Jack pushed some branches out of the way. "The feds think we had something to do with Shoemaker's disappearance when he fell off a boat. They also saw you drive me away from the fire. That puts you in the hot seat."

Wetterman's face was wet and dirty as a mud puddle. "How can any of this be happening? We're wanted men!"

"It could be worse."

"You think so?"

Jack stared into the night. In fact, things couldn't even be remotely worse. They were fugitives. "I don't have all the answers," he told Wetterman. "What I do know is that Lance Sheppard is involved. That means something illegal is going on."

"What do you think he's scheming?"

Jack picked up a rock and threw it at a tree. "I'm hoping the guy we're supposed to meet can tell us."

"Tell us what?" Wetterman's face muddled up with confusion. "Can't we just go home and pretend none of this is happening? We always pretended to be busy at work. Everyone bought that performance. Why should this be different?"

Jack considered Wetterman's proposal. The twisted logic almost made sense. People were gullible. Back at the office, when he complained to the HR department about being overworked, they'd send help to alleviate a workload that didn't even exist.

Unfortunately, that kind of reasoning wouldn't work here. The feds were convinced they were guilty. Agent Hill and his henchman Rupinski would rush in like a hurricane, incarcerate them, and then drip water off their noses until they confessed. If that failed, the feds would just shoot them in the head.

Jack stood up and sniffed. Dry timber crackled in open fires. Crickets chirped in the trees.

Turning off the main trail, they traipsed along in the woods where they'd be apt to attract less attention and wouldn't be seen by unwelcome eyes.

"Ouw!!" Jack smacked his head on a tree limb. "I can't see anything. Hand me your flashlight."

"What flashlight?" Wetterman asked. "All I have is some lip balm and a pack of sugarless gum."

Jack looked around. Every direction appeared shadowy and alien. Branches slapped him in the cheek as they trudged through the woods.

Wetterman tripped over a rock and fell headfirst to the ground. Cursing and muttering, he got back up and brushed off his trousers.

"How did I let you talk me into this?" He slapped at a mosquito feeding on his neck. "I should be home sleeping. We're completely lost."

Jack hoisted his leg over a fallen log. "Show some appreciation. If you weren't here, you'd wake up tomorrow working for a bottling company and trapped in a dead-end job. Does that sound like a happy existence?"

"You want me to thank you?" Wetterman punched a tree instead of Jack's face. "By now there's a warrant for our arrests."

"Why do you insist on blaming me?" Jack asked. "Can I help it that the feds think you're guilty?"

"I'm not guilty."

"I'm not either."

"You carried gasoline out of a burning building."

"What's that supposed to mean?"

"You're a firebug."

"Even if I were," Jack pointed out, "you helped me escape. You're an accomplice."

Grinding his teeth in anger, Wetterman launched himself at Jack and started choking him. Rolling on the ground, branches snapped and cracked.

"You've lost your mind!" Jack pushed him away.

A porch light flicked on from a house buried in the woods. Sam Bales stepped out the door with a shotgun cradled in his arm. He shined a flashlight into the forest; the light danced off tree trunks. "Who's out there?"

Jack scrambled behind a clump of bushes. Wetterman followed.

Moments later the kitchen door opened again. A women staggered out on the porch.

Wetterman's eyes widened. "Is that..."

"Shhh." Jack put a hand over Wetterman's mouth.

200

In the light of the full moon, the woman's long nose and thin features resembled a witch. Only instead of a broom, she carried a sloppy cocktail.

"It's Shoemaker's wife," Jack whispered.

"What's she doing here?" Wetterman was so disarmed by the sight that he nearly bit a hole in his lip. "Shoemaker is barely nibbled down to fish food and she's already out burning her braziers, the shameless slut."

Satisfied that nothing was amiss, Sam Bales set his gun down and groped Shoemaker's wife like a peach in the marketplace. She giggled when he pinched her ass. Slobbering and drunk, Sam Bales took her hand and walked around the rear of the house for a romantic stroll under the moon or perhaps a quick screw in the woods.

Jack watched them disappear in the dark and pondered what a momentous day it would have been for Ed Shoemaker to witness such a flagrant display of transgression. All his miserable life, he waited for a savior to arrive out of the ashes and extract him from the jaws of an overbearing wife with whom he shared as much wilted warmth as iceberg lettuce. Now that day finally arrived in the form of a campground proprietor named Sam Bales. Shoemaker, sunk at the bottom of some murky ocean, never lived to see the fulfillment of his dreams.

"She must have despised her husband," Wetterman said.

"I disagree," Jack answered. "They had a mutual disrespect for each other. Maybe this is her way of honoring his loss. Besides," he reminded Wetterman, "you saw the postcard from Fiji. Shoemaker's picture is on it. He must be still alive."

Jack stood up and brushed his trousers off. Looking around, an avalanche of night caved in all around them. "The boat launch is that way." He nodded in a direction towards the lake and looked to see if anyone else lurked around. "Be careful and quiet. That was a close call."

"Closer than you think," Wetterman whispered. "Look over there."

The bushes rattled. Something grunted.

Jack's heart jumped. He turned his head towards Sam Bales' house, wondering if the owner might have circled around behind them.

"Mr. Bales?"

"That's not Sam Bales." Wetterman gulped. "That's a bear."

The animal stood on hind legs and sniffed at them as if they were a rack of garbage.

Wetterman shivered. "The big one has her cubs with her."

Jack stiffened. "That can't be good."

The cubs stared at them. The mother bear, on the other hand, growled and scraped her paws in the dirt.

"Don't make any sudden moves." Jack took a slow step backward.

The mother bear paused as if deliberating. After a frozen instant, she let out a noisy growl and charged.

"Run!"

Jack dashed through the woods and Wetterman chased after him. The mother bear prepared to pounce just as a shot rang out in the night air.

"Pests!" Sam Bales, back from his jaunt in the woods with Shoemaker's wife, picked up his shotgun and fired. The bullet ricochet off a rock and nearly clipped Jack's ear.

Shoemaker's wife, the straps on her yellow halter top falling down over her shoulders, yelled drunkenly into the night. She picked up a lid from a garbage can and banged it loudly off the porch railing. "Beat it, bitches."

The mother bear stopped cold. Turning its nose up in a conceited sniff, the animal made a slow withdraw back into the forest while the cubs cried plaintively in the distance.

Jack and Wetterman retreated into the woods. They came to an abrupt halt when Wetterman, in the dark, thumped his head on the wall of a bait shop that sat adjacent to a nearby lake.

"Stop being so clumsy," Jack complained and pulled his friend off the ground. "You'll wake up the entire camp."

Most of the campfires were doused and campers snored like sleeping bears.

Tiptoeing down the path, they made their way to a boat launch at the edge of the lake that bordered the campground. Stars shimmered in the water. Outside of some young lovers floating in a paddle boat and sucking the face off each other, the place looked deserted.

Looking out over the water, Jack once again thought about the broken mechanics of his failing world. He found his thoughts slipping back to Paradise. He squeezed his eyes shut for a moment and wished she would materialize, her blue eyes reflecting in the moonlight. He'd take her by the hand. Run away to some far off tropical haven where federal agents like Agent Rupinski and bottling companies like Cool Caps didn't exist.

However, when Jack opened his eyes, no beautiful brunette appeared, and the only sound besides chirping crickets was a wet sneeze that came from the direction of the boat launch.

Shrouded in fine mist swirling off the lake, a shadowy figure stood on the dock. He wore a long grey trench coat and was illuminated only by a dim lantern anchored to a post. His face had a red scarf wrapped around it and in the faint light, it was impossible to discern whether he was a runaway circus clown or perhaps Boris Crane, the East Coast killer, coming to claim another victim on a lonely lakeside setting.

"Ahhh!" Wetterman nearly jumped in Jack's lap.

The stranger on the dock sneezed again and wiped his nose with a handkerchief. "The pollen count is killing me."

"Lance Sheppard sent us," Jack said. "You the guy we're supposed to meet?"

"What do you think?"

Jack eyed the stranger's shoes. "You're wearing orange moccasins. The only person I know who wears ridiculous shoes like that is Dan Rupert, the personnel director at Cool Caps. Are you him?"

"If I wanted you to know my name, would I wear this stupid scarf?" He sneezed again. "Before this is over, you're liable to get strung up by the balls and squeal like pigs to the cops. I don't need that kind of publicity."

"We need to know..."

"You need to know nothing." The stranger in the red scarf interrupted. "Every cop in town is gunning for you guys, not to mention the feds. We don't have much time."

Wetterman tapped Jack on the shoulder. "We should get out of here. This guy looks like he just bolted from the mental hospital."

The stranger glared. "Tell your friend to stow it before I stuff a Ground Guide down his throat."

Wetterman's jaw dropped. "How does he know about that?"

"I know lots of things." He dabbed a runner of sweat off his neck that dribbled underneath his scarf. "I don't have to be out here in the middle of the woods, saving your ass. This place is a far cry from Fiji."

Jack stared. "What made you say Fiji?"

"Does this sound like an inquest?"

Jack studied the stranger with careful scrutiny. He pondered the idea that the guy in the red scarf might not exist at all. Perhaps he was a hallucination brought on by mental stress. After all, only yesterday he sat at a desk reading a newspaper and drinking coffee on company time. But life changed in a heartbeat.

Just that quick, the feds were hunting him and wanted him dead. And now he found himself standing lakeside at midnight, seeking salvation from a stranger with a red scarf wrapped around his face who suffered from a pollen allergy.

"Your employer, Norman Cooley, has something we want."

Jack raised an eyebrow.

"He keeps it sitting on the corner of the desk in his office." The stranger paused. "It's a cigar box. The words, "*Daddy's Stash*", are written on the side of the box. We need you to steal it."

Jack laughed. "You're putting me on, right?"

"Does it look like I'm joking?"

Jack asked, "Why would anyone steal a cigar box? It's ridiculous! Even if we agreed, the police would arrest us before we ever stepped foot in the building."

"Don't pull that crap on me. Security at the company is about as tight as a jar of grease. It isn't like I'm asking you to steal the Mona Lisa," he said. "After you make the heist, head for Atlantic City and a casino called *Lots of Slots*. Here." He reached in his pocket, pulled out a cell phone, and tossed it to Jack. "You'll find a telephone number from a woman named Luanda in the contact list. When you get to the casino, call her. She'll give you further instructions on what you have to do."

Jack stuck the cell phone in his pocket. "But…"

"Face it." The man in the red scarf sneezed again. "You guys are sinking faster than Shoemaker after you allegedly pushed him in the ocean. If that's not enough motivation, there are always other factors to consider."

"What factors?"

"Such as that tomato you've been dogging on. Her name is Paradise. I'd hate to see someone like that get messed up."

"Don't touch her!" Jack lurched forward.

"That's up to you," he said. "Now get the hell out of here. This place stinks like fish." Clearing the phlegm from his throat,

205

he walked over to a car parked on a dirt road alongside the lake. Opening the door, he jumped in.

"Come back here!" Jack marched over to the car. "I want an explanation."

"We don't have time for talk." He turned the ignition key. "If you want to stay alive, not to mention keep Paradise breathing, stick to the plan." The stranger let out another wet sneeze and the red scarf fell off his face.

"Rupert!" Jack slammed his fist on the hood. "I knew it was you!"

"You didn't see me here." Rupert tied the scarf back on and stared down the reedy path. "You got company." He squealed the tires and sped away. The car's taillights bounced in the rutted road as it disappeared out of sight.

Jack turned his attention to the wooded path and gasped. Standing by the boat launch like a dark spirit, Shoemaker's wife clutched a cocktail with one hand and planted the other on her brutish hip. The woman's eyes dilated down to pencil points. "You threw my husband overboard." She hiccupped. "Murderers!"

"That's crazy," Jack shot back. "He probably jumped on purpose."

"You insensitive clod." She smashed her margarita glass on the ground. "What kind of thing is that to say to a woman in mourning?"

"What mourning? Rigor mortis barely set in on the guy and you're already flaunting your goods."

Shoemaker's wife's thin lips stretched like a rubberband and trembled with rage. She let out a loathsome scream and charged ahead like a bull.

The irate woman knuckled Wetterman in the head and he reeled backward.

Jack turned to run, but from behind a darkened corner of the bait shop, Sam Bales jumped out, wielding a shotgun. "You son of a..."

BANG!

Bales fired a shot in the air. "Don't move," he warned. "The police are on their way."

Jack froze just as Shoemaker's wife swung around and kicked him in the kneecap.

"Ouw!" Jack yelped, but his cries were buried under the sound of approaching sirens.

"It's the fuzz." Shoemaker's wife snickered. "You're dead now."

Jack looked down the path toward the entrance of the campsite. Flashing lights lit up the trees near the area where Wetterman's car was hidden. Several men with flashlights, undoubtedly cops, raced down the path.

"Run!" Jack shouted to Wetterman.

Sam Bales raised his weapon. Wetterman grabbed it and tossed it over by the bait shop.

Shoemaker's inebriated wife pulled her shoe off and repeatedly whacked Jack over the head with it. Jack pushed the irate woman, who standing near the dock, lost her balance and fell in the lake.

Hearts pounding like hammers, Jack and Wetterman ran off in the woods and disappeared into the night.

28

Daddy's Stash

(The Heist)

Norman Cooley leaned back in his chair. He puffed on a Cuban and stared out his office window. The sun shined like the heavens. It was a glorious morning.

Only yesterday the world looked bleak, but in one quick swipe, a horde of chicken livered troublemakers were eradicated from his life.

Nick Crowe got incinerated in a fire, Ed Shoemaker was shark bait in the ocean, and Lance Sheppard was being sought for embezzling money. Making matters even more desirable, Jack Snaggler and Bob Wetterman were on the run for arson and murder.

Norman often worried about the future of the company. Now, with so many agitators disposed of, the probability of failure had if not been eradicated, then at least depleted.

Life was perfect.

Norman's concentration broke when he heard the noise of someone unclogging their sinuses. It remotely sounded like a gorilla breaking wind. He set his cigar in the ashtray and straightened his tie. "Miss Puck." He smiled. "Please come in."

Harriet Puck walked through the door and sat down in a chair nearest the window. The sun explored the bottomless crevices of her aged face.

Norman grinned. "You're looking beautiful today."

"Flirt." Harriet snorted. She pulled a flask of the hard stuff from her pocketbook and took a slug.

Norman sighed.

Harriet had been a prized fish in the corporation since she first joined the organization. In her early years, the woman enjoyed a vigorous career in prostitution. Outside of her promiscuous past, the only shining moment in her inconsequential life, now over a half of century ago, was a brief career in nude modeling. In the aftermath of halfway houses, hard liquor and substance abuse, a once beautiful flower, she now withered like a dried weed in a waterless wasteland.

None of those particulars mattered to Norman. Looking into Harriet's eyes, now sunken like prunes in the hot July sun, his heart regressed into that same mischievous adolescent that once upon a time, hooked a jug of his father's homemade hooch, hid in the garage, and pleasured himself with the help of a pin-up picture showcasing Harriet in her once lush prime.

Norman glanced at his Rolex and took a last puff of his Cuban before dousing it in the ashtray. "It's time to make the rounds. I've got to ride the men like mules to keep them from taking advantage of me. Care to join me?"

"Bah." Harriet grunted.

Standing up, Norman took her arm and walked out of the door.

Jack Snaggler and Bob Wetterman hid behind a hedge near the front of the corporation building. Outside of a cat sniffing a trashcan, the place bustled with inactivity.

"Cooley walks through the plant at this time every day." Jack pointed. "Right on schedule."

In the near distance, Norman escorted Harriet out of the office. Opening a door, they walked into a side entrance that led to the production area.

Jack nudged Wetterman. "That's our cue. Let's go."

Keeping a low profile, they hurried along a row of high hedges.

"Wait." Wetterman grabbed Jack's arm. "Someone's coming."

The door opened. Puffing like a blowfish, a salesman walked out and shook a fat fist. He turned around and caught sight of Jack lurking in the bushes.

"What are you doing?" He raised a suspicious brow.

"Nothing?" Jack swallowed hard.

"Can you believe these guys?" The salesman pointed angrily at the building. "They think they're gods because they make bottle caps." He slicked back his hair and straightened his tie. "You know, this might be your lucky day," he told Jack. "What's my business, you might ask?"

"I didn't ask," Jack reminded.

"Gumballs," he announced proudly. "Who can resist the taste of a mouthwatering gumball. Kids lov'em. Adults crav'em. They come in all colors."

"I really don't want..."

The salesman popped a purple one in Jack's mouth. "For the low price of..."

"I don't want your stupid gumballs!" Jack spit the candy out. "Do you have any idea what I've been through? Do you?"

The salesman took a step backward. "Yes, but..."

"Shut up!" Jack shouted. "Between a fast food chef getting snuffed in a fire and federal agents chasing me, I'm ready to detonate. Now I'm supposed to steal a box of cigars. Cigars!" He glanced down at the salesman's hand and noticed he held a brochure about Fiji. Jack grabbed it and waved it in his face. "Where did you get this, from Shoemaker?"

"Now you're being rude." The salesman snatched it back. "Our company is based in Fiji. Everything from hairpins to dump trucks is made overseas and sold in the states for profit. It's the American way. "Confidentially," he paused, "there's a lot of things that might interest you in Fiji."

Jack eyed him with suspicion. "What do you mean?"

"You know exactly what I mean, Jack. Stop fighting the system."

"How do you know my name?"

"You're a legend, amigo. We're counting on you to make the big score." The salesman turned to leave.

"Stop right there!"

"Stick with the plan." Saluting, he hurried away.

Wetterman chewed nervously at his bottom lip. "What was that all about?"

"I don't know but he knew my name. He must be one of Lance Sheppard's moles. Forget him." Jack surveyed the grounds. "We have to stay focused. Cooley will be back any minute."

Jack walked over to the glass doors at the main entrance. Peering in, the only person in sight was Rosa, the receptionist. Nodding at Wetterman, they slipped inside.

Rosa Cruz sat at the front desk in a miniskirt and a purple top that looked more edible than a bushel of grapes. Wetterman's eyes glowed at the sight of her. He tried to speak but could only manage an inaudible squeak.

Rosa raised a questioning eyebrow.

"Straighten up." Jack grabbed Wetterman by the shoulders and shook him. "You sound like a squirrel with a mouthful of peanuts. We can't afford any slipups."

Footsteps came down the hall. Jack pushed Wetterman through an open door that led to the basement where Biddle's office was located. In the muddy overhead light, the place resembled a morgue.

Seated at his desk, Biddle examined the fishnet stocking that brought about his debacle in Ocean City. When he saw Jack at the doorway, humiliation scrolled over one half of his face and pleasure painted the other. He quickly tossed the contraband in a desk drawer and slammed it shut. "What are you doing here? The cops are looking for you. I figured you'd be on a plane to some remote corner of the world by now."

"We know about the cops," Jack said. He picked a file folder up from the clutter on Biddle's desk and tossed it on the floor, then stomped on it. "This place is a pigsty."

Biddle cowered in his chair. "What's wrong with him?" he asked Wetterman. "Is he crazy?"

"Isn't everyone who works here?"

"You used to work here," Biddle corrected. "Now you're just convicts. The feds were here. They went through your files. Cooley said he has enough evidence to put you guys away for the millennium."

Jack grabbed a tissue off Biddle's desk and mopped at his head. "I'll give it to you straight." He sat down on the edge of the desk. "Can you keep a secret?"

Wetterman warned, "That's like feeding a monkey a hand grenade. He'll blow his mouth off to everyone."

"We need to get to Atlantic City but the feds impounded our cars," Jack told Biddle. "We need yours."

Biddle chuckled. "Are you high on drugs? I'd be assisting criminals. That'd be insane."

"It is insane."

"You still can't have my car."

"I'm trying to be reasonable." Jack picked a folder up off Biddle's desk and swatted him over the head. "Didn't we pretend to be your friend when you got arrested at the shore for wearing women's clothes? Show some appreciation. Now hand over the keys before I have to kill you."

"You can't scare me." Biddle kicked his feet back on the desk. "I'm innocent."

Jack walked over and spun Biddle's chair around. "You really think you're innocent?"

"What do you mean?"

"If the feds arrest us, we'll name you as an accomplice."

"That's blackmail."

"Yes it is."

"Bastards." Biddle spat on the floor. "Your plane is crashing and you want to lock me in the cargo bay." He reluctantly pulled out his keys and tossed them to Jack. "If I get arrested, I'll have you passed around for cigarettes to every sexual deviate on the cellblock."

Jack glanced at the clock. Time was the enemy. Cooley would be back in his office at any minute. Walking over to a storage locker in the corner of the room, he opened the door. "Get inside." He motioned to Biddle.

"You serious? It's dark and cramped in there. I have claustrophobia."

"You can't be trusted," Jack told him. "The minute we leave, you'll call the feds."

"You really want me to get in there?"

"You really want me to kill you?"

Biddle's face shriveled like a prune. Grabbing a liverwurst sandwich off the desk that he packed for lunch, he stepped inside the locker. "You'll never get away with this!"

Jack slammed the door shut.

Jack hurried up the stairs from Biddle's office. Wetterman peeked from behind his shoulder. Looking down the hall, nobody was around.

"Now's our chance," Jack said. "Follow me."

Tiptoeing down the corridor, they found Norman Cooley's office. Motioning to Wetterman, Jack slipped inside the room.

Cooley's office mimicked the Oval Office at the Whitehouse, complete with a fireplace and oval interior walls. Three lavish windows sat behind his desk, and while there was no Rose Garden outside, a large flowerpot with a drooping cactus sat on the windowsill.

Wetterman grabbed a monogrammed handkerchief off Norman's desk and dabbed at his face. "This is breaking and entering. If the police get us, we'll have real crimes pending against us instead of all the pretend ones."

Ignoring his cohort, Jack honed in on the walnut cigar box sitting on the corner of Norman Cooley's desk. The words, '*Daddy's Stash*', were engraved on the side of it. He picked it up and stuffed it under his coat. "Got it."

"Are you listening? We're going to prison for this!" Wetterman pleaded.

"It's Cuban cigars, not the jewel of the Nile. Relax," Jack said. "All we need is to make it out of here without getting caught and we're home free."

Jagged lines of fear were inked on Wetterman's face. "Maybe we should head for Mexico. They're always sneaking over our borders. Why the hell shouldn't we return the favor?"

Brushing off his friend's insanity, Jack turned towards the door but stopped cold.

Harriet Puck, her face crumpled as dried up fruit, blocked the entrance. She planted her white knuckled fists on squishy hips. The old sow looked like she wanted to chew them like tobacco and spit them on the floor. "What are you doing here?"

"We were just leaving." Jack nodded and smiled.

"What's stuffed under your coat?"

Jack wrapped his hand tight around the cigar box. "Nothing."

"Thief!"

"Run!" Jack shouted to Wetterman.

Shoving the old woman out of the way, they bolted out the door but were quickly stopped. Norman Cooley rushed down one side of the hall. The feds hurried towards them from the other direction.

Rupinski clicked the safety off his weapon. He got down on one knee and targeted them. "Put your hands in the air!"

Trapped, Jack grabbed Harriet by the arm, pulled her in front of him and retreated back into Norman's office.

"Don't get stupid," Agent Hill said. "Release the woman. We promise to give you every professional courtesy."

"Dido." Agent Rupinski huddled on the floor in a sniper-like position.

Agent Hill took a few steps forward and stood in the doorway of the office.

"That's close enough," Jack warned. "Nobody needs to get hurt."

Agent Hill glanced at the bulge under Jack's coat. "What do you have under there, a bomb? Are you going to blow us up?"

"You really want me to answer that question?" Jack stared.

Not only didn't he want to answer, if the feds found out that the lethal weapon under his coat turned out to be nothing more than a cigar box stuffed with Cubans, he'd get more bullets to the head than a hot air balloon blasted with a machine gun. "I don't want any trouble."

Agent Rupinski stood up. Chewing on a piece of gum, he kept his weapon targeted. "Why don't we just shoot them and get it over with," he suggested to his partner.

"Too many witnesses," Hill whispered. "We'll give them a means of escape and pick up the trail afterwards. Once they're alone, BAM!" He turned to Jack. "Take it easy, cowboy. Hand over the woman and you can walk away."

Jack laughed. "You think I'm stupid? You'll open fire the minute I release her. She's coming with us."

Harriet crumbled into a mound of panic. Not since the days of the raid on her cathouses in the Bronx back in '65 had she felt so helpless. "Norman, stop him!"

Norman glared at Jack, whose undying determination to escape, refused to waver.

Things were falling apart. It was a bad day in the history of the company. When troublemakers like Shoemaker were assisted over the rail of a cruise ship in the middle of the ocean, Norman had assumed his problems were over. Then along came Jack Snaggler, irritable as a loose bowel, messing up the place.

Business already sagged and union representatives needled him about subpar working conditions. Things were so bad, he had to slash pension and retirement funds just to maintain his annual eighteen percent wage increase as acting CEO for the company. The men often faulted him for such actions, but waitresses got comparable tips in restaurants for serving coffee and salads. Why the hell shouldn't he get the same?

Like so many before him, Jack Snaggler had broken ranks from the mentally stable and the company was sure to fall under investigation. With the help of local unions, half the workforce would end up suing him for stress related illnesses. Healthcare premiums would skyrocket. It was only a matter of time before the doors of the corporation were finally nailed shut for good.

"Norman!" Harriet screeched again.

Norman pulled himself out the daydream. "I'm here, Harriet." He turned to Jack. "Guys like you give the industry a bad name. You'll never work in the business again!"

Given his present situation, Jack reasoned that he'd be lucky to escape without getting shot, or at the most, a fugitive working a backwoods farm in Georgia, picking cotton with a gang of illegal aliens for slave wages.

The picture would grow even bleaker if the feds arrested him. When they did a strip search, they'd find out that rather than a high grade explosive, he clutched at a box of Cubans. He'd be torched at the stake before sundown.

Thinking quick, Jack walked over to a closet in the corner of office and opened the door. "Get inside." He motioned to the feds.

Agent Rupinski didn't flinch. His finger jostled the trigger of the gun with all the stability of a kite in a windstorm; if the string snapped and he lost control, he might be inclined to kill everyone in the place.

"I'm not asking again." Jack bluffed.

"Norman!" Harriet yelled again.

Rupinski squeezed the trigger but Agent Hill stayed his hand before he could get off a shot. "Hold your fire." He glanced at Harriet, whose pruned face was baked with crevices of fear. "Too many bystanders and witnesses. Do as he says."

Norman glared at Jack, and Rupinski, ferocious by nature, nearly grew fangs.

Agent Hill reluctantly walked into the closet in the corner of the room. Norman Cooley and Agent Rupinski grudgingly followed him.

Slamming the door shut, Jack propped a chair against the handle. "That should hold them for awhile."

"Now what do we do?" Wetterman's eyes darted like overheated ball bearings.

Jack pulled Biddle's keys from his pocket and tossed them to Wetterman. "We make for the Atlantic City, just as we were told to do. With any luck we'll be able to find out what's going on and clear our names."

Seizing Harriet Puck by the forearm, Jack and his cohort hurried out of the office. In the main lobby, the janitor emptied a trashcan and Rosa polished her nails as she hummed a Spanish tune. She nodded and smiled as Jack, with a grumbling Harriet Puck in tow, hurried out the door.

Wetterman pointed to the rear of the parking lot. "Biddle's car is over there."

Running to the vehicle, Jack flung the door open and pushed Harriet into the backseat. Wetterman was already in the car, pumping the gas and turning the ignition.

Jack jumped in. "Get moving!"

Wetterman smacked the wheel with his fist. "She won't start."

Jack looked out the window. Near the entrance of the administration building, two brutish security guards stood by a soda machine. Their expressions were as compromising as a tractor trailer in a demolition derby. Recognizing Jack, they took off in a sprint towards Biddle's car.

"Hurry!" Jack shouted.

Someone suddenly jumped out from behind a hedge. It was the cranky gumball salesman that they encountered in the parking lot. He ran across the macadam and plowed into the security guards, headfirst. All of the men tumbled to the ground.

Quickly getting to his feet, the salesman brushed off his suit. "Watch where you're going, you idiots. This is a lawsuit in progress. By the time I'm done, this company will be buying me a condo in Fiji!" He craned his head around and winked at Jack.

Across the lot, Wetterman turned the ignition once more and the engine started. "Yes!"

Jack looked back at the guards who grabbed the salesman by the shoulders and flung him back on the ground like a sack of garbage. Nearly stepping on his head, they ran full force towards Biddle's car.

Tromping on the gas pedal, Jack and Wetterman fled the scene.

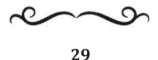

29

Drew Biddle

Minutes after the great escape, Walter the janitor, walked into Norman Cooley's office and emptied the trash. A rogue cigar sat on the boss's desk blotter. Looking to see if anyone was around, he picked it up and sniffed it.

"That's one damn fine after dinner smoke," he muttered and stuffed it in his shirt pocket.

A loud rap on a door made him jump.

"Open up!" someone yelled.

Thinking he might be hearing things, Walter slapped at his ears. God knows he wouldn't be the first employee at Cool Caps to hear voices. There were more crazy people at the company than there were rats at a cheese fest.

Another sharp thud pounded on the inside of the closet door.

"Are you deaf or just an idiot? Let us out!"

Walter the janitor walked over to the closet. A folding chair was propped up against the door. He pulled the chair away and opened it. Norman Cooley and the feds tumbled out the door.

Norman grabbed the janitor by the shoulders and shook him. "Which way did they go?"

"What are you talking about?" Irritation filtered in the janitor's voice.

"Don't play stupid."

Walter the janitor peeled Norman off him and stuck his nose in the air. Given his subpar pay and shoddy benefit package, he wasn't about to be bullied by a second rate CEO with onion breath. "Hands off," he grumbled and straightened his starched blue work shirt. "A couple of guys just ran down the hall, if that's who you mean. Just figured they were sneaking out of work early to hit the bar like everyone else. They're in Biddle's car."

Agent Hill glared fiercely. "How do you know that?"

"Dumbass. Open your eyes." The janitor pointed out the office window.

Outside, two security guards argued with a salesman. Pushing him out of the way, the guards ran through the parking lot just as Biddle's car pulled out and raced down the road.

Agent Rupinski kicked the wall. "Damn. They got away."

Agent Hill turned to Norman. "Where's Biddle's office?"

"In the basement, but..."

"Come on." Agent Hill snapped his fingers at his partner. The feds raced out the door.

The door to Biddle's office wasn't locked, but Rupinski kicked it open anyway. He spun around the room and targeted his gun in all directions.

"Biddle?" Agent Hill walked over to a desk in the corner of the room. Papers were scattered everywhere and littered with junk. He opened a desk drawer and fished around in it. Hidden in the back of the drawer behind some files, he found a black fishnet stocking and burgundy panties. Hill grimaced and flung the undergarments on the desktop.

A noise like someone shifting around came from inside a file locker in the corner of the room.

Agent Rupinski sidled over to it, unbolted the lock and opened the door. Inside, Biddle was squashed up like a rat in a pickle jar. He held employee files in one hand and a liverwurst sandwich in the other.

"Sorry, I didn't hear anyone come in." Biddle fidgeted. "I was updating some files of employees we're planning on firing."

Agent Hill raised an eyebrow and peered over his sunglasses. "From inside the file locker?"

Biddle gulped.

Hill grabbed Biddle's ear and pulled him out. "Sit down," he ordered. "Snaggler and Wetterman were here. They took off in your car."

"I don't know anything."

Agent Rupinski pointed a sharp finger."You helped them escape."

"That's crazy! I hardly know those guys."

"Really?" Agent Rupinski slapped Biddle in the head. "You went to a seminar in Pittsburgh with them but ended up at the shore. Nick Crowe was there too. That guy stinks worse than day old cat urine. You also used the company credit card at some sleazy hotel called The Sea Sprocket, and then got arrested for indecent exposure."

"Someone forged my name. It wasn't me!"

"More lies, eh?" Agent Rupinski slapped him again. "We got the arrest reports."

Agent Hill sat down on the edge of the desk. Pulling out a cigarette, he lit up. "You should make things easy on yourself. Tell us what you know, Biddle. We're only here to help. Hell, we'll even vouch for you at your trial. Maybe even drop some of the obstruction charges, along with the other crimes."

"What other crimes?"

"Does it matter?" He blew smoke in Biddle's face. "We'll make something up if necessary."

"You wouldn't."

"We're feds. That's martial law in this country. Trust me. We will."

Sweat ran down Biddle's neck and his bottom lip quivered. Things were getting ugly.

Biddle shivered as the feds stared at him. He thought about his many efforts to climb the corporate ladder. Even as far back as high school, he was shoved about by the masses and fodder for bullies. Towel slaps targeted at his manhood in the gym showers was the norm.

A ruddy complexion didn't help matters. A walking advertisement for pimple cream, women shunned him completely. Once in the lunchroom he mustered the courage to ask Debbie Abernathy for a date to the movies, but she laughed in his face and dotted her amusement by pouring tomato juice on his head.

Later on he enrolled in college. But after a failed stab at higher education, he landed a job at the Cool Caps Bottling Comapny as a file clerk. Advancement took time and determination. However, unlike the days of standing in the darkened corners of dancehalls like mismatched wallpaper, he gained the respect of his peers by alternate means. He talked to the boss behind closed doors and turned in coworkers for even the most meager infraction of the rules.

All of those indecent actions, like a train jumping the track, crashed in on him. With the criminal antics of Jack Snaggler, coupled with a suspect fishnet stocking from Pedro's Cantina in Ocean City, he was not only humiliated or in danger of being fired. He was on the verge of being arrested.

Biddle slumped down in his chair and ran his hands through his hair. "It's true." He thumped his elbows on the desk. "Snaggler and Wetterman were here. They said something about stealing a cigar box from Norman Cooley's office. Snaggler told me they were headed to Atlantic City. They stole my car keys. I tried to fight them off." He lied. "They beat me up and shoved me in that file locker."

Agent Hill stared. Rupinski pulled at the hairs on his chin.

"You want me to believe that?" Hill asked.

"I swear it's true."

"We'll talk about it at your arraignment." Hill pushed Biddle away and paced the floors. "None of this adds up. If Snaggler and Wetterman broke into the company trust fund or a security safe to steal money is one thing, but a cigar box?"

Brisk footsteps tromped down the steps into Biddle's office. Norman, his eyes burning with fire, materialized at the door. Turning his head, he glared at Biddle. "Does the little mole know anything?"

Agent Hill scratched his neck. "According to Biddle, Snaggler and Wetterman stole a cigar box."

Norman blinked uncertainly. "That's nonsense. Why would they do that?"

"That's what we want to know." Hill answered

"I have a handmade cigar box on my desk. It's a family heirloom," Norman said. "When my father, Clyde Cooley, opened the bottling business, it was given to him by a man named Marvin Caruso as a gift. It's hardly a gold block from Fort Knox."

"We know all about Clyde." Hill doused his cigarette in a coffee cup on Biddle's desk. "Your old man had more ghosts hiding in his closet than a haunted mansion. He was a bootlegger."

"And a shyster," Rupinski echoed and eyed Norman with distaste. "The nuts don't fall far from the tree."

"I resent that."

Hill walked over to the door. "No, you resemble that, but we don't have time to argue your family's psychological profile." He turned to Rupinski. "If Snaggler and Wetterman are headed for Atlantic City, we can still nail them on the expressway."

Agent Rupinski stuck a toothpick in his mouth and sucked at it. "I still don't get it. Snaggler and Wetterman are wanted for arson and murder. They're fugitives. Why come back here for a cigar box? "

"Use your brain." Agent Hill bopped Rupinski in the head with the heel of his hand. "Marvin Caruso was a mobster. He got arrested for moving hot merchandise on the black market." Hill crossed his arms. "What do you think is really inside that cigar box?"

Agent Rupinski's eyes widened. "You mean..."

"What else could it be?"

Norman's confused face reddened. A good Cuban was as enjoyable as hell, but that was the least of his worries. Snaggler and Wetterman managed to dupe him again. Even if the feds located and shot them, it still wouldn't calm the rising tide of degradation that he had already suffered at the hands of such irritants.

"You can't let them escape," Norman implored them. "I'll give a reward for their capture. Don't kill them. I want to skin them alive."

"Reward?" Biddle's eyes brightened.

"We'll find them," Agent Hill replied.

"Reward?" Biddle repeated. "I already told you. They're headed for Atlantic City. That should get me something." He held out his hand. Agent Hill slapped it away.

"Not so fast," Hill said. "How do we know you're not conning us? You could be making excuses while your buddies are headed for the Canadian border." He paused to consider. "You're coming with us."

Biddle laughed. "That's impossible. Can't you see how much work I have to do here?"

"What work?" asked Norman.

Biddle wordlessly sucked at his lips.

Agent Rupinski grabbed him by the shirt and hauled him out the door.

30

Life on the Expressway

Wetterman raced the car down the interstate. Crossing into Philadelphia, he veered off and made a detour on to the Atlantic City Expressway.

"Can't this thing go any faster?" asked Jack.

"The car is a piece of crap." Wetterman pushed down on the gas pedal and it backfired. "Biddle could use a tune-up."

Harriet Puck crumpled up in the backseat like a lobster in a fishbowl. She swatted Jack in the back of the head with her purse. "You won't get far. I worked the cathouses in New Jersey. The head pimps would have dropped you in the East River with the rest of the bottom feeders."

Wetterman gripped the steering wheel so hard that his knuckles turned zombie white. "Can't you shut her up or at least dump her on the side of the road? It's like being married to Shoemaker's wife."

Jack studied the rearview mirror, certain of pursuit. However, except for a couple of truck drivers pulling the nightshift, the road was empty. "We can't get rid of her," he told Wetterman. "If the feds talked to Biddle, they're already chasing us. If we get hemmed in we'll need her as leverage to escape."

Eyeing the cigar box seated on his lap, Jack opened it. A couple of Cubans, expensive no doubt, sat on red velvet clothe. Jack shook his head. "Why the hell would anyone go through all this for a box of cigars?"

"Never mind that," Wetterman said. "What do we do when we get to Atlantic City?"

Jack pulled a cell phone out of his pocket. "The man with the red scarf gave this to me when we were at Sam Bales' campground. He told me to call a woman named Luanda when we get to the casino."

A puff of grimy smoke unexpectedly billowed up from underneath the hood of Biddle's car. The engine sputtered. Red lights blinked on the dashboard and a loud backfire from the exhaust let loose like the blast from a shotgun.

Wetterman stared at the instrument panel. "You think she might be overheated?"

Groggy and tired, Jack watched as steam spewed from the engine. The car slowed to a crawl and truckers rolled down the highway, honking their horns, as the car clunked down the road. All the while, Harriet, an alcoholic prostitute who had never seen better days, croaked like a frog in a pond of alligators.

Life had fallen into decay.

"There's a rest area up ahead." Jack pointed. "Get the car off the highway."

Wetterman hugged the shoulder of the road and drifted down the off-ramp, into the rest area. As he hit the brakes, another spurt of steam jetted out from under the hood.

Jack stuck his head out the window and scanned the vicinity. A dim light bulb hung on the entrance door of a crummy restroom. Across the parking lot at Milo's Snack Shack, a nightshift cashier stood outside puffing on a cigarette and yakking on a cell phone. After a minute, he flicked the butt in the gutter and stepped back inside. Otherwise, the place was deserted.

From the backseat of the car, Harriet swatted Jack in the head again with her purse.

"Stop that!"

"I got friends in prison." Harriet said. "You'll be a party favor for every con on the cellblock."

"Stick a sock in her mouth!" Wetterman shook as if someone put a snowball down his shirt. He turned around and nearly crawled over the seat after her.

Jack latched on to Wetterman's shirt and pulled him back. "Have you lost your mind? You can't just go beating up old prostitutes. Keep your head."

Out on the highway, a car flashed its blinker and turned down the entrance ramp.

Wetterman's eyes blinked in fright. "Someone's coming."

"They're headed straight for us," Jack said. "Stay quiet."

The car rounded a curve and came to an abrupt halt, only a few yards away. A man with lopsided sideburns and a button down red plaid shirt hanging out of his trousers, walked over to a lone corner of the parking lot. Whistling a tune, he unzipped his pants and urinated on a tree. After a long stream of relief, he tugged his zipper shut. Looking up at the moon, he yawned tiredly and ambled towards Milo's Snack Shack.

Harriet poked her head out the car as the guy walked by. He stopped for an instant and looked in the car window. Jack sat still as a rock. Wetterman giggled nervously.

"You stupid louse," Harriet sounded off. "Call 911. I've been soiled."

Sniffing indifferently, the guy mumbled something and then continued on his way.

Wetterman wiped a trail of perspiration off his neck. "Maybe he's going to call the police."

"Forget him." Jack eyed a large billboard sign on the side of the road. It had a poster of a buxom blonde in a sunburst bikini holding a bottle of vodka and a deck of cards. Ironically, the ad was for the Lots of Slots casino in Atlantic City. "Over there. We can hide Biddle's car behind the billboard sign. We'll have to hitch a ride or call a cab."

Jumping out, Jack got behind the car and pushed. Wetterman stayed in the driver's seat and steered the vehicle behind a clump of wild bushes at the rear of the sign.

Jack picked up some sticks and bramble and threw it on the hood. "That ought to do it."

Wetterman exited the car and sat down on the hood. His face dripped of depression. "Our lives are ruined." He stated the obvious. "If we're going to get arrested, it should at least be for some legitimate charge like harassing Rosa in the workplace. Nope." He thrust out a pouty lip. "Instead I'm stranded on the expressway with a stolen car, an arsonist, and a defunct prostitute from the forties. That was a lousy decade anyway!" He shook his fist at the old woman then turned back to Jack. "You got us into this mess."

"You're blaming me?"

"Who else would I blame? Maybe you did start the fire at the diner. Everyone saw you run from the place with a jug of gasoline. "

"You're making a lot of accusations."

"Wouldn't you?"

"I didn't do anything wrong."

"Yeah, neither did the rest of the criminals in the penitentiary."

"Your problem is..." Jack stopped short and his eyes widened.

Harriet Puck managed to get out of the backseat of Biddle's car while he and Wetterman were squabbling. The old woman hobbled like a penguin on shaky legs towards Milo's Snack Shack.

"She's escaping!" Jack shouted. "If she gets to a phone, she'll call the cops."

Jack and Wetterman hurried after her across the parking lot.

Biddle fidgeted uncomfortably in the backseat of the feds' car. He tilted his head out the window and glanced up in the air. Police cruisers raced up and down the road. Helicopters with bright searchlights combed the night sky "That's the second chopper that went by," Biddle commented. "Snaggler and Wetterman must be big fish in the crime pond."

Agent Rupinski tromped the gas pedal to the floor as the car rocketed down the freeway. His unmoving face stared at the open road. Several times he took his hand off the wheel and stroked the handle of his pistol, almost as if it were a magic lamp that would grant him a wish not of fortune or fame, but a fresh kill before dawn.

Biddle cleared his throat. "I've got to go to the bathroom."

Agent Hill drained the last of a takeout coffee and passed him the empty Styrofoam cup.

Rupinski reached over and turned up a radio handset bolted to the dashboard.

"Are you guys copying me?" a voice asked. "We got a positive ID on that car you're chasing. The suspects pulled off at the North Gates Rest Area, about ten minutes outside of Atlantic City."

"That's just up ahead." Hill pointed.

Agent Rupinski floored the car and was already approaching the entrance ramp that led to the rest area. He turned out the headlights, glided the car alongside of the road until he entered the rear parking area, and then cut the engine.

Agent Hill pulled his gun out and unlatched the safety. Outside, the only person in sight was a vagrant over by a snack bar. "I'll take the area by the woods," he told Rupinski. "You circle around the rear of the snack building." Turning around, he glared at Biddle. "Stay in the car. If anything moves, bang on the horn. We'll come running."

The feds jumped out and took off in separate directions.

Biddle sat in the backseat of the vehicle and twiddled his thumbs. It was turning out to be a long night. Hill and Rupinski were antsy, and with any luck, Snaggler and Wetterman would be shot quickly so they could all go home and get some shut-eye.

Peering into the night sky, it was a beautiful evening. Stars glimmered like polished diamonds. The only smudge on an otherwise lovely night was a stream of grey smoke that jetted up behind a billboard sign in the corner of the parking lot. Squinting to see, Biddle noticed a car with some bushes piled on top of it.

"Good for him, the dumb bastard." Biddle laughed to himself. Some schmuck broke down on the road. If he didn't have the brains to check his oil before getting on the expressway, he deserved to get stuck.

Biddle tried to get a better look. Stepping out of the car, he walked toward the abandoned automobile. "Ha! The loser broke down and tried ditching the car in the woods behind a billboard, under some scrub." Biddle laughed to himself. "What an idiot."

Intent on vandalistic behavior, he opened his zipper and relieved himself in a steady stream on the side of the car. "Nothing like draining the old lizard." He sniggered as he thought about the poor sap that abandoned his car and got peed on.

However, a doughy look of alarm baked on Biddle's face as he looked down at the rear of the vehicle. A crinkled *Cool Caps* sticker was pasted on the bumper. His gloating expression turned to rage as he pulled broken vines and bushes away that were stacked up on the trunk.

Biddle's jaw dropped to the ground. "Snaggler!" He kicked the tire. "You wrecked my car!"

31

The Dimpled Green Pinto

The guy with lopsided sideburns and a psychedelic t-shirt walked out of Milo's Snack Shack. Chomping on a burrito, he burped, jumped in his car and punched the gas pedal. No sooner had he pulled out, he slammed on the brakes to avoid hitting Jack running across the parking lot.

"Sorry about that."

"No problem," said Jack, trying to get rid of him quickly.

The driver noticed the steam billowing up from a vehicle behind the billboard in the corner of the lot. "That your car?"

Jack nodded.

She's smoking like a banshee," the stranger said.

"We're having a little engine trouble."

The driver stuffed the remainder of the burrito in his mouth. Swallowing hard, he wiped away crumbs with his sleeve. "You should be careful out here. A couple of creeps with sunglasses are prowling around. Who wears sunglasses at night?"

"Federal agents," Wetterman, who stood nearby, answered.

"Shut up." Jack elbowed his friend.

"There's a service station a few miles down the road. Need a lift?"

Jack looked around the darkened corners of the rest area. If the feds were abroad, it was just a matter of time before they found Harriet Puck wandering around.

"We'd appreciate that," said Jack.

The driver pushed open the passenger door.

Wetterman tugged on Jack's arm and whispered, "What are you doing? This guy might be a cop, for all we know. We can't trust him."

"No choice. We need to get out of here. If Hill and Rupinski are around, the best we can hope for is a long jail term or a bullet to the head."

Jack called shotgun and jumped in the front seat. Wetterman reluctantly climbed in the back.

The driver hit the gas but made a sudden detour. "Look at that. Damn vandals! Some wiseacre is kicking the fender and punching the hood. A guy like that should be skinned alive."

Jack's eyes opened wide.

Biddle bounced up and down around the car as if he were doing a war dance. Shouting obscenities, he banged on the doors. When the driver pulled up alongside him, Biddle immediately saw Jack in the vehicle.

"Snaggler, you thief!" he ranted. "You ruined my car!"

"Keep your voice down."

"I won't!" Biddle shouted. "When I'm done testifying at your trial, they'll hang you. There's a reward for your capture. It'll take every penny of it to fix this thing."

"I don't have all day." The driver impatiently tapped on the wheel and revved the gas.

Biddle slapped himself in the head in disbelief. "Are you stupid? These guys are wanted men. They're dangerous. Look at my car!" He pointed at the gush of steam rising into the night air. "You're not going anywhere." He leaned in the passenger side and tried to grab the keys out of the ignition.

The driver expelled an irritable growl and latched on to Biddle's arm.

"Let go of me, you moron!"

Dragging Biddle over the top of Jack, the driver plunked him down on the gear shift console. "Now sit quiet and shut up."

"This is kidnapping!" Biddle punched the dashboard.

"Damn straight," the driver said indifferently. Sliding his foot off the brake, he sped on to the expressway.

The driver looked in the rearview mirror as he got on the highway. The two men in sunglasses ran through the parking lot of the rest area. A haggard woman followed them and pointed at the car behind the billboard sign.

"That old broad looks feral. Wasn't she with you guys?" the driver asked. "We could go back and give her a lift."

"No," they answered in unison, including Biddle, whose face was cemented into a permanent grimace.

From the rear of the car, police cruisers with lights flashing and sirens blaring made a rapid approach. The steady whoosh of a helicopter could be heard overhead.

"Lots of action on the road tonight," the driver said. "The cashier back at the rest area said the cops have roadblocks up. Someone didn't pay their parking tickets."

"Hello?" Biddle knocked on the windshield with his knuckles. "Are you blind? Look around. Do these guys look like they're selling magazine subscriptions? They're criminals!"

The driver shrugged and shifted his eyes toward Biddle. "You look familiar. I drove up the coast a few days back. Didn't I see your picture in a Maryland tabloid? Something about a riot at a beauty pageant."

Biddle stuck his nose in the air. "That wasn't me," he lied and changed the topic. "If you had half a brain, you'd be more worried about the derelicts you picked up instead of pageant nonsense." He glared at Jack. "That one in particular ruined my life."

"I'm no angel, so who am I to judge." The driver belched. "Where you boys headed?"

"Atlantic City." Jack answered.

"You're hitting the slots?" The driver's eyes brightened. "I love the boardwalk. Last time I was there, I made a killing."

"Who cares?" Biddle grumbled and sniffed. "Something smells rancid in here, like rotten eggs."

The driver reached under his seat and pulled out a pineapple scented aerosol can. He squirted it everywhere, including in Biddle's face. "That's probably me. I stopped by some crummy food joint up north a few days ago. I've had gas ever since."

Jack looked at the driver. The guy was familiar. He recalled seeing a man with lopsided sideburns and chili dribbling down his shirt. It was the same night that Lance Sheppard crawled out the bathroom window of the diner to evade capture from the police. "I remember you. You were at Alfred's Diner, right?"

"What's it to you?"

"The place burned to the ground last night."

"And they say there is no God." The driver chortled. He shifted his eyes to the cigar box gripped tightly in Jack's hands. "What are you hiding in there, a gun?"

Jack laughed nervously. "I keep my money safe." He rattled the box. "Crooks will hack you to pieces these days for a dollar."

"Now you're speaking my language." The driver sprayed another round of pineapple breeze. "Thieves are everywhere, not to mention punks on dope. At home I keep all my valuables locked up in a suitcase in a big freezer down the cellar."

Biddle raised an eyebrow. "That's ridiculous. Why would anyone put a suitcase in a freezer?"

"Why wouldn't they? Good luggage is airtight as a funeral drum. It keeps all your meats fresh." He nodded knowingly.

A police cruiser racing up the road caught the driver's attention. "Man, someone's in deep shit tonight." He tromped on the gas with all the grace of a gorilla stomping on a mouse.

A loud thump in the trunk of the car made Biddle jump. "It sounds like the spare tire is loose."

"That's no tire." The driver shook his head and chuckled.

"What then, groceries?"

The driver paused. "It's a body."

Biddle twitched in his seat. "That's funny."

"Is it?"

Biddle's widening eyes turned to look at Jack.

Whistling merrily, the driver flicked on the radio. The DJ played an old Stones' tune. The sound of the muffled car speaker reverberated off the interior walls of the vehicle.

The driver hummed in a gravelly voice and tapped his fingers on the steering wheel. "Yeah! I love the classics!" He nudged Biddle, whose chalky face, wired with fear, stared into the darkness.

The DJ suddenly interrupted the song. "We're rockin' and rollin' here on the Big Kaduna show. We got more info coming in from a listener about the big shakeup on the AC Expressway. This is Kaduna on WU81 FM. What's the scam?"

"Kaduna?"

"Yo man."

"Me and some of my buds are headed for the shore," the caller said. "There's a lot of crap going on."

"The news is reporting that police choppers are in the air and roadblocks are up," Kaduna said. "You see any of that action?"

"Cops are everywhere," the caller said. "We stopped at a rest area a few miles back. Two creeps with badges were talking about a guy named Snaggler. I think they were G-men."

"Sounds like a bust is going down," Kaduna commented.

"There's more," the caller continued. "We heard a rumor that Crazy Boris, the East Coast killer, is on the expressway. He was spotted driving an old dented up green Pinto. He has people with him."

Kaduna said, "Boris "the buzz saw" is on the road? Wow. Those passengers are dead as worms under a lawnmower and they don't even know it."

The driver reached over and flicked off the radio. "There's nothing but rubbish on that thing. Police helicopters and mass murderers? Ha! That makes me laugh. That really makes me laugh." He squirted the car down again with pineapple air freshener. "It's insanity," he concluded.

However, the continual swish of overhead aircrafts and a bright searchlight beaming down on the dimpled hood of the green Pinto, dictated otherwise.

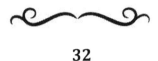

32

Boris 'The Buzz Saw' Crane

"STOP the vehicle. Come out with your hands in the air," a loud mechanical voice shouted from an overhead chopper.

Another loud thump from the trunk sounded out when the car drove over a pothole.

A look of horror, like the black plague, washed over Biddle. "You're Boris Crane!"

"Please! No autographs."

"Is that really a body in the trunk?"

"You mean Lou?" Boris sniffed and again squirted some pineapple aerosol. "Hot days wreak havoc on my hobby. Lou was a meat cutter at a deli in Asbury Park. Yeah, that's ironic." Boris sniggered. He pulled Lou's nametag out from underneath the visor and displayed it like a trophy, then put it back again. "When I got finished, there was nothing left but chopped mutton. The thing is," he paused and turned to Biddle, "I'm gonna do the same thing to you."

Biddle's eyes bounced like ball bearings.

Sitting beside him, Jack's mind reeled with the gruesome particulars reported in the newspapers about Boris Crane's life and adventures.

Boris, a drifter from the south, first burst on the FBI's most wanted list after a body turned up in a meat locker in upstate New York.

Since then, Boris worked his way along the eastern seaboard, claiming victims from Miami to Long Island. According to witnesses, he once even drove by the Outer Banks in a convertible with a cadaver wearing a sombrero in the passenger seat and calypso music blaring from the radio.

During his formative years, Crane's mother worked in a sewing machine factory before the government instituted NAFTA so that businesses could send all the jobs overseas and make the economy better for all the other countries. His father suffered a similar economic fate when steel mills bellied up and were reopened in foreign lands, allowing corporations to hire penny labor and fatten their stockholder's pockets. Boris and his family struggled, but unlike many of the other ninety-eight percent of the population at the mercy of the elite rich, they somehow managed to survive.

After high school, Boris relocated to Florida, where he got a job with an excavation crew near the everglades. He acquired the nickname, *The Buzz Saw*, not from moral misgivings, but from operating a chainsaw on a land clearing crew. Jack read one profiler's report that suggested it was Boris's most impressionable practice with an instrument of destruction. Coworkers later told reporters that whenever Boris picked up the chainsaw, his eyes glowed like a hyperactive kid in a candy shop. Only instead of a mischievous youth cutting up lumber, Boris was about to start stacking up the body count.

Boris eventually returned to his roots in New York. He got a job at a meat processing plant where he fell in love with Mindy Grable, a perky woman who worked in the mailroom. Unfortunately, Mindy was smitten by Max Becker, a shop supervisor who reeked of charisma and had trousers stuffed with testosterone. Aware of Boris's affection for the young woman,

Max taunted him about how Mindy loved to screw, a pleasure he'd never know.

Boris decided to pay Max a visit early one morning while he caught up on paperwork in his office. When Mindy later arrived for work, she found a note from Boris explaining that he decided to move on to greener pastures, but left her a parting gift in freezer number two. Upon opening the door, she found much more than a slab of beef in cold storage. Max, hung from a meat hook, was carved up like a holiday goose.

It was official; *The Buzz Saw* was born.

Even with a swarm of flashing lights from police cruisers and the whoosh of helicopters beating their wings against the sky, Boris drove boldly down the expressway, humming a tune and squirting pineapple air freshener every mile of the way.

"We're gonna get axed!" Wetterman scratched at the doors and windows like a man waking up to find he's buried six feet under the sod.

Thunderstruck, Jack looked over at Biddle, whose expression had all the horror of a kid on a rollercoaster that just jumped the track. If Crane didn't kill him, a coronary surely would.

In the distance, bright lights of casinos lined the boardwalk. But not all the illumination came from the glitz of towering gambling houses. Less than half a mile away, police cars were strung across the road like a bundle of Christmas lights. As they drew closer, Jack saw an army of lawmen ducked behind vehicles, targeting their weapons.

"Damn-it!" Boris punched the steering wheel. "The cops ruin everything."

Boris reached under the seat again. This time instead of an aerosol can, he pulled out a carving knife that to Jack's frightened eyes, looked bigger than the Taj Mahul.

The dire circumstances moved much too quickly across Jack's mind to register the magnitude of the situation. Boris Crane, a man who snuffed out more people than there were alligators in a Florida swamp, was about to gut them like a tuna fish. Barring the possible exception of Ed Shoemaker who fell overboard a boat in the Atlantic, forever evading a life of torment from his obnoxious wife, happy endings were sparse.

"STOP the car! You're surrounded," a voice again thundered from above. The rush of air from the copter's blades pushed the car around the road.

Jack considered the idea that God was giving one last command to mark the end of an impossible day. But when he cocked his head out the window to look up, rather than a Supreme Being, the only person he saw was a policeman with a helmet and bullhorn leaning out the side of a helicopter.

Only yards from the roadblock, Boris slammed on the brakes. The car spun in a circle until it came to a screeching halt.

An undercover cop with a scruffy beard and a faded green t-shirt ran around the car like a tiger circling a lamb-chop. "Give it up, Buzz Saw." He got down on one knee and pointed his weapon.

"You want a piece of me?" Boris waved his fist out the window.

"There's no escape. You're hemmed in."

Boris reached over and grabbed Biddle by a clump of hair. Biddle turned white with terror. "If anyone makes a false move, the beauty queen here gets flayed." He held up the carving knife. The edge of the blade glinted in the wake of police lights.

"Put down the knife and release the hostages," the cop said again. "Things don't have to end this way."

Boris laughed. "You got more punchy cops here than hunters at a duck shoot. They're ready to fire at the rattle of a branch."

"I'm not asking again. You gonna cooperate?"

Grinning like a shark, Boris stomped on the gas pedal. The car headed straight for the police blockade. A cop with a cigarette dangling out of his mouth jumped over the guardrails and rolled down the embankment. Another one hunkered down in his police cruiser, holding his breath and awaiting certain impact.

Jack braced himself. Trapped in a speeding vehicle, ready to be punched with bullets and crashed into by a squadron of police cars, the only thought that flashed across his ruptured mind was that of Paradise, the brunette from Eddie's Alamo. He pulled the girl's picture out of his shirt pocket. Judging by the backdrop of lawmen, coupled with a depraved killer intent on carving them up like squid at a sushi bar, it might be his last look.

"Yeah!!" Boris stiffened up and pushed the gas pedal to the floor.

Boris tried to thread the car between two police cruisers parked haphazardly on the road. The green Pinto slammed off the side of one car, bounced against the other, and then continued accelerating down the road.

Agents' Hill and Rupinski arrived on the scene minutes after Boris smashed his way through the roadblock. Seated in the backseat, Harriet Puck grumbled miserably.

Hill jumped out of the vehicle and flashed his badge at an undercover cop. "What happened?"

Red and yellow rotary lights from police cars pulsed on the undercover cop's face. "Boris Crane is on the road." A rush of adrenaline caked his voice as he paced back and forth. "We had him in our back pocket. We had him!" He kicked the side of a police cruiser. "He busted through the roadblock and took off. He had passengers with him."

Agent Hill stiffened. "Where are they?"

"Who knows." The cop lit a filterless cigarette. "Those guys would have a better chance of survival in a bathtub filled with acid."

Rupinski slammed his fist on the hood of the car. "The cashier back at the rest area swore he saw Boris and that he picked up hitchhikers. That had to be Snaggler. They got away again." His lip curled in irritation. "Bad call, Hill," he told his partner. "We should have shot them when we had the chance."

Agent Hill stared into the distance at the glittering lights of the casinos and pondered the state of affairs. Things would have gone easier if *The Buzz Saw* would have wrecked in a fiery crash. Then they all could have gone home, secure in the knowledge that everyone was dead. He might even have been able to take credit for Boris's demise. A promotion would have been in order. Maybe even a talk show interview. He wasn't sharing any of the glory with Rupinski, either. Screw him. He was an obnoxious crybaby with a gun fetish.

Rupinski rubbed at a ball of tension rising on the back of his neck. "Those losers could be anywhere by now."

Harriet stuck her grey head out of the back of the feds' car. "They're troublemakers. When I used to turn tricks in the Bronx we knew how to deal with people like that. They'd disappear. Nobody would ever hear from them again."

"This aint the Bronx," Agent Hill snapped at the old broad. "When we shoot people, it's all legal."

"Bah." Harriet made a noise that sounded like an irritable sheep.

Agent Hill scowled at the sound of the woman's voice. He wondered how beautiful she must have been in her provocative youth. What was once a tasty plum, aided by alcohol and substance abuse, had wasted into a shriveled peach.

"We'll never pick up their trail." Rupinski put his hands on his hips and spat on the ground.

Harriet grumbled, "Lots of Slots."

Agent Hill tilted his head. "What did you say?"

"You heard me, dumbass. They said they were headed for the Lots of Slots casino."

Agent Hill's muscles tensed into slabs of hardened clay. He gazed at the shimmering casino that towered on the boardwalk, just down the road.

"Let's get moving." Rupinski already had the driver's door open. He stopped briefly to look at Harriet in the backseat, whose face was as inviting as a bucket of road tar. "What do we do with her?"

"We can't just dump her on the road," Hill answered.

"Why not?"

Momentarily stymied, Agent Hill sucked at his lips. "Too risky," he finally concluded. "If she gets mugged or arrested for solicitation, it'll give the department a blackeye. We'll call Norman Cooley. Let him pick her up. He got a nice stash from screwing over all his employees on their pension plans. He can afford a taxi cab."

"What if he refuses?"

"I don't have all the answers." Agent Hill's voice muddied with irritation. He again glanced at Harriet who picked at her nose. "They send old horses to the glue factory, right?" He snapped his fingers. "Hit it."

Agent Rupinski revved the engine and flipped on the flashing lights. Stomping on the gas pedal, he sped around an obstacle of police cars scattered over the highway and took off toward the boardwalk.

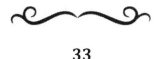

33

Lots of Slots

Glittering casino lights towered into the sky like glowing stars over the coastline. The rim of the sun, a red ball of melting steel, rose over the ocean, as the dented green Pinto pulled up in front of the Lots of Slots casino.

"Hell of a night, huh fellas?" Boris squirted pineapple air freshener again.

Jack glanced back at Wetterman, who looked paralyzed with fright.

"I don't want to die!" In the front seat, Biddle's lips trembled and he refused to open his eyes.

Boris gave Biddle a playful slap. "Hear those sirens?" In the near distance, a line of police cars, hot in pursuit, were already closing in. "Fortune smiled on you today, cupcake. I got to be moving on."

"You mean we can leave?" Jack shivered in his seat.

"You guys got bad karma." Boris picked at his teeth in the mirror. "No offense, but I don't like drama. A few weeks ago I met a bartender named Melvin in Margate. He asked me to stop by the next time I was in town. You know, have a drink of tequila with him." He curled the handle of the knife in his fingers. "He'll be feeding worms before I'm done." Boris turned to Biddle. "Now get out before I change my mind."

Wetterman bolted out of the backseat of the vehicle, and when Jack opened the door, Biddle literally crawled over top of him, fell to the ground and landed on his head.

Boris's eyes clicked over them, almost as if tabulating an unpaid debt. "I'll be seeing you boys again, real soon." He winked at Biddle.

Nearby, flashing police lights scattered the highway like spilled marbles in the sun.

Boris leaned his head out the window of the dimpled green Pinto. "Yo fruitcake!" He yelled at a cop standing on a curb and revved the engine. "Show a little respect for *The Buzz Saw*, right?"

The cop's jaw went slack and he dropped his takeout coffee from Starbucks.

"Giddy up!" Boris peeled out, clipped two parked cars and made a hard left down a one way street.

The cop jumped in his car, spun his tires in a circle and took off after him.

Jack stared at the Lots of Slots casino, a favorite among gambling addicts. The place bustled with wealthy tycoons who stood for greed, capitalism and the American appetite for taking risks with other people's money. Trimmed in bronze and gold décor, the casino served as one of the many entertainment meccas on the boardwalk. Advertisements of coming attractions, most featuring washed up '80s bands on wannabe comeback tours, lined the front of the building.

"That's impressive." Wetterman gawked at the towering structure.

"You idiot." Biddle glared. "We almost just got hacked up by a murderer and you're admiring the architecture?" He paced the road and muttered curses.

Jack sat down on the curb. His downturned expression was so miserable that a passerby mistook him for a bum and tossed him a quarter.

Wetterman plunked down next to him.

"This can't be happening." A dark shadow hung over his eyes. "We must have heatstroke. Right now we might be locked up in a padded room right next to Eileen Klump and don't even know it." He put his head in his hands. "I'm even still having nightmares about a dancing banana, for God's sake. Who does that?"

"Stop belittling yourself," Jack told him. "You're no more unstable than everyone else we know."

"Is that supposed to make me feel better?" Wetterman picked up a rock and angrily tossed it across the parking lot.

Regardless of their misfortunes, Wetterman was right. Nothing made sense. Days ago they worked at a bottling facility and made good money wasting company time. Now, sitting on a curb in Atlantic City, they were penniless vagrants waiting to be arrested by the authorities.

Biddle stopped pacing, marched over, and wagged an angry finger at Jack. "You got me into this mess!"

"Calm down. You got arrested for indecent exposure at a beauty pageant. That doesn't make you a hardened criminal like the rest of us. Why don't you go home?" Jack suggested. "Nobody wants you here anyway."

"How can I leave? You wrecked my car!"

Wetterman pleaded, "Why can't we run off to a deserted island like Shoemaker always wanted to do before his wife drove him to suicide? Is that too much to ask?"

Ignoring his friends, Jack stood up and looked around. Outside of a vendor selling shriveled hot dogs on a street corner, all remained quiet. "We can't sit here all day. We're open targets if the feds show up." He paused. "Let's go inside."

"I'm not going anywhere." Biddle's jaw snapped like a wild dog. "I didn't do anything."

Jack shrugged. "It's your neck, but the feds think you're guilty. If you go to prison wearing burgundy panties, you'll be every inmate's personal escort service and cheap thrill for the night."

Motioning to Wetterman, they went up the walkway and stepped in the rotating glass doors at the casino's entrance.

Biddle pursed his lips nervously and hurried after them.

Inside, mobs of gamblers huddled around poker tables. Most of the patrons were retirees, eager to give away what little money arrived in their mailboxes in the form of welfare and social security checks. Cocktail waitresses in skimpy red outfits delivered industrial strength drinks to wealthy clientele lining the blackjack tables. In the lounge, some joker with a flashy striped tie and big teeth played a piano and belted out songs about falling in love and getting laid.

A waitress with a bunny tail breezed by and Wetterman grabbed a drink off her tray. "The place is packed. You really think this is a good idea?"

"Wait here and stay under the radar," Jack told him. "I'm gonna have a look around."

Jack walked through the center aisle of the casino. Old ladies guarded their slot machines like soldiers standing a post. Security guards with stern jaws roamed the floor, leaving him imagining that he was being watched.

Turning right down the main lobby, Jack stood in an isolated corner near the back wall. Glancing up and down the corridor, he pulled out the cell phone that the man in the red scarf gave him at the campground. A number was programmed in the phone under the name *Luanda*. Taking a deep breath, Jack called it. After two rings, someone picked up.

"Hello?"

"Is this Luanda?"

"What if it is?"

"This is Jack Snaggler. I was told to contact you."

"You look ragged. Rough trip?"

"You can see me?"

"Stop looking so damn conspicuous. Stick to the plan."

"Where are you?" He growled. "Everyone keeps talking about some plan and..."

Jack looked in the lobby and froze. Standing behind a desk, a female in champagne satin pumps, a low-cut turquoise blouse, and hair stylishly pinned up, stared back at him. Regardless of her chic appearance, there was no mistaking the woman.

Walking over to her, he tilted his head suspiciously. "Eileen?"

"My name is Luanda." She tapped the nametag on her blouse.

"Do I look blind?"

"Are you?"

"Stop lying!" Jack pounded on the desk. "You're Eileen Klump. The last I heard, you jumped out of an ambulance on your way to a mental hospital."

"I don't know what you're babbling about." She stuck her nose in the air. "You need a Reward's Card to be in this line."

"You're crazy! You probably don't even remember me."

"Do you have a Reward's Card?"

"No."

"Then I don't need to remember you." She slammed a book shut that sat on a desk. Glancing around, she leaned down and whispered, "Someone's looking for you."

"What makes you think they're looking for me?"

"Is your name Jack?"

"Yes, but..."

"Then who else would they be looking for?" she said smartly. "Take good care of '*Daddy's Stash*.'" A smirk crossed her face and she slapped Jack on the cheek. "You would have made Marvin Caruso proud."

"Nick Crowe told me about Caruso," Jack said. "He was a mobster who turned state's evidence in exchange for a ticket into the witness protection program. He later changed his name to Alfred, bought a diner, and ran the place ever since. It burned to the ground the other night. What else do you know about him?"

Eileen said, "Only that the lawyers won't be happy. They made a fortune on gastritis lawsuits out of that place."

Jack leaned in and whispered, "What's going on here, Eileen?"

"You ask too many questions, Jackie-boy. Stick with the plan and everything will go off without a hitch, capuche? Now go mingle. Maybe shoot some craps." She pointed over towards the Tundra Bar. "Tell them Luanda sent you." She tapped her nametag and turned to leave.

"Wait!"

Balancing herself on her pumps, Eileen disappeared through a back door and into the employee lounge.

Jack's head pounded. Every answer brought more questions. Barreling towards the edge of a cliff with henchmen like Hill and Rupinski trailing him, it was just a matter of time before he skidded over the edge.

Out in the hall, Wetterman dumped quarters into an old-style payphone and repeatedly dialed the number at Cool Caps. When Rosa Cruz picked up the phone at the front desk, Wetterman's mouth turned to mush and he hung up. Unable to contain his appetite for rejection, he dialed again.

Jack pulled the receiver out of Wetterman's hand and slammed it down. "What's wrong with you? That's a public phone. Police can trace the number."

"My cell is dead." Wetterman pulled his mobile phone out of his pocket and stuffed it in an empty martini glass that sat on a window ledge. "It doesn't matter. In the end we'll be arrested and tossed in the slammer for the millennium."

"CRAPS!" someone shouted.

Over by the Tundra Bar, a crowd gathered around some hotshot at a High Roller's table.

Jack turned his attention back to Wetterman. "Pull yourself together and stay focused. If the feds aren't here already, they will be."

"CRAPS!"

"Shut up already!" Jack shouted, his nerves frayed and ready to pop like piano wire.

A couple of bouncers with muscles as big as lumberjacks eyed him distrustfully.

Driblets of sweat gathered on Jack's forehead. They were backed against a wall. Hell, they were cemented in it.

Back home, people were already at work. Word would have leaked out that he and Wetterman were fugitives. By midday, coworkers would scour through their desk drawers and steal everything from paperclips to coffee mugs. As the day progressed, office workers would quietly settle back into a normal state of depression. They'd read newspapers, ignore purchasing requisitions, and dream about hitting the lottery. Their ordinary world would continue. But for Jack Snaggler and Bob Wetterman, things were anything but ordinary. Life was as secure as a date with Boris Crane and his carving tools.

"CRAPS!"

"That's it." Jack cracked. "I'm going to kill someone."

A mob of partying gamblers cheered a shooter wearing a leisure suit leftover from the '70s era and a Hawaiian luau shirt. He tossed the onlookers a few dollars as a show of appreciation and financial supremacy. The crowd loved it. Throw a bunch of monkeys a banana and they'll beg for more.

Jack walked towards the shooter to take a closer look but stopped short. He rubbed his eyes in disbelief.

The shooter spun around, snapping his fingers to an old Troggs song called Wild Thing, and then kissed the inebriated woman beside him, who slurped at her drink like a bad drain.

Jack pointed an angry finger. "Nibbles!"

34

Nibbles Revisited

"CRAPS!" Nibbles hollered again and let the dice fly.

Onlookers clamored around the shooter who flaunted his gold Rolex and a wad of cash. With his smug attitude and dapper vintage clothes, he didn't seem to mind if a few economically deprived slugs skipped a side of flapjacks for breakfast because of an overnight rise in gas prices. Someone had to assume the position of poverty. As far as Jack could ascertain as he watched the scene unfold, it was critical to the preservation of capitalism.

A curvy waitress in high heels strutted across the room, balancing a tray of drinks in her hand. "Cigarettes. Cocktails." She handed Jack a glass of rum and whispered, "Compliments of the shooter."

Jack walked over to Nibbles and grabbed him by his coat. "What are you doing here?"

Nibbles pushed Jack away and dusted off his jacket. "Easy on the threads. Who are you?"

"Don't play stupid." Jack would have loved to punch that face in. "We met in Ocean City. I nearly made love to your wife."

"I resent that," said Nibbles. "My wife is as faithful as a Saint Bernard."

Floating on a waterbed of inebriation, Cecile hiccupped and swigged her drink, all the while slobbering over an Italian gentleman wearing an Armani suit.

Nibbles, a sensitive man dedicated to the simple pleasures of life, such as filming adult videos, would likely add to his proceeds before the night ended.

"I'm supposed to meet someone here," Jack said. "Is that you?"

A muscular galoot with a hotel security badge walked by and eyed Jack. "Is there a problem?" He sniffed like a coke addict with a deviated septum. Tilting his head suspiciously at the cigar box in Jack's hand, he asked, "What do you got there, steamboat?"

"I'm not sure it's any of your business," Jack retorted.

"Smart guy, huh?" The security guard crossed his arms. "For all I know that's a brick of hashish or a bomb."

"That's defamation of character," Jack warned. "Can't a guy walk down the street without getting accused of being a criminal? I thought this was a free country?"

"Don't be ridiculous." The guard scoffed. If this were a free country, less than two percent of Americans wouldn't have more than the other ninety-eight combined, right?" He poked a finger in Jack's chest. "You're interfering with all the paying customers who come here to have fun and lose money. It won't be tolerated. Move along."

"But I know this guy!"

Nibbles nodded at the security guard. "Yup. He's one of my gophers."

The guard glared at Jack and walked off.

A moat of irritation muddied Nibbles' face. "Instead of shooting torpedoes, you should thank me. If I didn't rescue you when you were in Ocean City screwing the company, not to mention my wife, the feds would have nabbed you. There's no telling what those goons would have done."

"What do you know about the feds?"

"I know they want to string you up by the balls." Nibbles glanced at the cigar box that Jack held. He dribbled at the corners of his mouth just looking at it. "Is that '*Daddy's Stash*'?"

Jack tilted his head. "What's so interesting about a box of cigars?"

"Finest smoke this side of Cuba." Nibbles sniggered. "Keep that thing safe." His voice turned serious. "We can't have anything happening to it, not to mention that tomato you've been dogging on. Paradise, right?"

"Nobody better touch her."

"You make the call." Nibbles winked. Straightening his tie, he jiggled a pair of dice and tossed them against the back wall of a gaming table.

"CRAPS again!" a wild-eyed spectator yelled.

Nibbles shook his head. "I'm unlucky as a declawed cat in a cage with a bulldog." He turned to Jack. "If I had half a brain, I'd head for the nearest exit and take the first pink taxi in the parking lot."

"Taxis are yellow," said Jack.

"Not the one you're looking for." Nibbles pointed out.

"Stop playing games." Jack pushed Nibbles again.

The security guard returned and put a hand on Jack's shoulder. "You sure this clown isn't bothering you?"

"He's becoming a pest." Nibbles glared. "This used to be a respectable casino. People could come here and help the casino make enormous profits at the expense of the little guy. Now all kinds of trash are walking around. This one in particular tried to screw my wife," he told the guard. "The next thing you know, he'll want me to pull out a camcorder and film the action."

Cecile belched. Sloshed as a wet sponge, she drifted from one potential lay to the next.

"He's a liar!" Jack hollered.

"I heard enough." The guard pulled out a radio and called for assistance. "I'm over by the Tundra Bar. We got a

255

troublemaker." The guard stopped talking and stared at a disturbance near the back of the casino.

A couple of suits wearing sunglasses rumbled through the aisles like bulldozers. They didn't look just irritated; they looked pissed. One of them held a badge up and pushed patrons aside as he steamrolled ahead.

"Hey you!" The guard shouted and then turned to Jack. "I'll deal with you later." He took off in the direction of the fracas.

Nibbles sipped his drink. "I'm thinking that's your cue to leave."

"FEDS!" Jack tugged at Wetterman's arm.

Wetterman pushed Jack away. His eyes were fixed on something across the room of the casino.

"Are you listening?"

Ignoring his friend, Wetterman walked over to a slot machine underneath an escalator. On the video display of the machine, a piece of yellow fruit in a blue bandana danced.

Wetterman's stare was so hypnotic one might have thought Rosa just strutted by wearing nothing but silk lingerie. "Paso." He sighed deeply. "The dancing banana."

Pulling out five bucks, Wetterman fed the money into the slot machine. He knocked his knuckles on the video display for luck and then pulled the lever.

Nothing happened at first. Then three bananas rolled up on the screen and bells started to ring. A light atop the gambling device shined the word JACKPOT, and Paso, that wild and crazy piece of fruit, began to rumba.

Wetterman gawked at the flashing JACKPOT sign. The dancing banana whirled around in a dust storm, spitting out hundred dollar bills. If the grin on Wetterman's face was any wider his jaw would have fallen on the floor. He raised his hands jubilantly. "I'm rich!"

Jack shouted," You idiot! The feds are coming. We need to hurry."

"Are you joking?" Wetterman blinked stupidly. "I just hit the jackpot!"

Across the aisle, Agent Hill jumped over a barstool and took off in a full sprint. Agent Rupinski knocked a tray of cocktails out of waitress's hand and pressed forward.

"Don't move!" Agent Hill pointed.

"We didn't do anything," Jack implored him.

"Who cares? Hand over the cigar box." Agent Hill gripped his gun.

Jack blinked stupidly and raised the cigar box in the air.

A geek with crooked teeth and a gaudy striped shirt shouted, "He's got a bomb!" The geek crouched underneath a blackjack table to avoid a spray of bullets.

The floodgates of chaos broke loose. Gamblers hid behind roulette tables and under the counter at the Tundra Bar.

Jack pulled Wetterman away from the slot machine, buried himself in the crowd and headed for the exit.

When the Agent Hill and his partner arrived on the scene, they ordered Harriet Puck to stay in the car, but the old souse was stubborn as a blood stain on white linen.

Minutes after the feds left, she got out of the vehicle. After taking a nostalgic walk and reliving memories of one of her old stomping grounds where she turned tricks for cash – and in some cases cheap whiskey – she meandered into the casino.

Inside, people ran around like cockroaches being sprayed by insecticide. Some nerd in a plaid shirt yelled something about a bomb in the building.

"The hell with it," Harriet grumbled.

It was a long day. A veteran of backstreet motels and stained bedspreads, she wasn't used to spending much time on her feet. Harriet plunked down on a stool at a slot machine that sat underneath an escalator. The machine made a horrendous racket. "Stop it!" She slammed her bony fist down on it, hoping to make the idiotic banana stop dancing.

A security guard in a trim uniform rushed across the floor. "Over at the Paso machine," he jabbered on his headset. "Someone hit the jackpot."

Digging into her memoirs of the good old days, Harriet recalled a bust at Ugly Jim's Pub, back in the fifties. She spent the night taking the wind out of the sails of a spry sailor on leave in Atlantic City who looked a little like the security guard, or at least a close cousin, when the cops burst in and hauled her off to jail. Memories were golden.

Across the aisle, the floor boss hurried over to Harriet. "Don't worry lady. We got some trouble but it's under control." He glanced up at the jackpot sign. "This is your lucky day."

"Ass-wipe," Harriet insulted. "This damn thing makes too much noise." She eyed a half empty cocktail sitting by an ashtray beside the slot machine. Picking it up, she guzzled it down.

"You don't understand." The floor boss grimaced at the old hag. "You just hit the jackpot."

"Bah." She passed him the empty cocktail glass. "Just bring me another drink, pinhead."

Jack raced through the casino and headed for the exit. He turned around to see Agent Rupinski grab a barmaid by her bunny tail and toss her out of the way.

"Hurry!" he hollered to Wetterman, who lagged behind.

Biddle shot out of an aisle and chased after them. Twice he latched on to Jack's shirt and twice he was swatted off like a pesky fly. "Agent Hill! Rupinski! Over here!"

Slipping through rotating glass doors, Jack and Wetterman exited the building into the parking lot. Across the road, a mud-spattered pink jeep with an Alfred's Diner bumper sticker was parked against the curb. It was the same vehicle that Nick Crowe drove when he sputtered into the Sea Sprocket in Ocean City.

The driver honked the horn and flashed the lights on the jeep. "Snap it up. The meter is running," he hollered out the window.

Jack marched across the street and flung the passenger door open.

"Crowe, you pompous ass, what are you..." He stopped short.

The driver wore green army fatigues, a backwards Las Vegas baseball cap, and a fake beard that looked as if it were purchased at a dime store.

Jack looked closer. "Greene?"

"You guys need a written invitation?" He spit a wad of chewing tobacco out the window. "Get in."

Jack turned his head to see the feds barrel out the exit door of the casino. Despite the consequences of a crowded parking area, Agent Rupinski pulled out his gun and locked on his target. Panic overcame the clientele, frightened by the danger or perhaps annoyed at losing their favorite seat at the blackjack table. Trying to get out of the way, they jammed the casino's glass entrance doors like fistfuls of worms in a shot glass.

Wetterman quickly crawled in the backseat of the jeep. Jack sat down in the front but was pulled back when someone grabbed him.

"You're not going anywhere!" Biddle's stubby little fingers clung to his waist.

"Let go!"

Biddle shouted, "Rupinski, over here!"

Rupinski turned to look and put Biddle in the crosshairs.

Biddle's eyes swelled like a river. "Not me, you klutz. Shoot them!"

Rupinski squeezed off a shot. The bullet landed in the side of the jeep with a thud. Gasping, Biddle let go of Jack and dived in the open door of the jeep. Jack jumped in and slammed the passenger door shut.

The driver spit another wad of chew tobacco out the window. "Arrivederci." He blew Rupinski a kiss. Squealing the tires, he took off down the highway.

In the parking lot, the feds pushed the valet attendant so hard he rolled over the hood of a Mustang. Waving guns and badges, they watched as the pink jeep made its hurried departure.

Aside from Agent Hill and his partner, Jack noticed other recognizable faces in the crowd. He involuntarily reached up and touched the crinkled photograph that he kept devotedly in his shirt pocket.

"We need to go back!" Jack grabbed the driver by the shirt.

"What?"

"You heard me. Turn around!"

"Are you on drugs?" The driver laughed and dusted his hand away. "Sit back. Enjoy the ride. You guys are in for the long haul."

Jack scanned the parking lot again and frowned. Near one of the entrances of the casino, he saw the blue-eyed brunette with an overnight bag getting out of a car with some friends. Paradise was checking in.

35

Slum's Air Service

Jack glanced at the driver. The fake beard he wore vaguely resembled a bird's nest strapped to his chin. The guy looked familiar, and as far as Jack could ascertain, he was last seen making an escape through the air duct at the Cool Caps administration building.

"Greene, is that you?"

"It isn't me." He kept a firm grip on the wheel and stared straight ahead at the road.

"Thanks for the lift." Not knowing the game, Jack played along.

"Trust me. I'd rather be in Fiji instead of chauffeuring losers whose lives revolve around a bottling company."

Jack raised an eyebrow. "Why does everyone keep talking about Fiji?"

"Forget it." The driver scratched at his fake beard and it nearly fell off his chin. He spit another wad of chewing tobacco out the window, half of which blew back in Drew Biddle's face.

"What the hell!"Biddle wiped the slimy brown spittle off with his sleeve.

The driver eyed him in the rearview mirror. "Shut up, mole. You're lucky to be here at all."

The pink jeep crisscrossed the backstreets of Atlantic City until they reached the open highway. The driver kept his foot planted firmly on the gas pedal. He turned right and headed south on the Garden State Parkway.

Jack leaned his head against the window. Outside, the sun's light rippled off the ocean water, but couldn't penetrate his surreal world that swiftly liquefied into a black pool of mud.

He glanced at Wetterman, whose expression looked as confused as a man stuck in a snow globe. It was impossible to distinguish whether he dreamed about making love to Rosa on a nude beach in the tropics or perhaps pondered spending the rest of his life behind bars. Whatever the circumstance, a quiet but certain intensity settled on his face as he stared ahead at a road sign:

Welcome to EGG HARBOR
A sleepy resort town in Gloucester County

On the bottom of the sign in bold orange spray paint, someone had written: *Make like the rest of the chickens... GET LAID in EGG COUNTRY.*

Wetterman stiffened. The color dripped from his cheeks like wet paint left out in the rain.

"Egg Harbor?" Jack sucked on his lip and turned to Wetterman. "Isn't that the place Eileen Klump mentioned when you were locked in the supply closet and almost made love to her?"

Wetterman crunched up in a corner of the jeep and cringed. "This has to be a hallucination."

Rings of sleeplessness circled Jack's eyes. Maybe Wetterman had the right idea. Brought on by the non-pressures of his every day work habits, he could have suffered a nervous breakdown. The men in white coats might have already transported him to a padded room and he merely imagined his

262

entire fugitive existence. Jack giggled to himself, further supporting the theory that he had cracked up.

Veering left, the driver drove down a wooded dirt road, pocked with holes and overgrown with shrubs. Empty Budweiser cans were strewn around from teenagers sneaking a few brewskis in the woods. After a few miles a sign that read, *Slum's Air Service*, appeared as they neared a dilapidated private airfield. Walls of trees surrounded the airstrip, perhaps constructed by drug cartels. An aged airplane hangar sat near the entrance and looked like a bunker leftover from the last war.

To the left, just inside the front gate, a man with a straggly beard, sucking on a pipe, leaned against a rusted tractor.

The driver slammed on the brakes and the jeep skidded to a halt.

"Where are we?" Jack asked.

"Does it matter? This is your stop. Now get out." The driver scratched at his fake beard and it fell on his lap. Opening the glove compartment, he tossed the phony fuzz inside.

"Greene!" Jack pounded the dash with his fist. "You're not fooling anyone. What are you guys scheming?"

"You'll know soon enough," he paused, "if you live."

The old man leaning against the tractor ran over to the jeep. "What's wrong with you louts?" He kicked the driver's door. "This pink monstrosity you're driving is about as conspicuous as a load of manure in a field of flies. Hide that thing in the hangar and take up your positions."

Jack crossed his arms defiantly. "I'm not going anywhere until I get some answers."

Greene pulled a pistol out from underneath his seat. "You might want to reconsider." He pointed the barrel of the gun at the door. "Vamoose."

Jack, Wetterman, and Biddle reluctantly climbed out of the jeep. Greene hit the gas, did a donut in the dirt, and disappeared behind the airplane hangar.

Jack eyed the man with the pipe. "Are you Slum?"

"What's it to you?" Sweat dribbled down the old coot's sunburned neck. A sloppy t-shirt hung out of his overalls that were pulled up over a roll of fat on his waist. He sucked at his pipe like the nipple on a baby's bottle. "You guys are late." He checked his wristwatch and suspiciously eyed Biddle. "Who's the dweeb? He's not on my guest list."

"Perfect," Biddle paced. "I'm stuck in Hicksville USA with a backwoods redneck and a couple of felons. I'm going home."

Slum picked up a pitchfork and waved it at Biddle. "You're going nowhere."

Biddle backed up and cowered behind a tire of the rusted tractor.

"What do you want from us?" asked Jack.

Slum turned his head towards a prop plane that sat on the runway. Like a car with a flat tire, it leaned dangerously to one side. "Happy trails."

"I'm not getting in that thing." Wetterman shivered. " I'm afraid of flying."

"Not half afraid as you should be." Slum chortled. "That plane is about as airworthy as a pigeon with frozen wings in a snowstorm." He stuck a finger in a rusty hole near the propeller.

Jack planted his feet firmly in the dirt. "You can't make us do anything."

Slum shrugged. "That's up to you. I get paid whether you clowns are dead or alive, but you better take a look over there." He pointed off into the distance. Dusty pillars lifted off the road as a car raced towards them. "That's the feds. Forget about taking prisoners. They want you dead."

"You're bluffing," Jack replied angrily. "How would the authorities even know we're here?"

Slum fanned himself in the stagnant air. "I called them."

Jack's eyes widened. "Why?"

"How else would I get you blokes to climb onboard that bucket of junk? Besides, that repulsive pink jeep you came in is about as discreet as a dinosaur meandering around Manhattan. If somebody saw you, I'd be implicated in whatever muck you guys have been slopping around in."

The car drew closer.

Jack chewed his lip. They were mice led to the cheese and the trap was sprung. One thing was certain. The feds weren't looking for a bottle of wine and sparkling conversation. Rupinski in particular would like nothing better than to empty a loaded magazine in their heads.

Biddle unexpectedly ran to the middle of the road and jumped around like a rabbit on steroids. "Agent Hill! Rupinski!"

Jack looked in all directions but escape seemed impossible. With all exits closed, he grabbed Wetterman by the shirt and pulled him to the entrance of the prop plane. Pushing him through the hatch door, he turned around just as the feds slammed on the brakes.

Agent Hill vaulted out the driver's door. Rupinski exited the other side, hit the dirt, and twisted around the ground with his gun thrust out in front of him. Firing off a shot, a bullet punched a hole in the side of the prop plane. The heat of another round nearly singed Jack's ear.

Jack squirmed through the hatch door but was hampered by Biddle who clung to his leg.

"Get off, you little leech!" He kicked him in the ribs.

Biddle lost his grip and fell to the ground. Jack tumbled in the door and slammed it shut as sporadic gunfire echoed outside the plane.

Inside the cabin, a guy wearing a Hawaiian shirt walked down the aisle and yelled to the pilot, "Roll the engines!"

The prop plane began to move and rumbled down the airstrip. Jack looked out the window to see Biddle get up off the ground and start chasing the aircraft down the runway. Waving his fist and screaming, he took off his shoe and hurled it at the plane.

Clunking along, the aircraft picked up speed and lifted off.

Breathing a sigh of relief, Jack turned and shouted, "For God's sake, has everyone gone mad? What are we doing here? I want some answers!"

A stiff fist hit him in the back of the head. He fell to the floor with a thud, knocking him out cold.

Once again, the chaos engulfing his life washed from his mind like a dark tide that had blemished the shores of his recent past. Jack began to dream. He found himself in a simpler world. It was a night of bright stars, bright enough to light up every darkened corner of his heart. It was the night he found Paradise.

36

El Morocco en Paradise

An old Buddy Holly song, *True Love Ways*, played on the radio. The green glow of dash lights spilled over the girl's face and her perfume lingered in the air like a field of flowers in a warm breeze. In tune with the 50ish theme of Eddie's Alamo, she wore a beehive hairdo, white cotton blouse and a wiggle skirt with red hearts imprinted on it. A lock of brunette hair fell across her face and her eyes sparkled like tropical water in the sun; they were inescapable.

Jack sat speechless behind the wheel of the El Morocco that was parked inside Eddie Alamo's Bar. When he was a kid, the closest thing to love he had ever known was snowball fights with girls or teasing them in the halls at school until they cried. It wasn't until he turned the corner into his teens that he discovered the marvelous potential romance had to screw up his life.

After he got his driver's license, a night out meant slapping on some of dad's Aqua Velva and cruising the tires off a car on a Saturday night. Youth was a wonderfully irresponsible time filled with tubes of pimple cream and awkward dates at drive-ins where teenagers fumbled their way into love.

Now, years later, seated in the El Morocco showcased in Eddie's Alamo Bar, Jack froze into a cube of apprehension as he glanced over at the girl who sat next to him. He met her twice in his life. Once as a snot-nosed kid while he fired apples at unsuspecting bystanders from a tree and another time during a high school football game. On both occasions his heart nearly thumped out of his chest.

"Paradise?" Jack gulped.

"Yes." She smiled like the stars.

A blonde waitress on roller-skates with a Polaroid Instant Camera rolled across the floor and knocked on the car window. "Take your picture, Romeo?" She cracked a wad of gum in her mouth.

Before Jack could answer, she raised the camera and snapped a shot. The self-developing film popped out of the front of the camera and she handed it to him.

"Chow," the waitress said and skated away.

An image slowly emerged on the photo. Paradise sat close to his shoulder. Her face was beautiful. Just the sight of it took Jack to another universe.

"Nice," she remarked as she gazed at the picture. A distant look of nostalgia played in her eyes . "Remember that football game back in high school?" Paradise asked.

"How could I forget?" Jack blushed.

The Boomerangs were in a dogfight against the Hoods, a rival school famous for cheating. When the Boomerangs star fullback left the field with an acute case of gastritis, Jack got unexpectedly thrust in the game. He failed to score the winning touchdown. Still he managed to meet Paradise, even as he lay on the ground, smashed in the dirt and only inches away from the goal line. "I guess I blew that one, huh?"

"You were almost brilliant." Paradise sighed.

Euphoria gripped Jack's toes as certainly as an ocean at high tide. He found himself frozen in the moment, the one that strikes like a hammer and smashes every morsel of emotional fiber in the soul. It was that brief minute in which life might go either way, lead to ruin or salvation, and could be shattered, crushed, and eradicated, all over the sake of a woman.

It was wonderful.

He glanced at Paradise. Her lips were full and inviting as plump strawberries.

"What do you think we should do now?" she asked shyly.

Jack's mouth was like a ball of cotton on a hot dry day. He was speechless. With just one look, somehow he knew all about the girl. It didn't matter what kind of movies she liked or if she preferred Italian or Chinese for dinner. It also didn't matter whether she was a waitress at a fast food diner or a ballerina on Broadway. In the end, the only thing real to Jack was when he looked in Paradise's bright blue eyes. He saw forever.

Leaning over, they bumped *noses* when they kissed, but with all the awkwardness, the anticipation of their lips pressing against each other had all the magic of a shooting star. Pausing for just an instant, Paradise's lips, tender as freshly peeled oranges, parted open and they explored every crevice of each other's mouth. Falling off a cliff that danced with waves of emotion, Jack and Paradise were both lost inside the moment, so they knew they were getting it right.

Jack backed away after a minute and dabbed at a droplet of perspiration on his forehead. "Sorry. I don't know what came over me."

Paradise smiled and whispered, "Could we do it again?"

Jack kissed her. This time deeper. Longer. Her lips had all the warmth of a fire on the edge of an ice field, melting away his every inhibition. It was love, and if the driver's door of the El Morocco wouldn't have opened at that precise moment, he might have lingered there forever.

Stinky Mason pulled Jack out of the car by his ear. "Think you can hide, punk? You were outside making time with my girl." He glanced at Debbie Abernathy, who powdered her nose in the reflection of a beer cooler. "Debbie told me you tried to slip her the tongue in the backseat of Wetterman's car. I hate that crap. You want to get castrated or something?" He poked Jack in the chest.

Debbie marched boldly across the dance floor. "He doesn't know how to treat a lady." She stuck her jaw out defiantly and pretended to cry. "He tried to maul me."

"I didn't do anything!" Jack shouted.

"He's lying, Stink." Debbie fluttered her eyelashes at the bully.

Jack curled his fists. The freaking girl had the morals of a shark in a public swimming pool.

Wetterman walked over and tried to defuse the situation. "Everybody calm down. There's no reason to fight. How about I buy you a drink?" He offered and then inadvertently glanced at Debbie's breasts.

Stinky pushed Wetterman with a fat knuckle. "Snap your eyes back in your head!"

"I wasn't looking at her!" Wetterman looked again.

Stinky's head grew so big and red it looked like it was being inflated by an air pump. Balling up his fist, he punched Wetterman squarely in the nose and knocked him against the bar.

"Loser!" Jack shouted and launched himself at the bruiser.

Shoving and punching, both men lost their balance and tumbled to the floor.

Eddie the barkeep raced out from behind a keg of beer with a baseball bat. Swinging it like a club, he smashed a tray of glasses sitting on a table. "There won't be any roughhousing here. I run a decent establishment."

Jack and Stinky, like two lobsters in a clench, rolled on the floor.

"Do you hear me!" The barkeep yelled. He swung the bat again and shattered a plate of hot wings that Ed Shoemaker chewed on at a corner table. The sauce splattered on his wife's dress and she slapped her husband in the head for being a clumsy oaf.

Jack peeled himself out of Stinky's grasp. He tried to get up but the brute shot a stiff elbow into his gut that sent him crashing to the floor again.

Eddie the barkeep grabbed Stinky by a tuft of hair and pulled him to his feet. He shook the guy around like a particularly difficult clump of crab grass that sprouted up on his property.

Still on the floor, Jack blinked the stars out of his eyes. When his vision finally cleared, he looked up to see Paradise standing over the top of him. Her blue eyes swam with concern.

"Are you hurt?"

Jack leaned up on his elbows and offered a timid smile. All through his life, he had endured a steady stream of endless flirts, superficial romances, and a downpour of eccentric friends. Now, sprawled on the ground like a boxer who just took a hook to the jaw, he was forced to adhere to one of life's greatest triumphs and fears.

It was love.

"You're not catching me at my best." Jack rubbed a bump on his head.

"Why were you fighting with that guy?"

"Idiots grow on trees." He took a deep breath and paused. "This probably isn't the best time to ask, but maybe we could do something together sometime?"

Paradise smiled. Her eyes were magnetic. "That would be..."

Eddie the barkeep marched over with his wooden baseball bat. He shoved Paradise and the rest of the crowd back. "Damn troublemakers." He still clutched Stinky by the scruff of the neck. "I told you no rough stuff." He slapped him in the head. "Get lost." He pointed at the door.

Jack got off the floor and looked around. "Paradise?" He turned to Wetterman, who nursed a bloody nose with a handkerchief. "Where did that girl go?"

"Forget her." Wetterman fingered a welt on his head. "You already caused enough trouble. Besides, you'd fall all over her. Women hate that kind of stuff. If you want their love and respect, you have to learn to ignore them. Take it from someone who knows. I treated Rosa like an Egyptian princess and she hates me." His glum expression grew like a weed.

On the stage, the band's singer grabbed the microphone. "We're gonna do a sappy love song for all you lovers in the house. Grab your potential screws and start turning those bolts." The drummer counted four and the sax player blew his lungs out to the slow beat of a blues tune.

Jack looked around the dance floor. For an instant he glimpsed Paradise standing by the El Morocco. He took a step forward but was quickly intercepted by Eddie the barkeep.

"Lousy bums!" Eddie nudged Jack out the exit with the tip of the baseball bat and then slapped Wetterman in the head as he left the property. "Stay out!" He slammed the door shut behind him.

Staring stupidly at the closed door, Jack reached in his shirt pocket and pulled out the Polaroid that the waitress took while he was in the El Morocco with Paradise. It was a face he'd never forget. Standing there, he wondered if he'd ever see her again.

A whisper from a darkened corner of the building caught his attention. Turning to look, he saw Lance Sheppard talking to Nick Crowe.

Sheppard's eyes shifted towards Jack. "We'll talk later." He shook Crowe's hand then disappeared into the dark.

Crowe walked over and eyed Jack's fat lip and Wetterman's busted up nose. "You guys look like you were in a war. What happened?"

"Nevermind. What were you doing talking to Sheppard?" he asked suspiciously. "That guy is a shyster."

"You talking to me?"

"Who else would I be talking to?" Jack rubbed his temples. "We're headed home. You still need a lift?"

Crowe breathed the night air. His expression was so satisfied you'd have thought he just won the million dollar lottery. "The only lift I'll ever need some day will be on a yacht in the South Pacific. It's a momentous day." He motioned towards the car. "Let's go."

The ride home was tense. Wetterman was too upset to drive and handed Jack the keys. He climbed in the backseat. Holding a handkerchief on his swollen nose, he complained about how much he hated Stinky Mason and how much he loved Rosa Cruz.

"I can't stop thinking about Paradise," Jack confessed as he drove down the highway.

Crowe put his hands behind his head and stared out the window. "You mean the hot looking brunette? What makes you think she'd even consider dating you? Face it," he said. "Why would a beautiful woman like that tend to a mule when she can ride a stallion? Besides, there are more important things to worry about."

"What do you mean?" asked Jack.

"I'm talking about economics." Crowe brought his hands from behind his head and slapped them together briskly. "You got to get your priorities straight. Plan your future. You can't spend your entire life behind a desk, doing nothing, and dreaming about women who want nothing to do with you."

"Ha!" Jack scoffed. "You should be the last person to talk. You're the company's network administrator and can't even get management to sign a stupid requisition for new computers. Not to mention you got shady friends. Everyone knows Lance Sheppard is a thief."

Crowe shook his head and sniggered. "Lance isn't a bad guy. We got a few business deals simmering in the pot. One day when I'm rich, I might even offer you clowns a job. By God," he slapped his hand on the dash, "by the time I'm done, you'll be out of the bottling business for good."

Jack pulled the car up along the curb outside of Crowe's house. "And when can I expect all of this to happen?"

"Don't sweat it." Crowe jumped out and shot him a sly glance. "You'll know. Now if you'll excuse me, I need some shuteye. I have to go to work tomorrow."

"On a Sunday?" Jack tilted his head.

"The computers need maintenance."

"You're crazy."

"Most of the great ones are." Crowe slammed the door shut and walked into his house.

Jack stepped on the gas. Two blocks down the road, he pulled into Wetterman's driveway.

Wetterman sat in the backseat, snoring soundly. "Rosa baby," he said, caught up in a dream. Then, "Dancing bananas..... Paso!" He screamed and then started snoring again.

Jack cut the engine and got out of the car. Leaving Wetterman in a restless sleep, he walked the rest of the way home. A soft summer rain began falling and the sidewalks glistened under the streetlamps. Still, thoughts of Paradise swayed in his mind like the soft hips of a Hula dancer under a lover's moon. Looking up in the sky, he saw a shooting star and made a wish.

37

Goodbye Blue Skies

A cold slap in the face pulled Jack from a dream to wakefulness in zero point two seconds flat. He opened his eyes, still smelling Paradise's perfume, to find an unshaved guy wearing a Hawaiian shirt, khaki shorts, and bright red flip flops, standing in front of him. He held the cigar box stolen from Norman Cooley's office.

"What happened?" Jack rubbed his head.

"Sorry about that pal. We didn't have time to talk politics. The feds were on us." He rubbed his knuckles. "You got a skull like a brick."

Jack stood up and looked out the window of the prop plane. They were traveling over the ocean.

Standing alongside Jack, Wetterman clung so tight to the back of the passenger seat that his fingernails nearly tore a hole in the fabric. He peered at a door that stood ajar and led into the cockpit. A familiar woman leaned against the instrument panel and giggled at a passing cloud.

"Eileen Klump!" Wetterman pointed and shouted.

Jack's eyes widened. "There's a crazy person in the cockpit," he told the guy in the Hawaiian shirt. "She spent more time in mental facilities than a lumberjack in the woods."

The guy in the Hawaiian shirt flopped down on a chair. Reaching under the seat, he pulled out a bottle of Bacardi, unscrewed the lid, and took a slug. "Tell me something I don't know." He passed the stolen cigar box to Jack. "This belongs to you."

"What's the big deal with the box?"

"That's not for me to say." The Hawaiian shirted guy tapped his fingers on the armrest of the chair. "The only thing certain is that Marvin Caruso would have choked if he ever knew what was in that thing. Ha! It probably served him right. Marvin would pimp his own mother out for twenty bucks, not to mention after he changed his name to Alfred, he bought that fleabag diner and had half the town sick with his subpar meats." He took another slug of rum, rolled it on his tongue, and ingested it. "That's a hell of thing, right? The guy goes from being one of the most feared mobsters in New York to selling hamburgers. Life is never predictable, eh?"

"Stop dodging questions," Jack griped.

The Hawaiian shirted guy opened up a lunch bucket that sat on the seat next to him. Pulling out a bologna sandwich, he unraveled the cellophane and took a chomp. "You're too tense Jack." He spoke with a mouthful of bologna. "Stress is the leading cause of heart attacks according to the Surgeon General." He swallowed and paused. "I used to be a pawn in the business world, just like you. Know what changed my life?"

"I don't care."

"I was a trial lawyer in Philadelphia," he forged ahead. "Most of my clients were people with phony back injuries who were poised to sue the balls off corporate America. In a world of Neo-Nazis, white nationalists, black separatists, cross burning klansmen and border vigilantes, making off with a few bucks for a fake spinal twinge is about as criminal as stealing peanut brittle from a candy shop. I was simply performing a public service with the benefit of kickbacks, right? Trust me." He took another sip of rum. "All kinds of derelicts are determined to live the American dream and go on workmen's compensation and disability benefits. Bribing judges to give it to them isn't a small feat."

"You're a crook," Jack charged.

The Hawaiian shirted guy nodded. "Not only that. I smoke cigarettes and drink rum like it's gushing from a fire hydrant. Hell," he laughed, "in the end I'll probably be in court defending a deadbeat and fall flat on the floor from a heart attack or brain aneurism. It's just a question as to whether they'll call 911 or leave me decomposing on the floor until garbage night so the janitor can deposit me in the dumpster." He took a deep breath. "Anyway, I was at the breaking point. Then I met some guy in this stupid looking Alfred's Diner t-shirt who smelled like a commode."

Wetterman, standing alongside Jack, grabbed his friend's arm. "Nick Crowe."

"Yeah." The Hawaiian shirted guy crossed his legs. "That's the name. He came to my office and wanted to retain my services. Said he had a business plan. At first I was skeptical as a rat circling cheese in a mousetrap. But he convinced me he knew the ropes about being a crook. The next day I resigned my position at the law firm, bought a boat, and went fishing. Fishing!" He threw his hands in the air, almost as if unable to believe it himself. "Outside of cleaning up some legal crap for a new resort opening in the islands, I'm on vacation all the time."

Jack took a closer look at the guy. "You look familiar."

"I should," he said. "I litigated a case against the Cool Caps Bottling Company on behalf of Lance Sheppard. What a fiasco that was. Sheppard did everything from stumbling in the courtroom with a cane to bawling like a baby on the witness stand. That bastard deserved an Emmy." He nodded his head in envy.

"You're Fritz Heinberg." Jack's eyes lit up. "Half the disability recipients in the county that are leeching off the system have you to thank."

Fritz leaned back in his chair and crossed his legs. "Don't be so sensitive. Politicians in DC steal tax dollars every day. Most of it goes to the fat cats on Wall Street who made off with everyone's pension funds. With all that revenue floating around, why shouldn't I get a share of the green stuff? It isn't as if my clients aren't better off."

"You're a thief."

"It's called free enterprise. Consider Lance Sheppard's position." Fritz jiggled the bottle of rum in his hand. "When he worked for Cool Caps, he scraped to pay the rent. Now he's pouring in revenue like an open spigot. He drives a BMW and visits exotic ports all over the world. The sky is the limit." He pointed his finger. "You won't get those kinds of returns on a 401K plan."

Jack gripped the back of a chair. "None of that explains anything."

"You're on a need to know basis, Jack. I'll tell you one thing." He leaned forward. "Nick Crowe was awfully fond of you. Before he went up in flames in Alfred's Diner, he swore he'd get you out of a dead-end future at Cool Caps, even if it killed you."

Jack stared at Fritz for a moment and then started laughing wildly.

Wetterman eyed him warily from behind a headrest on a passenger seat. "Are you crazy?"

"Aren't we all?" Jack snickered. "You said it yourself, Wetterman. This is a hallucination. Maybe even mass hysteria. Tell me the truth. You really think we're on an air, land and sea chase from federal agents, hmm?" He turned to Fritz and laughed. "The next thing you'll tell me is that Gary Greene is hiding in the bathroom."

Wearing a backward baseball cap that said Vegas or Bust, the pilot popped his head out of the cockpit. Crusted glue clung to his chin from the fake beard that he had been wearing. "I'm up here, Dumbass." He slammed the cockpit door shut.

"See what I mean?" Jack shook Wetterman by the shoulders. "This can't be real!"

Reaching over, Fritz slapped Jack in the head. "Does that feel like a mirage?" He slugged at his rum again. "Straighten up and get your game face on. Don't you see the kind of risks I'm taking by being here?" He reached in an open bag of tortilla chips and crunched.

Jack looked at Fritz uncertainly. "You still haven't told me what you want from us."

Fritz sighed and fingered the handle of a pistol sticking out of his khakis. "Like I said, you're on a need to know basis. You're a carrier pigeon, my friend. Don't make me clip your wings."

"Are you going to kill me?" A cold chill snaked its way up Jack's spine.

"We're going to do what's best for everyone." Fritz nodded sympathetically.

Jack slumped down in his chair. The uncomplicated and simple life he once knew was gone. He gazed out the window of the plane into the blue waters, thousands of feet below, and wondered what could possibly happen next to eat away any remaining morsels of time. A few moments later, he found out.

The cockpit door flew open. Chewing on a toothpick, Greene stuck his head out. "We're almost at the drop point. Suit up."

Fritz shoved a last bite of the bologna sandwich in his mouth and licked his fingers. Leaning down behind a seat, he picked up a parachute and tossed it at Jack's feet. "'You'll need this."

"You want me to jump?" Jack backed up. "You must be crazy."

Fritz shrugged. "Some people think so. Not everyone walks away from six figures at a law firm to go fishing."

"This is suicide. We can't dive into the middle of the ocean."

"Hold on there, cowboy." Fritz waved his hand in dismay. "WE aren't jumping. There's no way in hell you'd get me out of this plane. Those waters are shark infested." He paused and licked his lips. "That's what I want you to do."

Jack's face shattered like broken glass. He wondered where all the madness of his life would finally end. As it turned out, it would be at the bottom of a murky ocean.

Even with disaster creeping in all around him, thoughts of Paradise still flashed in his mind. In a simple world, he'd be walking with her in the sunset on some secluded beach. Instead, he was buzzing around in a rundown prop plane, ready to be jettisoned out the hatch door, all the while conversing with an inebriated lawyer turned fisherman.

Standing in the plane's aisle, Jack refused to move. "There's no way I'm taking the dive. You'll have to kill me."

"Don't tempt me." Fritz winked. "You sound bitter."

"Wouldn't you be?"

"You got trust issues, Jack." Fritz gulped his rum, swished it in his mouth, and swallowed. "I'm thinking something bad must have happened to you along the way. Confidentially, the trouble usually starts in puberty. I don't wanna brag, but I had a few psych classes in college. Talking about it might help." He passed Jack the rum.

Jack reluctantly took the bottle and swigged it. A moment later, he started pouring out his life history. He talked about working in a dead-end job at a bottling company and attending a bogus Ground Guide seminar. He rattled on about Nibbles, a feisty old man, who wanted him to make love to his brazen wife Cecile in Ocean City. He shivered while relating the harrowing run-in with Boris Crane and cringed at the feds' obsession to arrest him on fraudulent charges. In the end, he imagined he'd be condemned to a dank cell behind penitentiary walls and bounced around from criminal to criminal like catnip for tom cats. Most of all he talked about Paradise, the girl he fell in love with at Eddie's Alamo, and in all likelihood, would never see again.

"Can't you see the dilemma I'm in?" Jack pleaded.

Fritz pulled a handkerchief out of his pocket and blew his nose. "You think I don't have a heart, you dirty bastard?" Sniffing, he shoved the hankie back in his khakis and then slapped his hands briskly together. "Okay then. It's ShowTime. Remember to hold your nose when you hit the water. The salt stings like hell. If you don't believe me, just ask Ed Shoemaker."

"Don't you have any compassion?" Jack shouted.

Fritz snorted. "Of course not. I'm a lawyer. Now lose the training helmet and get in the game. The feds saw you board this plane. They probably already have an interceptor jet in the air. If they find you, it'll be my ass hung from a hook. You can't expect me to get involved in that crap. I've got a reputation."

Curled up in a passenger seat, Wetterman's teeth chattered like a jackhammer on a slab of concrete.

Fritz pulled a pistol out of his khakis and aimed it at them.

"Take it easy!" Jack raised his hands and backed up.

"Eileen? Do your stuff, woman." Fritz hollered up to the cockpit.

The door of the cockpit swung open. "Bulla Bulla!" Eileen yelled and beamed at the mouth.

Marching down the center aisle of the plane, she carried a belly pack and tied it around Jack's waist. Grabbing the cigar box from him, she tucked it securely inside the pack.

"You can't do this!" Jack insisted.

Eileen pulled a scrawny orange life preserver out of an overhead compartment. "Nice day for a swim." She pulled Jack's arms through the sleeveless vest.

"Now put the parachute on him." Fritz waved the gun dangerously.

Picking the chute up off the floor, Eileen forcibly put it on Jack.

Her eyes shifting to the other side of the aisle, Eileen walked over to Wetterman, planted a wet kiss, and then slapped him on the cheek. "Have a nice dip in the pool, hot stuff," she said, then disappeared back into the cockpit.

Fritz pointed his gun at Jack's belly pack. "Whatever you do, keep that thing safe. I'd hate to think we went through all this just to have it get stuck in the tummy of a fish."

"You're throwing us to the dogs!" Jack yelled.

"You mean sharks," Fritz corrected. "That reminds me." He snapped his fingers. "We got a minor glitch. Slum, the stupid lout, only loaded one parachute onboard the plane. He was probably looking to save a buck on expendables. Hell, with inflation rates, who can blame him." He shifted his sights to Wetterman. "Hold tight to your buddy on the way down. With any luck the chute will support both your weight." He scratched his head uncertainly.

"I can't swim!" Wetterman pleaded.

"Then doggie paddle," Fritz recommended. "Bon voyage."

Opening the hatch, he pushed them out the door.

38

Splash!

Falling from the blue skies, Wetterman clung to Jack's waist like a lover in heat.

"Pull the rip cord!" Wetterman pleaded to his friend.

"You moron, I don't even know where the ripcord is!" Jack fumbled with the parachute, searching for the string.

Plunging downward at speeds exceeding 120 miles per hour, wind pounded their ears.

Jack's thoughts whirled. In the waning moments of what he assumed would be the final ones of his miserable life, he thought about things. Mundane things. He remembered sitting at his desk at work, reading newspapers and eating blueberry bagels for breakfast on company time. He grimaced at a fleeting vision of Biddle prancing around in fishnet stockings at a seaside bar. He pondered Nick Crowe's obsession for clean urinals and pictured Cecile, the drunken woman from Ocean City, who tried to make love to him while her husband Nibbles videotaped the action.

Most of all, he thought about Paradise. As he and Wetterman fell from the sky like a meteorite, she probably drove down some highway with her hair blowing in the wind, listening to the radio. The newscaster would report on still another sighting of Boris Crane terrorizing the East Coast while she powdered her nose in the rearview mirror.

Wetterman clamped himself around Jack like a koala bear. Stricken with visions of his own mortality, he shouted incantations of love to Rosa Cruz, a woman who in all likelihood had no idea that he even existed.

Struggling with the parachute and his own doubts of survival, Jack finally latched on to the ripcord. He gave it a firm yank and welcomed the sight of a red and white striped chute flowering open in an otherwise deep blue sky. It snapped like a pistol shot, caught a passing wind, and a tug in the airstream slowed their fall. Jack and Wetterman began a slow descent into the rippling blue water. In the distance, the plane carrying Fritz Heinbeck and his renegade crew faded into the seascape.

Wetterman's strewn hair blew in the warm wind as he clung to Jack. His face, pocked with shock and remorse, looked as if a bomb just detonated under his feet. "We're finally alone," he said. "I never thought it would end this way, and certainly not with you. If we weren't going to die, I'd probably have to kill you for putting me through this."

Jack peered down at the water. "Shut up and hold your nose." He embraced the stolen cigar box tucked firmly against his gut in the belly pouch.

With a gasp and a scream, he and Wetterman splashed into the ocean. They hung underwater for an instant before the life preserver dragged them back to the surface. Spitting up mouthfuls of sea water, they bobbed like apples in a Halloween tub. Miles of endless ocean spread out before them in every direction.

Wetterman hugged Jack's neck like a wrench. "What do we do now?"

Jack peered from side to side. Ripples of sunlight bounced off the water as they drifted in the current. "Maybe the tide will float us ashore."

"We'll never see dry land again." Wetterman coughed. "Rosa probably won't even come to my funeral if they ever recover our bones."

Even in such dire circumstances, Jack was surprised at the things that pass through someone's mind when confronted with impending doom. He stared at Wetterman, amused in spite of himself. Lost at sea with little hope of rescue, Wetterman's utmost remorse in a life filled with lonely nights and late night sitcoms, remained focused upon Rosa Cruz.

"Do you think we're being punished for our sins?" Wetterman asked.

A salty wave rolled by and smashed them both in the face.

Jack spit out a mouthful of water. "What sins? We led just as unproductive lives as everyone else. Why should we be singled out?"

"One time I walked up to the reception desk at work and started talking dirty to Rosa." Wetterman's half-lidded eyes were dabbed with shame. "She smiled dumbly because she couldn't speak English. All the while I asked if I could squeeze her tomatoes. Do you think that's what this is all about, squeezing tomatoes?"

Jack was speechless. Wetterman's confession served as a further declaration of guilt that made him all the more conscious of the ill fate that awaited them both. Wetterman needed atonement.

"I'm not a priest," Jack told him.

Furthermore, Jack didn't care. He had his own problems. For one thing he needed to avoid drowning. For another, regardless of his dilemma, his thoughts remained fixated on Paradise.

Digging in his shirt pocket, Jack pulled out a sopped picture of the brunette. Long ago he realized that Paradise would forever haunt his dreams, and that forever, as it turned out, would be a very limited time in the middle of an ocean. Jack kissed the photo and stuck it back in his pocket.

Floating on a scrawny orange life preserver, Jack pondered this and the many questions that beset his unusual universe as he awaited whatever black fate the rolling sea might deliver. That wait was short-lived and came in the form of a large circling fin.

"Shark!" Jack cried.

Wetterman gulped. "It's just a little seaweed, that's all."

"Is your brain soaked in applesauce?" Jack shouted. "That thing has a fin the size of Godzilla!"

"No it doesn't," Wetterman insisted. He stared at a passing cloud and even whistled gingerly.

Jack watched as his friend attempted to apply one of the many critical lessons learned during their tenure at the Cool Caps organization. Wetterman pretended that if he didn't see anything in the water, it wasn't there.

Despite the comfort zone of his own denial, Wetterman's defiance of the obvious soon turned to dread. He started to twitch as the fin circled in the water. As time wore on, he paddled, kicked and splashed uncontrollably.

"Quit it," Jack warned. "You're aggravating him."

The large fin dipped, resurfaced, and then grew closer.

And closer.

Wetterman finally settled down and took a deep breath. "So this is how it all ends. People like Lance Sheppard get filthy rich and drink margaritas on a beach, and we get eaten by sea monsters." The shark made another pass as Wetterman eyed him closely. "He's probably the one that got Shoemaker."

Jack raised his head when he heard a reverberating noise rumbling in his ears. "You hear that?" He listened again. "It sounds like an engine."

In the near distance, a small fishing boat bobbed in the water and steadily moved towards them at a deliberate pace.

"HELP!" Jack's arms thrashed in the water.

"Don't move!" someone on deck yelled. "Sharks!"

"Do we look blind?"

The fish, only yards away, made another slow pass and sniffed its dinner.

"Hold on!" a voice hollered.

In what wasn't more than minutes but seemed like an eternity, the fishing boat moved in close. In the bright gleam of sunlight, someone stood on deck, peering at them through binoculars. "We'll throw you a line. Grab hold."

Wetterman clutched Jack and spit up more foul water. "These guys could be drug smugglers or pirates."

Jack said nothing. Wetterman's logic was about as twisted as a gerbil picking a fist fight with a Doberman. A shark had them on the lunch menu. In the grand scheme of things, getting enslaved by drug cartels, terrorist regimes, or even catching a ride with Boris Crane, paled in comparison.

"Would you prefer getting chomped by a Great White?" Jack splashed Wetterman. "We need to get out of the water now!"

Someone on deck tossed a rope off the starboard side of the boat. Jack tried to grab it and missed, but managed to snag it on a second attempt.

"Hang on tight. We'll pull you aboard."

A couple of gruff sea hands hoisted them up over the side of the boat.

Jack fell face down on the deck, coughed up bad water, and rubbed the sting of salt from his eyes.

"You lugs were almost breakfast for a bottom feeder."

Jack shielded his vision from the sun and stared up at his rescuer.

Contrary to Wetterman's fears, there were no pirates, drug lords, or even foreign militants ready to take political prisoners. Nonetheless, there was one recognizable person leaning against the side of the boat.

"Ahoy, mates!" Nick Crowe grinned as he slurped a margarita.

39

Crowe's Captivity

"Ahoy, I say." Nick Crowe raised his hand in a hearty salute. He wore hush puppies, orange Bermuda shorts, and had a dark tan. "It's a brilliant morning on the high seas. You must be famished." He pointed at a couple of steaks sizzling on a grill near the side of the deck. "Grab a plate."

A cold drip of water fell off Jack's nose and his waterlogged shoes swished when he moved. Taking one off, he marched across the deck and batted Crowe over the head. "What are you doing here? I saw you run inside Alfred's when the place caught fire. You're supposed to be dead!"

"Maybe we're all dead and don't know it." Crowe nodded.

Drenched and stinking of sea salt, Wetterman scratched his head uncertainly.

"Don't you realize what we've been through?" asked Jack. "The feds are after us. We almost got shot!"

Crowe picked up a spatula and flipped a steak over. "No sense rehashing things. You should get out of those wet clothes. There's a change of underwear on the lower deck, but don't mess the place up." He wagged his finger. "I just shined up the commodes in the bathroom." Crowe glanced at the belly pouch around Jack's waist. A gush of excitement flooded his cheeks. "Is that it?"

"Is it what?"

Crowe breathed deeply. "*Daddy's Stash.*"

"We almost got eaten by sharks and you're worried about a box of cigars?"

"Well," Crowe sniggered, "they are Cubans. Besides, none of this is my fault. If that cheapskate, Norman Cooley, wouldn't have fired me from Cool Caps, things might be different. Maybe I would have been satisfied sitting at a desk and pretending to work like the rest of you schleps. But he had to pick a fight."

Jack slouched down in a deck chair and rubbed his fingers over his eyes. "What the hell is this all about, Crowe?"

Fanning himself, Crowe leaned against the boat's rail. "It goes back some years."

"Remember that night at Eddie's Alamo when you met the brunette?" Crowe asked.

Paradise's face shined in Jack's mind. She was the one constant, an unbroken circle that revolved around his life like a rocket circling the planet.

"Lance Sheppard was in the bar that night. He was happier than an alligator that just swallowed a possum. Sheppard won a huge settlement from Cool Caps after faking a spinal injury and was celebrating his newfound wealth." Crowe sipped his margarita. "We started talking. When he found out I was the network administrator at Cool Caps, we struck a deal."

Jack raised an eyebrow. "What deal?"

"It took some persuading, but I agreed to reactivate Sheppard's payroll account on the mainframe computer," Crowe confessed. "I also tripled his salary and gave him an unlimited expense account."

Wetterman toweled off his hair and glared. "You can't do that."

"I did do that." Crowe differed. "Sheppard's lawyer, Fritz Heinbeck, hid the money in a private offshore account. If anyone got suspicious, I immediately deleted Sheppard's name from the payroll. When things quieted down, I added it again. Usually I gave him a fat raise, just for the inconvenience."

"And what did you get out of it?" asked Jack

"My services didn't come cheap. I demanded half the profits. We had one hell of a business."

"Business?" Jack slammed his fist on a table and Crowe's drink spilled on the deck. "You're a thief! The feds have you pegged. They know you're working with Sheppard. If you're so smart, how did you get caught?"

Crowe grabbed a napkin from the wet bar and cleaned up the mess from his spilled drink. "Sheppard had an appetite for exotic living. He wanted to see the world. Hawaii... Australia... he even had a condo in Guam. There's no way I could hide those kind of expenditures in toilet paper and turnpike receipts. Somebody got suspicious and called the authorities. Don't they know I could go to jail for some that?" Crowe's cheeks burned with resentment.

"That still doesn't explain what any of this has to do with me."

"None of it does. The money we extorted from Cool Caps was chump change." Crowe poured himself another drink. "After Norman Cooley fired me, the real scam began." He glanced at the cigar box. "That's where you came in."

Crowe picked up a tube of sun-block and dabbed it on his neck. His expression was smug as a black bear that just raided a garbage can and found a slab of beef with all the trimmings. Stretching his arms in the warm sun, he sat down beside Jack.

"Not long after I got ousted from Cool Caps, I took a job at Alfred's. It wasn't glamour work, but hey, it had its moments. Before the place burned down, we had the most sanitary commodes in the state." His cheeks, the size of marshmallows, puffed up with pride. "One night while I was closing up, I grabbed the keys to Alfred's private office to snoop around."

Wetterman walked over with a beach towel wrapped around his neck and his hair mussed up like a rooster. "That's invasion of privacy."

"Yes it is." Crowe agreed. He squinted up at the sun, pulled a pair of Ray Ban sunglasses from his shirt pocket and put them on. "I went through Alfred's desk. Talk about a slob. The guy had everything from dirty socks to stale pizza crusts stuffed inside. I've seen desecrated toilet seats in less deplorable condition." He grimaced. "I was about to go back to work. Then underneath a girlie magazine stuffed in one of the drawers, I found something."

Jack stared blankly.

"Alfred kept a diary." Crowe said. "I started reading it. What I found changed my life and it's the reason we're all standing here today."

"I don't understand," Jack said. "What's so exciting about a slumlord diner king?"

"All the rumors are true," Crowe continued. "Years ago, the guy was a mobster. His real name was Marvin Caruso."

"So what?"

Crowe removed his Ray-Bans and leaned forward. "According to the diary, he got his hands on some hot diamonds. He was supposed to sell them on the Black Market but double-crossed the mob and kept them for himself."

Jack tapped his foot anxiously. "Get to the point."

"The feds got wind of the stolen rocks and were closing in on him. Marvin gave the diamonds to Clyde Cooley for safekeeping until things quieted down. But Clyde got emphysema and died. Nobody ever knew what happened to the missing diamonds.

"The feds eventually arrested Marvin on money laundering charges. He struck a deal with the state attorney's office. He agreed to turn state's evidence against the mob in exchange for his freedom and a ticket into the witness protection program. Marvin changed his name to Alfred. He's been working the fast food business ever since."

"You really want me to believe this?" Jack laughed. "Alfred sells hamburgers, for God's sake."

Crowe took a deep breath of ocean air and raised his glass. "Gentlemen, ignorance is bliss. Rummaging through Alfred's desk, I also found a letter from Clyde Cooley. It was stuffed in the back of the diary. Judging by the postmark, Clyde wrote it just before he died." He pulled the letter out of his pocket and handed it to Jack.

The letter said:

Hey Marvin,

Haven't heard a word from you since the feds squeezed you. In case you're wondering, the BLUE ROCKS are tucked away securely in my STASH. When the air clears, stop over and collect. I know how you got a fondness for cigars, and I got a box of Cubans that'll make you feel like a couple of mil. Trust me on that one.

Hope everything is good. Aside from that little bastard Norman who keeps stealing my hooch and has the brains of his mother, life is a hoot.

Arrivederci, Clyde

Standing alongside Jack, Wetterman stared at the letter. "I don't get it."

"You're stupid as a rock, aren't you?" Crowe stood up. He pointed at the belly pack strapped around Jack's waist. "Give me that thing."

Jack took the pack off and tossed it to Crowe.

Pulling the cigar box out of the pouch, Crowe's eyes were eager as a hungry vulture. Opening it, three soggy Cubans were tucked inside. He pulled one out and sniffed it like a dog nosing a pork bone. Sticking one of the cigars in his mouth, he lit up and blew a smoke ring in the air.

"Wet or dry, these babies are hot fire." Puffing away, he knocked his knuckles on the side of the cigar box. "This is the *STASH* that Clyde wrote about." He pointed at the words, *Daddy's Stash*, written on the side of the box.

Jack blinked and stared. "What makes you so sure?"

"Are you blind?" Crowe asked. "Clyde had the words *"Daddy's Stash"* engraved on it as a clue. However, he died without ever revealing the secret to anyone. Norman, his son, inherited the business but never discovered what was inside the box." Crowe shook it.

Jack let out a loud belly laugh. "Take another look inside, Dick Tracey. The only thing I see is a couple of squelchy cigars."

Digging in his khakis, Crowe pulled out a pocket knife. He peeled up the red fabric lining of the inside of the box. A thin but deliberate slit was cut across the flooring of the wood. Jimmying it up, the wood was hollow underneath.

"Mama!" Crowe's eyes glimmered like stars. He tugged at a small purplish sack stuffed into the empty gap. Pulling the sack out, he opened it and poured the contents in his hand. A petite fistful of diamonds sparkled in the sunlight.

"Daddy's Stash," Wetterman whispered and sighed.

Jack's jaw dropped open wide enough to stuff a rabbit down his throat. "Those must be worth a million!" He put his hand out to touch the loot. Crowe batted it away.

"That and more," Crowe said. "They're blue diamonds from India. Very rare. Even more expensive." He rolled them in his fingers. "All these years Norman Cooley had a fortune sitting on his desk and was too stupid to know it."

Crowe looked smug as a man who just guessed a sixty-four million dollar question. He leaned coolly against the side of the boat, picking his teeth.

"What makes you think you can get away with this?" Jack asked.

"I already have." Crowe said. "I got incinerated in an arson fire that you started, remember?"

"I didn't start that fire!"

"That's not what the feds say."

"You ruined me!"

Crowe took another sip of his drink, swished it in his mouth, and then spit it out on deck, most of which landed on Wetterman's shoe. "I tried to avoid putting a wrecking ball in your life."

"Seriously?" Jack face twisted in different angles of anger. "Tell me how."

"That's easy. Remember when Greene took Dan Rupert hostage in the Cool Caps administration building?"

"What about it?"

"Greene works for me," Crowe said. "The plan was for him to create a diversion so I could sneak into Norman Cooley's office. But the feds sealed off all the entrances. Making the heist was impossible. I had to resort to other tactics."

"What tactics?"

"I burned down the diner, or I should say you did. At least that's how the feds see it." Crowe smirked. "When I faked my death, the authorities forgot all about me and concentrated on you. Slick, huh?" he boasted.

Infuriation dented Jack's face. "Why involve me? What did I ever do to you?"

Crowe sucked thoughtfully at his lips. "You tried to save me from getting toasted when up in flames. I admire that, but business is business. Someone had to be the goat. Why not you?"

"I tried to save you from the fire!"

"Is that my fault?" Crowe defended himself. "When you started waving around the gas container I used to light the place up, the feds instantly pegged you for arson. Since everyone thought you were guilty, I thought we could do each other a favor. What the hell, Jack, all I needed you to do was steal a lousy cigar box."

"You framed us!" Wetterman spouted off.

"Why all the complaints?" Crowe kicked his feet up on a chair. "Did you really want to spend your life working in a bottling factory?" He slapped his head in disbelief. "I don't think so. Besides," he pointed out, "you weren't in any danger. Spies were everywhere."

"What spies?" asked Jack.

Crowe walked to the bow of the deck. Wind blew in his hair as he stared across the horizon. "Finding recruits was easy. Cool Caps has enough disgruntled employees to fill the San Andreas Fault."

"Like who?"

"Dan Rupert, the personnel director, for one. Norman Cooley made his job about as pleasant as a ballerina dancing in a sewer. I convinced him to join my team." Crowe beamed. The bastard enjoyed hearing himself talk. "Rupert wore a stupid red scarf wrapped around his head and met you at a campground in the middle of the night. Now that's devotion."

"Who else?" asked Jack.

"Eileen Klump," he said. " She's crazier than a cat in heat, but she needed a change in her life. I took her under my wing. She still swears she's going to make love to Wetterman on a deserted beach in the South Pacific."

Wetterman cringed.

Jack stared a hole in Crowe's head.

"Remember Nibbles in Ocean City?" Crowe pulled a compass out of his pocket and fiddled with it. "I first met the guy in Long Island. He tried to sell me a porno business. We kept in touch over the years. When he found out about my plan to steal the diamonds, he wanted in.

"The feds trailed you guys to the shore because they were convinced I was doing something illegal and that you worked for me. When they got brave and were about to haul you in for questioning, Cecile coerced you back to her hotel room." He slapped his knee and laughed. "You should have seen the look on your face when Nibbles pulled out a camcorder and started filming you in bed with his wife."

"You watched that video?" Jack gasped.

"Wouldn't you?" Crowe sniggered. "I didn't laugh like that since Biddle modeled fishnet stockings at Pedro's Cantina."

Jack drooped like a wilted flower against the starboard side of the boat. Everywhere he turned, conspiracy surfaced. Only instead of international spies, the cast of players were disgruntled office workers led by a janitor with a fetish for dirt free toilets.

"Even the gumball salesman in the parking lot on the day you made the heist was watching your back." Crowe added.

"He works for you?"

"Bingo!"

"What about Rosa Cruz, the front desk receptionist for the company. Is she here?" Wetterman sounded hopeful.

Crowe gave him a sympathetic slap on the cheek. "Afraid not. Rumor has it she's an illegal alien. The government is cracking down on that stuff. You understand."

"But..."

"We'll talk about it later." He pushed him off.

Wetterman thrust his bottom lip out in remorse. Grabbing a bottle of booze off the table, he took a long swig and walked over to the boat's rail, staring into the endless sea. Like

Shoemaker before him, it appeared certain that he'd take the plunge.

Jack gazed into the ocean. Crystal water lapped at the boat and wind tugged at his hair. A spray of salt water splashed in his nostrils.

What was there left to say? Crowe exploited the system and rode the mediocrity of corporate America like a mule. He threw his friends to ruin and damnation, all in the name of greed. Instead of clandestine organizations like the mob that were practiced in the art of thievery, in the end, it was a simple case of a urinal concierge with a dream.

Jack punched his fist on the side of the boat. "You threw me to the dogs!"

"I did what was in your best interest."

"You're an arsonist!"

"That's not how the arrest report reads." Crowe differed. "You are."

"You probably even dumped Shoemaker overboard!"

"Now you're talking like a drunken sailor." Crowe turned his head to the ship's bridge.

Seated in the captain's chair on the upper deck, a guy with a scraggily beard steered the wheel with one hand and held a bottle of rum in the other.

"Ay, mates!" he shouted and took a slug from the bottle.

Jack shielded his eyes from the sun. "Shoemaker?"

"Don't be surprised." Crowe shook his head. "Shoemaker had issues. Could you imagine living with his wife? One night when I was cleaning the grease fryers at Alfred's, he stopped by. The guy was drunk and in tears. I offered to help him. So when he went on a cruise with his wife, he fell overboard. The authorities assumed he drowned or got eaten by sea monsters. But minutes after he took the dive, we picked him up." He glanced at Shoemaker who sang something about Captain Kid and waved his rum bottle in the air. Crowe whispered, "He's a fantastic bartender when he isn't drinking up all the profits."

"Ay mates!" Shoemaker shouted again from the captain's chair.

Jack folded his head in his hands. His world hadn't just fallen apart; it smashed to pieces. Everyone from a pauper like Shoemaker to crazy Eileen worked for Crowe and got rich.

Everyone that is, except for him and Wetterman. Instead of basking in the glow of fortune, they were held in a dank hole of desperation, destined to a life behind bars.

Jack lunged at Crowe and grabbed him by the throat. "I'm a wanted man!"

"You brought it on yourself." Crowe jiggled his drink.

"What?"

"Remember that night at Eddie's Alamo, the same night you fell in love with the brunette? I told you I was starting a business. You wanted in when I got rich. Well here it is." He shook the diamonds in his fist. "The mother lode!"

On the ship's upper deck, Shoemaker jumped out of the captain's chair. His tan cotton shorts and tropical shirt blew in the breeze. He took another slug of rum. "Hey man, what's the hold up? Fiji is waitin' on us."

"Fiji?" Jack blinked.

I'll collect a fortune for these diamonds on the Black Market. I'm opening a business in the islands. Operations will be up and running within weeks." Crowe sniffed the salty air. "There's nothing like seeing your dreams come true." He left out a long sigh. "Welcome to the good life."

Jack stared into the water. The mystery, like a roll of toilet tissue, had finally unraveled. Crowe was a thief. But instead of plundering unsuspecting fishing boats or happy vacationers on jet skis, he was stealing corporate crooks blind.

In a wave of anger, Jack grabbed Crowe by the scruff of the neck and lugged him to the edge of the boat. "You call this the good life? The feds will crucify me! Give me one good reason I shouldn't feed you to the sharks."

Crowe sniggered and said, "Because I can get her for you."

Jack kept a firm grip on Crowe's neck. "What are you talking about? Get who?"

Crowe grinned. "The brunette, of course. Paradise."

40

Welcome to Paradise

(Six Months Later)

The plane touched down in Nadi en route to a tropical paradise and the vacation of a lifetime.

Paradise studied a pamphlet of the islands. Fiji, located in the heart of the trade winds in the South Pacific, was made up of nearly 322 islands and over 500 smaller islets, 106 of which were inhabited. A majority of the land masses were formed through volcanic eruptions millions of years ago. Vatulele, about thirty minutes south of the Nadi airport, was one of them.

The island of Vatulele sported one of Fiji's newest resorts and was celebrating their grand opening. The place had already become one of the chief hot spots in that little corner of the world. Despite a fashionable design and rich décor, the brochure said the resort wasn't the product of wealthy investors, but rather the dream-child of an unknown entrepreneur, rumored to have started out as a restroom concierge at a fast food diner.

From Nadi, Paradise boarded a puddle jumper en route to Vatulee. Setting the vacation pamphlet down, she looked out the plane's window at the deep blue sky. Only two passengers were onboard the flight, both females, and one of Mexican descent.

"I still can't believe it." Paradise flipped her hair over her shoulder and again gazed out the window of the plane. Surrounded by shimmering water, the island of Vatulele came into view. "I don't remember entering any sweepstakes for a Fiji vacation. Then a few weeks ago, I got a letter in the mail that said I won an all expense paid trip to *The Crowe's Nest*, a luxurious resort in the islands."

Beside her, the Mexican woman in an orange sundress smiled and nodded, but said nothing.

The ride in the commuter plane was bumpy. The cockpit door stood ajar and the pilot, wearing green army fatigues and a *Vegas or Bust* baseball cap, cursed the controls. Even stranger, a stewardess toted around a feather duster and repeatedly talked to the luggage in the overhead compartment.

"Buckle up," the pilot announced in the intercom. "We're about to land. On behalf of Crowe Express Flights, have a pleasurable stay, and don't forget to tip the waitress."

"Bulla Bulla!" the stewardess shouted in the intercom just as the pilot flicked it off.

Paradise pulled her sweepstakes ticket out of her purse and again wondered about how she won the contest.

Lifting a quizzical eyebrow, the Mexican woman seated beside her reached into her sundress and held up a matching ticket.

"You won too?" Paradise's eyes widened. "That seems impossible!" She held out her hand. "It's nice to meet you. I'm Paradise."

Shaking Paradise's hand, the Mexican woman nodded but still said nothing.

"I'm sorry. " Paradise blushed. "You don't speak English, do you?"

The Mexican woman smiled and then began to laugh out loud. "No apologies necessary. Yes, I speak English, but please don't tell anyone. Back in the states, I'm employed as a desk receptionist at a bottling company. Nobody asks me to do anything but look pretty because they're convinced I don't speak the language. Confidentially," she said, "I grew up in Jersey."

Paradise giggled. "That sounds crazy."

"It is crazy," Rosa answered. "Sometimes it's also amusing. The men talk dirty to me because they think I can't understand them. One in particular, Bob Wetterman, used to call me on the phone and hang up when I answered because he was too afraid to talk to me. He had some trouble with the law and I haven't heard from him for a long time." She sighed. "Maybe he lost interest."

"Something similar happened to me," Paradise confided. "Years ago, I met a guy and crossed paths with him over and over, almost as if it was supposed to be. He once even kissed me in an El Morocco. I fell for him instantly. Then one day he just disappeared." Her eyes grew dreamy and distant. "I suppose things fall apart."

The plane hit the runway with a jolting thump and glided down the landing strip until it came to a stop. Again the intercom blipped on.

"Thanks again for flying Crowe Express Flights, the finest ride in the blue skies. Included in your fabulous island vacation package is a complimentary dinner for two at Nick's Pizza Palace, fashionable fast food for all occasions. You've also been assigned a personal escort to take you around the island's exotic ports. Have a great day. Now get out." The pilot stood up and fanned himself in the heat.

"Bulla Bulla!" the stewardess yelled once more before exiting the plane.

Paradise and Rosa stood up and grabbed their luggage from the carry-on rack. Stepping out into the aisle, they walked off the plane.

Outside, the sun cast a bright glow of warmth on their faces. Much like a Hawaiian greet, a contingent of hula girls in grass skirts put yellow orchids in their hair. Asian lily flowers and ginger snaps were all over the place. Colored balloons spiraled up in the bright blue sky and a rainstorm of confetti was tossed in the air by a welcoming committee.

"This is like a dream!" Paradise laughed, but froze when she saw a familiar person crossing the landing strip. She rubbed her eyes and looked again. "I can't believe it."

Making his way alongside the exit ramp, Jack Snaggler held a rose in one hand and a margarita in the other.

Wetterman stood beside him and looked as out of place as a panda bear on a Bermuda beach. Regardless of the hot tropical sun, his face was lily white. Colored love beads were strung around his neck as he held up a sign with letters written in big blue magic marker that read, *ROSA CRUZ*. When he finally got the courage to glance in Rosa's direction, he had the expression of a man lost in the Sahara who just stumbled on an oasis.

Jack fidgeted uneasily. Regardless of his rising emotions, experience taught him that life often rolled like a rollercoaster; reaching the top had sometimes been doable, but the trip back down wasn't always the thrill ride that it was cracked up to be. Back in the states, he had endured being chased by federal agents and framed for arson and murder, compliments of a fast food worker with a fetish for sparkling toilets. Where was the optimism in it all? It was hard to believe that another interlude with Paradise, the same brunette dreamboat he kissed in an El Morocco so long ago, would turn out any differently.

From around the opposite side of the plane, Nick Crowe rushed over to greet the women. "Welcome to the land of bliss!" He uncorked a bottle of champagne and raised a glass.

Rosa walked over to Wetterman. Tilting her head, she smiled coyly at him.

Hot flashes and cold sweats condensed on Wetterman's face. If one didn't know better, he could have been mistaken for a woman in the throes of menopause. By the look in his eye, he immediately wanted to make love to her. Bundling his courage, he took Rosa's hand and strutted away like a proud Brazilian playboy.

Paradise stepped off the exit ramp and approached Jack. Her perfume, the same as she wore when he kissed her so long ago on one magic night at Eddie's Alamo, drifted like lilacs in the breeze. Her eyes, big and soulful, glistened in the sunlight.

"I'm Jack." He handed Paradise a rose. "We've met before."

Paradise's brunette hair blew in the warm wind. "How could I forget that night in the El Morocco?" She looked at him through pensive eyes. "How could you be here?"

Jack didn't answer. A rockslide of sentiment collapsed on his heart. Unlike Wetterman, whose yearning for Rosa was as obvious as a cat's whiskers sticking out of a mouse hole, Jack was speechless. Memories of that night at Eddie's Alamo swung in his mind like an open gate. When he first tasted her lips in the El Morocco, the moment was a masterpiece that grew more priceless with each passing day.

Crowe slurped his drink. "You two know each other?" He snapped his fingers and turned to Jack. "Maybe you could give the lady a tour of the island and the resort." He stuck his chin up with pride. "We have excellent restroom facilities."

A knot the size of an orange stuck in Jack's throat. He glanced over at Paradise and offered a timid grin. "Would you mind?"

Paradise's face painted over with the warmth of summer and brightness of the moon.

Hand in hand, Paradise and Jack walked out towards the shore where the sunlight and waves meet the sky.

Epitaph

Life in Fiji

The Crowe's Nest quickly evolved into one of the best vacation spots on the globe. The resort's big selling points were beautiful beaches, luxurious accommodations, and first class restroom facilities.

Norman Cooley and Harriet Puck took a romantic hiatus to the island. The vacation was cut short when Norman developed a severe case of gastritis. The *Lobster ala Crowe* served in a hotel restaurant by a suspicious waiter in orange moccasins was thought to be the culprit. Curiously enough, he looked like a former personnel director at Cool Caps.

Harriet jilted Norman sometime after pocketing a hefty jackpot in Atlantic City. In an attempt to resurrect the glory years of her tainted youth, most of her winnings were squandered on trying to re-establish an unprofitable cathouse in the Bronx. She was last seen working as the world's oldest cocktail waitress at *The Flamingo Bar* in Ocean City.

Ain't life grand?

Drew Biddle was ultimately cleared of all wrongdoing by the feds. He later pursued a career on the Vegas strip as a female impersonator and in due course made his way to the Fiji Islands. Crowe signed Biddle to a long term contract. Mindful of his roots, he closed every show with the same fishnet stockings that launched him into the winner's circle at Pedro's Cantina.

Biddle's one other crisis in life came in the form of Boris Crane, the East Coast killer, who for unknown reasons stalked the male prima donna from city to city. Crane was eventually apprehended during one of Biddle's performances at Radio City Music Hall, and is resting peaceably in a mental facility in Tucson.

Unlike Biddle, Lance Sheppard continued to ride high on the FBI's most wanted list. He'd sometimes go on trips to exotic ports around the world and take in the sunset, or in some cases, file phony lawsuits after slipping and falling in shopping malls.

Gary Greene also remained on the FBI's hot register. Green changed his name to Pierre Rombosci and drawing on his piloting skills from the Gulf War, took a job heading up airline operations at Crowe Enterprises. He routinely took trips to Las Vegas for reunions with his old army buddies to knock back a few cold ones and meet promiscuous women.

That's life in the fast lane.

Agent Rupinski, bent on shooting someone, finally got his wish when during a drug bust in downtown LA, accidentally shot his own toe off and had to retire from the force. His partner, Agent Hill, took a desk job in Washington. To this day he keeps a picture of Jack Snaggler on his bulletin board and often refers to him as the *Great White Whale,* vowing that one day he'd find him and take him down.

Dan Rupert retained a position as personnel director for Crowe's company. His lifestyle wasn't as lucrative as Greene's adventures in Sin City, but he did have a private restroom, complete with his name spelled out in gold letters on his favorite stall.

Nibbles became a confirmed bachelor after his wife Cecile ran off with an Italian gentleman in an Armani suit. Relocating to Fiji, he opened a nude beach in Vatulete. He later expanded operations to include mail order bribes. Sometimes referred to as the Guru of Love, he is considered by many to be the foremost authority on the oral history of romance.

Speaking of romance, Rosa Cruz fell in love with Wetterman, although she never did tell him she spoke English. She resigned her position at Cool Caps and moved to Fiji. In due course, Wetterman convinced Rosa to elope. They tied the knot in Hawaii during the monsoon season and hiding in a basement as the seasonal storms raged, they made love and in the coming months, a new Wetterman arrived in the world.

Hallelujah.

News of Wetterman's romance with Rosa dealt Eileen Klump a crushing blow. She sought counseling in the states and later returned to Fiji with renewed vigor in her soul and forgiveness in her heart. Eileen took a job as hostess at one of Crowe's restaurants, but was soon confined to kitchen detail after customers caught her talking to a tray of breakfast bagels. She eventually fell in love with a native islander from Taveuri and got married, as was their tradition, on top of a volcano. To this day she's sought by head tribesmen for spiritual advice after she was seen talking to a statue of an ancient goddess in the center of town.

Of the many happy endings in life's quagmires, Ed Shoemaker stood at the head of the pack. His belligerent wife, a nagging monkey perched on his shoulder, was gone. Head bartender at the resort's main hotel, he drank up most of the profits. When he was sober enough to reflect on his past life, playful as a pussycat, he'd send an anonymous postcard to his wife that simply said, *"Eat your own liver and onions."*

After an elaborate prenuptial agreement, Nick Crowe, CEO in charge of operations, married Jodi Frick, an old flame from high school. With a new love in his life and a sparkling commode in every room of his house, life was ecstasy. In Crowe's world, even orchids grew in manure.

As for Jack Snaggler, despite an investigation, the feds never found any evidence of his guilt and all charges were dropped. He remained in Fiji and sometimes took long walks under the sunset, pondering the old days. It occurred to him that life was never about bottling companies or even diamonds stuffed in cigar boxes. Life was about the moment all the pieces fit together. That instant when everything a person does, all the memories, the magic, no matter how good or bad, brings someone back to the place he or she was always supposed to be. Life was about that first kiss, the one that makes you fall in love forever.

Jack married Paradise on a beach in Fiji and honeymooned onboard the Lovebird, the same fabled ship where Ed Shoemaker found freedom from his overbearing wife. They have two small children, both spoiled, and destined to inherit a fortune.

Late at night, Jack and Paradise often watched the sunset over the ocean and made love on the beach to the sound of the crashing waves.

Life was about Paradise, and paradise never ended.

About the Author

Jeff Davis lives in Jim Thorpe, a small tourist town and gateway to the Poconos in northeastern Pennsylvania. Currently he's working on his next novel.

Joryd,
Welcome to Paradise
and.
The American Loon's Nest!